Praise for *The River Warren*

"Entertaining and brilliantly written first novel . . . As stunning in its use of language as it is touching in its human revelations, *The River Warren* is an impressive debut from a writer entirely at home in what may still be America's greatest single resource—its magnificent, if embattled, unspoiled rural landscape."
                    —Howard Frank Mosher, *The Denver Post*

"Intelligent and intuitive—a very promising writer."
                    —Peter Matthiessen

"His descriptions of the river at night are seductive, and his spare and affectionate accounts of farm life never miss the mark."   —*Minneapolis Star Tribune*

"Somewhere between the weight of Faulkner and the ease of Kesey, Kent Meyers brings to American fiction a tenaciously gripping story that moves with the subtle subterfuge of an aging river current. . . . *The River Warren* is a seductive and dark tale that closes with a welcome sense of light and fulfillment."   —*ForeWord*

"Kent Meyers uses his first novel to dissect Cloten and its citizens as they try to make sense of the disaster. While they do ... [Meyers] moves cleanly from the event itself to an insightful inspection of local life and its discontents."
— *The New York Times Book Review*

"Skillful and sensitive."   — *Publishers Weekly*

"A muddy, turbulent tale filled nonetheless with strong moments and singing sparks."   — *Kirkus Reviews*

"Meyers writes with refreshing sensitivity, drawing countless analogies from the river, which is both a soothing respite and a turbulent force to be reckoned with."
— *The Grand Rapids Press*

"A moving tale of families, friendships, and the uses of silence."   — *Booklist*

"A luminous first novel."   — *City Pages* (Minneapolis)

The River Warren

≈

The River Warren

≈

A NOVEL

Kent Meyers

A HARVEST BOOK
HARCOURT BRACE & COMPANY
San Diego   New York   London

First published by Hungry Mind Press

Library of Congress Cataloging-in-Publication Data
Meyers, Kent.
The river warren: a novel/Kent Meyers.—1st Harvest ed.
p. cm.
ISBN 0-15-601062-3
1. City and town life—Middle West—Fiction.
2. Young men—Middle West—Fiction.
I. Title.
PS3563.E93R58 1999
813'.54–dc21 99-26983

Text set in Adobe Caslon
Designed by Wendy Holdman

Printed in the United States of America
First Harvest edition 1999
A C E F D B

To Zindie, who has been with me from the beginning.

≈

THANKS

To my family, for their love and support.

To Bill Schulz, Paul Higbee, Temma Ehrenfeld,
Al Masarik, Stuart Kenny, and Scott Howard,
who read early drafts of this novel,
and encouraged and advised me.

To the National Endowment for the Arts,
for time to work.

To Noah Lukeman, my agent, who revived me.

To Dallas Crow, who edited this book with
insight and understanding.

To Tom Herbeck and Wendy Mendoza, who taught me,
and whose voices reside in all that I write.

The River Warren

≈

Angel Finn

≈

ON THE NIGHT RIVER, everything seems far away, so far away it's come back around to being close, and a man can need nothing and want everything, and wonder what his life's all about at the same time that he knows. You can't see your line in the dark. It's all sound and feel, and I swear there've been times I smelled a strike coming before it came, a bigfish smell rising up to the water's surface from down in the real dark. Sometimes a baitfish'll go frantic before a strike, trying to swim away from the mouth opening behind it, hooked through the back and dangling in the current, and still something else kicks in when a big blue or channel cat comes gliding up out've the murk.

You got to start with the river, with its drop and slope and attention to gravity, and with the land out here that it drains. You got to start, far as I'm concerned, with the river's heart in the big freeze and thaw, and how time piles up on the land, and how sometimes you'll see it all there, nothing lost, shining through the moment. A man drives a semiload of cattle downhill and crashes through town and wrecks things and kills himself and his wife and the cattle, most people'll start with that. But I'm thinking it's surely funny how stories run backwards and how there's nothing like a death for starting them. No story in this town ever followed time well.

I'd come off the river that morning, and the town was as quiet as it's ever been. I parked the boat and went in to sleep, the sun barely thinning the dark in the east, and the next thing I know my neighbor'd walked right into the house and was standing over me and shaking me because I wouldn't answer his pounding on my door. I followed him downtown and couldn't believe what I saw. Leo Gruber was working within the sounds of the dying cattle, winching them off the truck, wordless and steady, the only person there who seemed to know what he was doing, everyone else standing around or just following orders. I did some repairs to the store, then couldn't see sense in listening to everyone guess at what'd happened, so I went back to the river.

Course if stories in this town don't follow time too well, maybe that's because time doesn't follow itself too well. It's like the river, with its back currents and side channels and backwashes, and its floodings when it doesn't know its own banks and has to rise up over them to take a look around and sort of remember what it once was. Talk's the same way. It loops and circles, gathers and runs, flows into something bigger than it knows, everyone pouring his own little stream in, till you can't tell if there's a beginning or an ending, or if you're in the main channel or a backwash or've gone over the banks with the flood.

The talk goes around and around about Two-Speed Crandall, but the talk's all about something else, like a whirlpool still in its center and everything going around it.

It's like Two-Speed, now that he's dead, and dead's about as still as you can get, he's drawn other stories to him, and they're all whirling around, and people're trying to see it all. There're two ways to look at a whirlpool. You can watch the whole thing, and it'll go smooth and won't seem to be moving at all, just standing there, a hole in the surface of the water. The other, you can watch one point go around, and you'll see the movement then, but you can't see the whole whirl. Apply that to Two-Speed Crandall and take it for what it's worth, which maybe isn't much, and you've got what's going on in this town.

You can look down the river at night and see the moonlight or starlight on the surface, and that surface can look hard and solid, and you can think that's the whole river, just what meets your eyes. Sometimes, even, just for the fun of deceiving myself, I'll think it, that the moment I'm seeing is everything, and the river's got no depth or current or creatures or snags or old, invisible waters.

Course it ain't true, any more'n it's true that all the stories going around this town are about Two-Speed Crandall. Why he hit my store I surely don't know. Maybe it was an accident, maybe not. It's easy to say it was, and maybe that's the best reason to believe it, but I've never yet met anyone who wanted to stay with the easy thing once he got started talking. Two-Speed was acting strange the last time I saw him, and I've heard he and Leo Gruber never got along, so you've got to wonder about Gruber's cattle being on the truck, though I don't know what it was made the bad blood between them.

Truth is, I know the sons better'n the fathers. The first

time I saw Luke Crandall and Jeff Gruber down on the river together I thought it was an odd thing: Luke a skinny kid, a year younger than Jeff, looking about as substantial as a spiderweb next to Jeff, and with a kind of hot, surprised look on his face most of the time, like he didn't know what to expect of the world but he was determined it wouldn't be good, and then Jeff Gruber, solid and square as a cutbank when you come around a bend, and always looking like he knew what he was about.

But there they were, down on the river together, jabbering like old friends, and I took a liking to them and started to teaching them things, and I never figured it was my business, even if I was curious, how they came to be friends when their fathers had such a reputation for not getting along. They had the kind of interest in the river they ought to've had, weren't down there just to drink and screw around, and that was enough for me, enough to take them fishing and show them what the river was and tell them what it'd been and still is in the right chances, when it lies on the land its old self, nothing ever disappearing, just falling into a different kind of seeing.

Anyway, you can look at Two-Speed Crandall all you want and figure what happened and guess and conjecture, you can be like Skeet Olson thinking the truth is in the events, and you can tell it over and over, thinking that if you just tell what actually happened enough times you'll get somewhere—but that's just looking at the surface of the river and thinking you're seeing the whole thing, forgetting it has a shape and form from way back.

Talk often enough starts with the end of something,

then circles around and finds itself, until people're satisfied and settle down. But if you're going to start at the start, you'd have to go clear back to who knows where? To why things freeze and thaw, including the heart sometimes, and why it sometimes won't thaw. People don't know half themselves. That's why I go fishing. I know I don't know myself on the river, but I swear that it knows me. And sometimes it'll let you in, and then you'll realize how big and old it is, and how long water can flow.

It happened to me once. Since then I've been less worried about beginnings and endings, more kind of thinking there isn't much difference. I wouldn't start with Two-Speed at all. I'd go as far back as you care to go, to the ways people know or don't know the deepest waters, and do my guessing from there.

Skeet Olson

≈

I'M THE ONLY ONE ACTUALLY SEEN IT. Since they reamed out my veins I been walking every morning. I go out of my house down to Main Street, then head south out of town up the hill to the section road, then west a mile, north a mile, east a mile back. I was at the curve on Highway 4 where it becomes Main Street when I heard the grunt of diesel above the hill. I looked up and could see smoke, a big thinning cloud growing into two black lines as they reached the edge of the hill.

You've seen how a semi looks coming over a hill. Like it's coming out of the earth, some chrome and smoky bug emerging. There it was then, flat and big, the sun all of a sudden whambright on the windshield. And I stopped walking. He came over the hill, and the diesel smoke kept right on pouring out of the stacks. Kept right on pouring. I stood there and thought, What the hell? What the hell? It was one of those things where you can't even name what's wrong, but your whole body knows it is. I didn't put it together like two plus two equals four, but more like the answer came first, four equals two plus two, except that the answer didn't make any sense, and the equation could have been a lot of other things, like three plus one, or two and thirteen-sixteenths plus whatever. New corn was growing in the fields, and a meadowlark sang on a fence post, and that diesel smoke went straight up into the sky, and I knew what was going to happen before I quite had the reasons I knew why.

"Jesus," I said. "He's not slowing down."

I stood on the curve, halfway up the hill, on the shoulder of the road, and watched. The sound of the engine came down at me like it was hard and heavy enough to knock me off the road.

It grew bigger and bigger, the cab red, the chrome stabbing me with sunlight. Coming down, coming down. Then over the sound of the engine I heard what if you go to hell and hear ghosts you'll hear, I imagine. My wife, Grace, tells me not to think such things. She keeps her mind on heaven, she tells me, because that's where her salvation lies. And sure. But I intend to appreciate salvation by knowing what I'm being saved from.

And I don't want to hear that sound again. When I fell on the floor that time and felt like death had a nail in its hand clawing around inside my chest, I thought not much could be worse. But I know now what's worse—to have death creep into you without a notice or muscle twitch and just sit there and stop your blood. When I heard that mooing, all those cattle—and don't ever tell me animals don't know something about the future, all those cattle bellering and lowing, like some big off-key organ with a soul—when I heard that coming down to me, my heart stopped entirely. I couldn't've run if there'd been a fire built under me. Couldn't've run if there'd been a flood.

Down it came, and I did this: I turned and looked behind me. I did. I looked to see if the town was still there, as if I thought maybe it'd up and move when it saw this riot roaring down. But there it was all right, sitting like always. There it was, covered in trees, hardly none of the houses visible, just a couple of the church steeples sticking up. The St. John's bells started ringing when I turned. Right then, they started ringing—and this thing roaring down.

I turned back. It was only a couple hundred yards away from me, and still gaining speed. "I can't believe," I said. "I don't. Who the hell?"

Then I knew.

I knew the way the cattle knew.

Then there he was, going by me, not even seeing me, I don't believe. I was lucky enough to be on the outside of the curve, because he took it like a race car driver, swinging wide at the beginning and cutting across the center to the inside shoulder and never once letting up on the accelerator. Two-Speed Crandall—as if anyone doesn't know.

And LouAnn beside him on the other seat. Flick, and they were gone. Gone, and I was looking at the back end of the thing, the road ditch grass whirling in the eddies, and the cattle's bellering coming back, and the meadowlark still singing, and the bells still going, and the diesel smoke curving over the trailer like two black horns and coming down to where I breathed.

But there was a moment when they went by that I'm not likely to forget. The sun left the windshield, and it was like I was staring into a dark, cool cave, and inside the cave were two faces that I knew, but they weren't like I'd ever seen them before. Two-Speed was looking out, but all he saw was the road. He didn't have a look on his face. He didn't have an expression. It was like his face was the road itself, like he was so intent on it that it ran right up the windshield and into his face. And that's what he had there—an expression without an expression, just lots of empty miles, like a road that goes nowhere and gets there too fast.

LouAnn was sitting sideways in her seat, and she had her hand on the air-horn pull, and she was looking right at Two-Speed, who wasn't looking at her, and she was ... well, I don't know. Her mouth was moving, so I guess she was talking to him, but he wasn't listening or caring. I got it like a photograph, that scene. Flick, and it's there and gone, and not a chance to change it. I'm gonna remember it for a long time.

I'm gonna remember it like this: Like they were carrying their own world down that hill. Like the space behind the windshield was something different than the space I was standing in. Like I didn't have nothing to do with them and them nothing to do with me. It sounds strange to say this, considering what was happening, considering what was going to happen, what did happen—it sounds real strange—but I can't think of nothing to make it clear but goldfish.

Grace has a goldfish bowl, and I'll be danged if I get it. Those fish just frustrate me. Stare at them long's you want, they still got nothing to do with you. They ain't in the world, not really. Once every day some food drops onto them from the world, some flecks of stink they eat. But that's it. They're in their own world, and they got their own space, and they don't care about you, and I'm not sure they care much about each other.

Take it for what it's worth, I don't know. But sometimes I get the feeling, watching them fish, that if they could pick their world up they'd smash it in your face—just to do it. And suffer the consequences. Suffer the gasping and dying. Just to do it. Just to spite your face.

Dr. Piersoll

≈

I THOUGHT I'D COME OUT TO the sticks after medical school, or what I thought was the sticks, and do some good for people instead of going after the bucks in suburbia. My med school pals thought I was crazy. By the time I figured out that I hadn't come here so much to do some good as to bless the people of the sticks with my suburban presence, I was too entrenched to move. I'd brought babies into the world and watched them grow, and I knew their parents and had kids of my own who were their friends. And I knew all the stories. So I bought some land, and my wife and I promised each other we'd go to Minneapolis once a month for theater or art, and we never kept that promise. Instead I learned to hunt ducks and pheasants and got pretty good at skeet shooting, and I trained my voice singing with the Lions Club at their Wednesday meetings. I can't tell you what's at the Guthrie this week, but I can probably tell you what became of most of the children I helped birth, or I can tell you what I've heard of them.

I know the talk that goes around as well as anyone, and I'm as ignorant of the events. The truth is, there's not much that anyone really knows about this last thing. We know this: Two-Speed Crandall came down the hill on Highway 4 with a semiload of Leo Gruber's cattle. He made the curve into town and threaded the semi between two trees and hit the mayor's new house with the swing of the trailer, opening up the living room, scattering two-by-fours and siding. He roared on down across the lawns of the entire block, leaving tracks in them all, then found another hole in the trees lining the sidewalk and emerged to descend on Main Street like a bowling ball among pins.

You can imagine all this from the evidence. You don't even need Skeet Olson's story, though he's a celebrity here lately, the only eyewitness—if that's any claim to the truth. But the only thing he knows that you couldn't figure out some other way is that Two-Speed was accelerating. And that just leads to questions, and guesses as to their answers. But the rest, what really happened, what we know—well, a semi isn't subtle. The truck hit the bank, smashed its automatic teller, destroyed its facade, its plate glass, its plants inside the windows. Then it went back across the street to smack Angel Finn's hardware store, sending files and hammers and hip waders spewing across the sidewalk. A twelve-pound maul, through some strange physics, flew across the street and embedded itself in the wooden front of the pool hall, where Walt Latham, the proprietor, had the good sense to leave it, as a draw to customers and an aid to conversation.

Mooing and roaring, the truck left the hardware store, straightened out, and hit the brick barbershop at the T on Main head-on. A little more speed and it would have gone right through and out the other side, but the bank and hardware store had slowed it down. The cab penetrated and came to a stop inside the building. Two-Speed Crandall was ejected through the windshield. He came to rest upside down over the second and never-used barbershop chair. There's some symbolism there. In death as well as life he didn't quite fit the places where he landed.

LouAnn was with him. She remained inside the cab. And that's all anyone knows for sure. By the time I got there the police and firemen had extricated her and Two-Speed and were placing them inside an ambulance, needlessly. I checked them, but then climbed into the ambulance anyway and went with them to the hospital in Clear River. I'd helped to birth their sons, and even here anymore, you've got to protect yourself against any claim to carelessness.

Through the back window of the ambulance I saw the firemen washing off the street. They didn't know what else to do. Nothing in their training had prepared them for anything like this. They were used to hooking up hoses and turning nozzles on problems, so that's what they did. The water crashed out, white with air, and hit the mass of blood flowing from the cattle in the semi, and ran in pink froth down the gutters. Only later, when Leo Gruber arrived, would he see what had to be done. The firemen, I've heard, shut off their hoses when he stepped from his car. They watched as he walked to the wreckage of the semi and peered through the slats, and in the silence they heard for the first time the hoarse breathing of cattle. Until then no one had stopped to listen. Leo turned and walked to the fire chief and asked for a four-wheel-drive pickup with a winch.

But you see how quickly you move from the evidence. Already I'm telling what I've been told.

Pop Bottle Pete

≈

SOMETIMES THE SUN'S REAL HOT. Sometimes it's real hot. It's real hot like fire, and I feel like an egg. I fry. Just like an egg.

But the bottles're cool. They're in the grass. In the ditches in the grass. People throw them away. Cans too. Sometimes I see them. But not usually. I usually don't see them throw them away. If I saw, I'd know where to look. Usually I just walk and look. Because they do it at night and always. Even in winter, when I stay home. So I have to walk and look.

When the sun's real hot I feel like an egg. I sizzle. I sizzle with my mouth. Sizz-z-z-z-z-le. Like an egg. But I still look.

The bottles're cool. The cans aren't cool, but the bottles are. They're both in the grass, but the bottles are always cool. Sometimes there's something in them. I'll sometimes taste. If no one's coming on the road. So they don't think. Especially Coke. It's the real thing. It sticks at my mouth. I'd like to play volleyball on a beach. With girls. That'd be the real thing.

People wave to me. They honk their horns. I wave back.

They wave and honk their horns. If a semi goes by, I raise my fist and go up and down with it. Sometimes they pull the big horn. Wa-a-a, wa-a-a-a. Like a ship. Like fog. When they do that, even if it's hot, I don't feel like an egg. I feel like lost in a fog. Like I wish they would pull the big horn always and make me feel fog lost.

He always did. Wa-a-a-a, wa-a-a-a, wa-a-a-a-a, until I couldn't hear it no more. I didn't have to raise my hand for him. He'd start way before. Before I even saw him. Wa-a-a-a-a, wa-a-a-a. I always knew it was him, cause he'd start way before. Wa-a-a-a-a-a-a-a-a-a-a, he'd sometimes go.

I'd shut my eyes. I was a ship and he was a ship. In the cool fog. But we weren't going to hit.

Then he'd yell my name. Not Pop Bottle like most people. He'd yell Pe-e-e-e-eter-r-r. Big and loud. Out his window, going by. He'd stop his horn so he could yell. My name. I'd open my eyes, and there he'd be. Grinning at me. Waving. I'd yell back and wave. Si-i-i-i-im-o-o-o-n. Not Two-Speed like most people. His name. Simon.

We'd yell our names at each other and wave and laugh.

Then, when he was past me, he'd throw a bottle out. One I could return. They're worth a nickel. People throw them away. But all you have to do is take them back, and they'll give you a nickel. Or a dollar if you have enough. He threw it out because we yelled our names at each other.

Then he'd wa-a-a-a again until I couldn't hear it no more. I never felt like an egg then. I felt cool and good.

He was just feeling like an egg. Like he was sizzling and sizzling, and he couldn't find something cool. Sometimes if

I don't find a bottle for a long time, and the sun's real hot, I'll feel like smashing myself. Just to let the hot out.

That's what he did. Because he couldn't find something cool. You can't feel like an egg all the time. You have to smash yourself.

I never sold the bottles he threw. I got them on a shelf. I probably got enough, I could buy a Walkman.

But I'd rather have the bottles. He always wa-a-a-ed and waved and called my name. And I called Simon.

Leo Gruber

≈

DUMB BRUTE EYES, WAITING.
You do what you have to do.

Arlene Schuh

≈

PRAYERS. THAT'S WHAT IT WAS. I been living across from that house for twenty-two years, and I seen some odd things go on there, I'll admit I like to stand and watch. I know the jokes, how people say I know what people've done before they've done it, so that they got to hear the gossip I tell about them to find out what sin they're supposed to commit next. All right. But I've seen myself through the gossip too, had it come swinging around behind me, like when my first husband left me, turned into something I didn't recognize, turned into my fault and shame.

So I've earned the right to talk, maybe, the right to stand at a window and watch. My children are gone except for the holidays, and my second husband's dead, and what is there to do but watch and talk? And anyway, people talk about my talking, That Arlene, she has more stories than anyone I know. So I give back as much as I take, and maybe there's a balance in that.

And anyway, what's better? What's better for an older woman living alone? To cry over soap operas? I know some women do that, people they don't even know acting out lines that writers they know even less have written, and they'll, some of them women, talk about their soaps like they were talking about real people. That happened to me once, I heard Thelma and Janet outside the Super Valu talking about what'd happened to some people, and I perked up my ears while I was putting groceries in the trunk. Finally I couldn't stay out of it no more so I went up to them and asked who they was talking about, and when they give me names I didn't know I wasn't quite sure for a second who I was. Then Janet said, "You know, on *Days of Our Lives*?" and I got so mad, I said, "You mean you've been standing here talking about a *soap opera*?" It made me mad. You tell me who has a better hold on what's real, them women who can talk that way about a soap opera, talk like you'd think it was their next-door neighbor had the abortion or the affair, or me who when I talk at least have something outside my window to talk about? You tell me what's better, to stare into a fake window at fake people and think it's real, or to stare through a real window at real people and wonder where they're fake?

So I don't care, you can believe all of what I say or none, you can pick and choose at your own liking. I'm saying it was prayer. Skeet Olson seen her mouth moving when they went by him, him on one of his walks, I think he just wants to get away from Grace, she's so trying-to-be-holy it must drive God nuts. I can't imagine what she and Skeet talk about together—how much further along she is? Like heaven's at the end of a ladder and she's skittering up the rungs? Anyway, Skeet was out on the highway when they come down the hill, and he saw the whole thing from start to finish, and he says she was looking sideways and her mouth was moving when they went by. She was praying, that's what she was doing. If the humble and the miserable inherit the kingdom then LouAnn Crandall is receiving her own. She was praying them both into heaven, if anything could get that man into heaven, which I doubt.

Twenty-two years I lived across the street from them, and I seen how it was in that house, her raising them three boys alone, if it's possible to do what you'd call "raise" with boys like that. Though Luke turned out all right, him and Jeff Gruber was such good friends, and maybe that had something to do with it, and here it's Leo Gruber's cattle Two-Speed took down with him. After he left that night to go out to Gruber's to load them cattle, LouAnn come out of the house, I hardly seen him go and there she is. More and more she'd leave like that after he went on a run, going to her sister's place in Clear River for the night, I guess. Ever since Frederick died right in bed beside me I been troubled by insomnia. I think it was that I woke up and he was cold. I slept right through it, and when I woke I reached over to shake him and get him going, and when my hand touched his shoulder it was like when I was a girl and we was playing, running to a brick wall and touching it and running back, and I run too fast and couldn't stop myself and put both hands against the wall, and then it was like the wall pushed back, my elbow locked and I heard a snap, and just like that I'd broke my arm. That was almost the feeling when I reached out to push Frederick's shoulder, it was so hard and solid and stiff, he must've died almost as soon as he went to sleep, that my push come back up my arm and pushed my heart right down to my feet.

Sometimes it feels to me yet that it's still there. Ever since, I've had trouble sleeping.

So I seen a lot of their comings and goings. She never left the house when he was around, anybody in town knows that. LouAnn Crandall if she'd been seen any less would've been invisible, and him down at the bar every other night carousing and who knows what all, but making sure she stayed home in that house that who knows what it must have been like on the inside, if how he let the outside fall apart is any sign?

Sometimes I don't know why women put up with men. Maybe I shouldn't be talking, the way I put up with my first husband, the less said about him the better, and when he finally does leave me, everyone says it's me chased him away, me who had the problem. But all right, Arlene, let's be honest with yourself, that's how you felt, too. Sometimes I think the gossip gets told about ourselves just the way we want it told, then we turn around and blame the stories for being nasty, and blaming makes us feel better even though we think we're feeling worse. I don't know. I felt like something bad'd been done to me, and it was my fault, too, and then I turned around and got mad at the ones who said just what I was feeling. So I don't know, maybe we're in control all the time.

Well, of course, Arlene, she'll say anything to defend gossiping. That's what the ones who think they're too good for a story would say about that. But I've never quite trusted them's won't listen to a story. Makes me wonder how people run their lives so perfect if they won't listen to how other people've screwed up theirs. I surely don't know, though, how LouAnn Crandall put up with Two-Speed long's she did. Hope's pretty deep, I guess. Pretty deep and wide, and there's nothing a woman can drown in easier, and that must've been what it was with LouAnn—treading water in a lake of hope. And every time Two-Speed got drunk, every time he come home raging, just adding another stone to the dam, which ought to be the reverse, ought to be that'd break the dam down and hope'd flow away and leave LouAnn standing high and dry on something solid, even if it'd be barren and full of rocks, just a drained, dead lake bed. But it don't work that way with some women, and maybe I better include myself, though I finally got over it. I finally realized two years after I got rid of my first husband that I was re-lieved, and all the guilt and shame I'd let hang on my heart was nothing but disguise, because I didn't want to admit I was relieved he was gone. I was relieved—and this is the hard part—that I didn't have to hope no more.

Women're scared of not having nothing to hope for. So they'll grab onto the worst kind of hope, which is hoping for what's hopeless, but it's also the best kind because it never ends, so it's always there. So LouAnn, every time Two-Speed'd do something that ought to've blown a hole in that dam, she'd be over there treading water and patching it up, building the dam higher and thicker, and the hope getting deeper and wider under her, until she can't see no way of ever swimming out, can't see nothing but this big lake of hope, can't see grass or trees, until she thinks this is what life is, these waves of hope running toward her, and this fear that if she lets the dam fall apart she'll be swept away to nothing.

Well, even for me I got carried away there. What I was saying was that she come out of the house that night, and I knew something was up. She almost followed him out the door, it was that soon after he left, and she went to that big green car of theirs, and I could see her reach over and lock all the doors, just enough light from the street lamps for me to see that. She backed out of the driveway onto the street and just sat there, looking at the house, and I knew it then. She's finally leaving him, I said to myself.

I wanted to open my window and yell at her, Way to go, LouAnn, but of course I didn't, I just stood there and watched her watch her house, me standing back away from the window in the dark, way back, but even then wondering if maybe she knew I was there and almost hoping she'd look up and wave at me so I'd know for sure. But she finally drove away without looking up or nothing, and who can blame her, I never did nothing for her really, and maybe she never realized I was awake up there at all.

He must've known she was leaving him, though, because he had to've gone and gotten her after he had the cattle on, because she was sure enough on that truck when it come down, though why she'd get into that truck with him I don't know. Maybe she looked at her life and thought, I've come this far, why not go the rest the same way, what's the difference?

Anyway, all I meant to say was that she was praying when Skeet saw them, that's what it had to be, prayers for herself and for him and maybe for this whole town that never once did anything for her. Let's all take some blame here, and I'll be the first, living across the street for twenty-two years and at the last just watching, waiting for her to make some decision, and not even yelling that I approved. We all got some blame, and that's partly why we talk like this, trying to pin down the blame in ourselves.

But, too, what're you going to do? We got two dead people, we got a funeral, we got half the town wrecked and the cattle dead. Those're things we can say, They happened. But before that, what? Rumors and guesses, things that might've happened and might've not, in a house that holds people who're not relatives and not friends and who might just be different, and everything can be explained that way—they're just different.

It's not polite to intrude on someone's strangeness, not polite to even let on you notice. And even if you had proof for everything you wondered, what could you do? People live their lives the way they're going to live them. So if I had gone to LouAnn and said something to her, and she hadn't seen it as an intrusion, which she most likely would've, even then what difference would it've made?

Of course, Arlene, I got to say to myself, that's all just excuses, too. The difference between what might just happen and trying to make it happen is too big for words. So yes, I'm to blame, the old gossip who lived in the house across the street and never did nothing. And this whole town, too, who counted them as not quite neighbors, people who never fit in even if their kids went to the same school with the rest and lived in the same place. Not quite neighbors— that's who they were.

But even in the end, I bet, praying for us all. I'll give up gossiping in heaven if it was anything else she was doing.

That man knew she'd finally got the downright guts to leave him, and he crawled under that semi and did something to the brakes just in case he chickened out when the time come. And then he went to Clear River with that load of cattle and got her out of her sister's house. Then he come back to Cloten, because he had to do it here on that hill and in this town, make it a big production, make it a show, and it wouldn't surprise me if he told her he loved her, and that's why all this was necessary.

Then he hit that hill fast, just like Skeet says, and the rest is known. Except that LouAnn was praying, holding the air-horn pull and praying, and behind her the steers were bellering, and the road running underneath, and the morning sun coming through the windshield, and the town rushing up at her. But she'd blocked it all out, looking right at Two-Speed and praying, and him pumping the brakes, wishing he'd never done what he'd done. But there she was, taking his revenge—or whatever it was—away from him with her prayers, forgiving everything ever done to her, and everything ever not done for her, calm as ice, praying him into heaven even while he was killing her. Praying him into heaven whether he wanted it or not.

Luke Crandall

≈

YOU SPEND YEARS LIVING WITH other people, you'd think you'd know them like the back of your own eyelids. And you do. But what you know still surprises you. You can map them out. You can say, When this happens, that will too. You can put a red dot in your mind, the point they will reach. It's you that you don't know. It's that your mind's color-blind as a deer's. It puts the red dot there, and then can't see it. So one thing happens, then the next, right like you knew it would. But you're surprised. It's like lights are shining in your eyes, and all you can do is stare.

There are a lot of ways to bullshit yourself. If there's one thing he taught me, it's that. In biology class in high school, we learned the taxonomy of living things, three major divisions back then—the plants, the animals, and what I called the fink-outs, the ones left over they couldn't classify, so they lumped them all together and told everyone they'd done it.

In class one day the teacher was defending this whole scheme. I thought: This is bullshit. Then I thought: How about a taxonomy of bullshit?—the kingdoms, the orders, the classes, the families, the genuses, the species. The gradations and nuances of bullshit. The three kingdoms I saw right away: Bullshit of Yourself, Bullshit of Someone Else, and Bullshit about Bullshit. The third one wasn't actually a category at all. It was an example of itself, what was left over when you couldn't figure out your own bullshit.

I worked two weeks, using the taxonomic system in the back of the book as a model. When I was done I had five pages outlined and organized. I found a place for it all: Bullshit by Drinking, Bullshit by Forgetting, Bullshit by Fighting, by Doing, by Not Doing, by Not Listening, by Not Caring, by Too Much Silence and Too Much Talk, by Doing the Opposite of What You Say You'll Do, by Doing Something Only Close to What You Say You'll Do, Bullshit by Religion, by Politics, by Argument—and Bullshit by Classification.

I had it all down clear, like a straight road in the daylight. It was all bullshit, but there it was. I never actually studied for biology, but I got so familiar with the taxonomic system that when we took a test on it, I scored 100 percent. Didn't miss a single question. The teacher didn't believe it. He accused me of cheating—he didn't know how and he didn't care—and he gave me an F. I had to add Bullshit by Testing to the system after that.

I said to the teacher, Screw you and your test. Ask me anything you want. Ask me this. Then I started asking him questions about taxonomy, and when he didn't have the answers, I gave them to him. I went on shouting Latin names while he wrote out the slip to the principal's office. I called him the Latin name for a lemur when I went out the door, but he never figured it out. On the way down the hall I laughed. He'd gotten rid of me, but I'd taken him, and we both knew it.

Then I stopped in the middle of the hall. Holy shit, I thought, how'd I know all that stuff? I started in again, testing myself. I jumped around the taxonomic system but couldn't find anything I didn't know. I was standing there when the principal came by and asked me what I was doing out of class. Running through the taxonomic system, I said, handing him the slip. He laughed. He thought I was joking—Bullshit by Confusing Serious with Funny.

In his office he asked what'd happened, and I told him straight and all of it. He said, It sounds like you know the material, son, and though you shouldn't be yelling at the teacher, I can understand why you were angry, and would you be willing to take another test, here in my office, where we can prove to the teacher that you weren't cheating?

No, I said, I wouldn't be willing to prove anything to anybody.

But Luke, he said, ready to launch into a speech.

I held up my hand, and he went silent. I thought, My God, this is a magic moment if ever I had one. Learn something well, and you got everyone paying attention.

Look, I said to him, I don't have to prove anything. If I cheat, and you ask me if I cheated, I'll say yes. All you got to do is ask. And if you ask and I haven't cheated, I'll tell you no. And if you accuse me without any evidence at all except who I am, then I'll say, Screw you. He never asked, but I'm telling you I didn't cheat, and I'm the only one in that class who got this kind of treatment, and I'll be fucked, sir, if I'll take that test again.

That kind of language isn't appropriate, he said, can't you see I'm trying to help, I'm on your side? I'm trying to find a way to make things work for everyone.

You want to help me, I said, you go tell him you believe me. Tell him, just on who I am and what I've said. Then let him make up his mind. I won't care what he decides. That's how you can help me. Say you believe me.

But he wouldn't do it. He was operating under Bullshit by Compromise. Nothing bugs a compromiser more than someone who won't see the wisdom of the middle way. As if someone isn't actually right. Sure I could've taken another test and proved myself, but he thought that was the whole issue. Bullshit by Compromise is the species, Bullshit by Seeing Only Direct Opposites the genus, Bullshit by Mistaking a Part for the Whole the family, Bullshit of Yourself the kingdom. The principal couldn't see that the issue wasn't the A or the F. If it was that, and we're compromising, why not just give me a C?

I wasn't about to take another test—Bullshit by Giving In. I wasn't about to say, OK, I want the A and I can get it—Bullshit by Changing Your Priorities. I wasn't about to let them think that just because they had the power they had the right—Bullshit by Confusing One Thing for Another.

I got the F—but they were wrong. And I learned that when you really know something, people listen to you. They may not get outside their own bullshit to do something about it, but they listen. I'd been right before on things in school—been in detention for no reason, even gotten kicked out just for being in the wrong place at the wrong time, and someone took a look and said, Ah, there's that Crandall kid.

But those times no one'd listen to me because all I had was right. I didn't have the knowledge to go with it.

I realized that all the stuff I'd convinced myself I couldn't learn was a snap, nothing to it, and if I didn't learn it, they were going to use it against me all my life—Bullshit by Holding the Cards. I decided then and there, sitting out the class in the principal's office while he pretended to work, pissed off as hell—You're just being stubborn, son, he said, and if you won't help me out then I can't help you either. To which I replied, You don't need my help, sir, and I guess you never will, and while I could use yours I've got to have it real, not some fake appearance of it. At which point he ended our conversation, Bullshit by Stopping a Conversation You Haven't Been Listening to Anyway. I decided then and there I was going to learn things; I'd been bullshitting myself and everyone else about being stupid.

The wanting to learn was still a problem. Once or twice, just to see, I studied a little and got A's on tests. It made Mom happy, but still I felt like I was giving in to something. The third time I almost felt sick looking at that grade, a big A from a teacher who had this note next to it that said, Way to go, Luke, I'm proud of you. I looked at that and thought, What, she thinks I got this grade for her? What's she mean, she's proud of me?

There are entomologists in jungles constantly finding new insects. There are people who get up at three in the morning during a new moon to discover comets that've been circling the sun forever. And the same way, once you start to classify bullshit, your whole day becomes a discovery. Just when you think you have a closed system, you find a new one: Bullshit by Learning What You Don't Want to Learn.

I looked at that A and that note and felt disgusted with myself, like I was the biggest bullshitter of all. My God, I thought, she thinks this stuff matters to me. I reached out and crumpled the test up. My hand seemed to do it by itself, move over and lay on top of that test for a moment and then slowly gather it up and crush it. I watched the paper fold and bend, the creases creeping up on the A until it buckled and deformed and disappeared into creases within creases. Multiple choice, hell. It came to me while I watched the correct answer to question fourteen, a C, disappear, that multiple choice means no choice at all, that if you're given the question and have to choose from someone else's answers, you're not choosing anything. It came to me that if you get to think about an answer and come up with it yourself, you're close to choosing something, but beyond that, even, is asking the questions. Only the person who asks the questions has any choice in anything.

I'd thought in the principal's office that knowing things was power and freedom but realized as I crumpled that test that it was just another form of bullshit—Knowing the Right Answers to Someone Else's Questions. The people asking the questions wanted the ones giving the answers to just go on giving answers. They spent so much time trying to convince us that knowing the answers was important. And no wonder: If they could just convince us of that, they got to go on asking the questions.

Not that they all even knew they were doing it. I looked away from my hand up to the front of the room and saw my teacher watching me. Her face sagged like a wet sheet that'd been billowed out by the wind and then the wind drops and the sheet just hangs there on a tight line, damp and limp. That A'd been some kind of wind for her, and when I crumpled it into the paper and lifted my face, she sagged. It reminded me of my mom's face, sometimes, looking at Dad. My own face felt like one of those cottonwood snags that've been sitting in the river for years, and the sun has bleached it, and the current has worn it, but it just keeps getting grimmer and sharper and snaggier from it.

I saw her face fall like a damp sheet, and I realized, She doesn't even know she's doing it. She thinks she's helping me go somewhere. She looked like it was something personal against her, like I was crumpling up and throwing away her hopes.

She didn't know all this was bullshit, because her questions were just answers to someone else's questions. I stared at her face up there at the front of the room, and I thought, Shit. How far back does this go? Who really gets to ask the questions? Where do you find those people?

When I wrote that taxonomy of bullshit, I was just a novice. I'd done five pages and thought I'd catalogued it all, thought no one in the world knew more about bullshit than me. And now I saw that I hadn't even tapped it, that bullshit doesn't just coat the surface of things but was the things themselves, the structures, the way things get done.

I'd never realized that most people couldn't help but b.s. I'd thought people knew they were doing it when they did it. But looking at that teacher's face, I felt sorry for her. We were in the same boat, none of us knowing anything but answers to questions asked by someone so far back in the scheme of things we couldn't ever reach him.

I finished crumpling the paper, then got out of my desk—the Bullshit of Neat Rows—and walked to the front of the room. The teacher watched me all the way, never saying a word, that damp-sheet face fixed on me. I went up and dropped the test into the wastebasket near her desk. I felt like I was walking through a kind of light that my own mind was producing. I'd always liked this teacher. She was young, and I liked the way she looked at me and leaned over my desk.

So I wasn't trying to hurt her or put her down. It was more that I was walking in a space created in my head, this world I saw of factories and office buildings and farms and stores and grain elevators. And there were all these people working in them thinking they're in control of their jobs and lives: putting notes into suggestion boxes and forming committees and having discussions and solving problems and nodding their heads and looking earnest, and all of it just answering questions that their bosses have given them. And then the bosses going back to their offices and writing notes and letters and buying and selling and making decisions and asking questions about this and that and quizzing their employees and writing memos and thinking, by God, they're the ones who get to ask the questions, sitting in their smug and smiley worlds and never figuring out that their questions are just answers given to them by someone even higher up, multiple choice: A, B, C, D, and all or none of the above.

I saw it like tiers of people going up the outside of a

pyramid, and every tier thinking they're the ones with the choices, they're the ones with the questions, just because they get to ask them to the tier below. But way up at the top, so high I couldn't even see him, there was someone who handed them all down, big questions that disintegrated tier by tier into smaller and smaller questions that were nothing but answers, really.

And then I couldn't tell if there was someone up there with questions or if the pyramid itself was made of bullshit, piled and packed so solid that it'd support any weight you put on it. And the only way to find out would be to somehow get to the top and find whoever did the asking, or else get to the bottom and off the thing and walk away from it entirely.

I threw the test in the wastebasket and stood by the teacher's desk for a moment. I didn't know what to say to her, because I knew she was doing what she could. Finally I just shrugged and tried to smile. Thanks, I said. For trying, you know. But it's all bullshit. I mean, really—all of it.

She didn't understand. I saw her face go doubtful, wary with that look teachers get when they're not sure if a student is trying to make them look stupid or not. I took another try. Hey, I said, I know I can learn. I know that.

Nothing changed in her face, but I couldn't do any more. Maybe some day she'd understand that I was trying to say she'd done good work by me, as far as she could. I turned around and the whole class was watching me, figuring I was up to something. I almost gave them all the finger, but then I felt sorry for them, too, sitting in their tiers and seeing only the tier above them and the tier below and not even knowing they were on the pyramid, thinking that kicking around the people on the tier below and having the chance to graduate to the tier above was some kind of freedom.

I saw the truth of all the cartoons I'd ever watched, saw my classmates as Wile E. Coyotes and Elmer Fudds and Daffy Ducks, falling down big holes and throwing off rocks they could jump onto, thinking they were saving themselves, and thinking they were going up when they were going down, because everything was going down around them. Or holding double-barreled shotguns bigger than they were, weady to bwast something, or quacking around in a frenzy, and all the time running down roads and chasing something someone else had drawn within a set of rules someone else had made that weren't even rules, that could change whenever the chaser was close to getting what he wanted. Jesus, I thought, you gotta step out of the damn cartoon.

Fuck it, Dad, I thought. I won't be a rock for you anymore. You and that goddamn cattle prod. I won't even be a coyote like you are. All your threats and promises. And I'll be screwed if I'll be a roadrunner, sticking out my tongue at the poor bastards who have no choice but to chase me and no chance to catch me, no matter how well they fly. If you won't step out of the damn cartoon, I sure as hell will, or at least I'll try. If I have to go right through the cartoon to do it, I will. Maybe I'll do like Mom says and become one of those college-educated bastards you're always complaining about. Of course Mom never stepped out of the cartoon either.

I didn't flip the class the bird. I could feel the teacher's eyes on me as I walked back to my seat and took my place. I took my place. Looking at all those faces as I walked back, I thought, Hell, they don't even want to ask the questions, maybe. They think a question is something that if you make a mark on a piece of paper, it's over, done with. I took my place, but I took it knowing what it was and where it was—in a row of desks in a square room in a square building in a square town in a square section, tiers going out. I took my place, but I thought, I'm asking my own questions from now on. If I have to go on giving answers for a long time, fine. If I have to go right through the bullshit, fine. But I'm getting off the pyramid and out of this cartoon, and I'm going to quit chasing the roadrunners someone else has drawn for me and quit falling down the holes they've drawn, too.

I sat down hard in my place and stared at the teacher, but I didn't really see her. Dammit, Dad, I thought. Dammit, Mom. Why couldn't you do it, too?

And now, good God, they have.

Jeff Gruber

≈

ON THE PHONE MY MOTHER asked me if I was coming back for the funeral.

"Should I?" I asked back.

"They were the parents of your best friend," she said.

"I haven't talked to Luke since we moved here," I said. "He's not going to miss me."

"But he might notice if you're there."

"Maybe," I said. I began to think of reasons I could give for not going. But before I could think of more than a couple, my mother said, "I don't know why I'm talking. I'm not sure I'd care if they buried him and no one came."

I couldn't say much to that. Her Christian understanding was generally pretty boundless.

"All those cattle," she said. "You wouldn't believe the mess."

"Pretty bad, huh?"

"Bad. Your father . . ."

"What?"

She didn't answer right away. The line snapped and buzzed.

"Not all of them died," she said. "He had to go through the semi and shoot quite a few of them."

Becca watched me over Jenny's head. Jenny grabbed a handful of her mother's hair and pulled. Becca winced, took Jenny's hand in hers, and squeezed until Jenny released the hair.

"That had to be tough."

"It was. On both of us."

"Two-Speed Crandall," I said, "what a strange thing."

"I never liked him hauling cattle for us. But I never thought he'd do this."

"*Do* this? What do you mean?"

"You hate to say it, don't you?"

"Mom, I don't know what you're talking about."

"That Two-Speed killed those cattle to get back at your father. When he's dead himself. And LouAnn. It sounds selfish. They're dead, and here I am thinking about our cattle, and your father."

Becca picked Jenny up and carried her into the living room. I watched them go, Jenny's fat face wrinkling in a smile at me as she receded.

"But I suppose it could have been an accident," Mom said.

"Quite an accident."

"The sheriff is saying he doesn't know. A bad brake line, maybe. Things were such a mess, it's hard to tell."

"Do you really think so, though?"

"It's possible." She paused. "No, I don't," she said. "Skeet Olson, you remember him? He says he saw Two-Speed accelerating down the hill. He won't talk to the police, though. Says what's the point, probably have to go to Clear River and sign a statement, and what difference would it make? But no one else saw it. Everyone was in church."

"He should've had those cattle delivered by then," I said. "What was he even doing in the county yet? That's no accident."

"Maybe he was drunk."

"Two-Speed Crandall? He wouldn't be drunk and driving."

"I suppose."

Then she said more quietly, "If he were, it might make me feel less bitter."

I made up my mind then. I'd go down, to the funeral, to whatever. My mother, I could tell, wanted me to come. And I'd see Luke. But as soon as I decided to go, an old renunciation gripped me. It was as if the land I'd put behind me still throbbed inside my heart, saying yesyes yesyes yesyes, while my helpless mind said no.

"It's up to you, Jeff," Becca said. I knew she'd say it, and yet hoped she wouldn't. I wanted her to give me a reason to stay in Duluth, some small expression of disappointment at my absence, or some sense that she could use my help with Jenny. Out on the lake three ore ships sat gray and motionless. They'd been sitting that way for two days now. They looked like rocks out there, floating on the hard surface of the water like strange, stone castles.

"I know what you're thinking," Becca said when I didn't reply to her. "We've been through this before. Personally, I like your father. I'd just as soon you got along with him. If you don't want to go down there, don't. But if you're going to ask me, I'm going to tell you to go."

She gazed at me, her eyes only slightly bluer than the lake. "I'll go," I said. "For the funeral. Just for that."

"Sure."

"What rule says I have to get along with my father? What rule says I have to want to see him?"

"None."

Jenny watched me. For a moment I had the sense that she could understand my words. I sat down on the couch and held out my arms for her. She toddled over, and I picked her up.

"All right, then," I said.

"All right." Becca stood for a moment watching me. "It's your home. Your family. You do what you want."

She started for the kitchen. Then she turned back to me. "Dammit," she said. "Maybe I do care. You really want my advice? Go back there and work it out. Because it's not just you anymore. It's Jenny. And me. We've got a daughter, and she's got grandparents. And it'd be nice if she knew them a little better. Yeah, Jeff, maybe I'd like that."

I had my arms wrapped around Jenny. I realized I was touching the scar in my right palm with the fingers of my left hand. I looked down, then closed my hand into a fist. Jenny, thinking I was hiding something, tried to pry my fingers open. I showed her I had nothing there. She reached out and touched the scar, her fingers soft and warm against it.

I looked sideways out the window at the three ships in the distance. Then I glanced at Becca. "He shouldn't have put him on that tractor," I said. "Never should have put him on that tractor."

"It was years ago," Becca said. "And anyway, you were driving tractor at that age."

"Not like that," I said. "Not that job."

She held my eyes for a moment, then shook her head. "I'd like to understand, Jeff," she said. "And I do, a little. But you've got your own child now. And a child makes it now. It can't be then anymore. That was years ago. Jenny's now. It's all I've got time for."

She turned and went into the kitchen. I gazed out the window, with Jenny on my lap, at the cold water, the gray ships.

The lake was so flat it looked convex, as if it sank toward the horizon. Jenny calmed in my arms, put her head against my shoulder, shut her eyes. She resisted sleep, though, and opened them again to stare at me. Even in her open eyes I saw the daze of sleep. She blinked, gave in, melted against me. I put my face into her silken hair and gazed at the flat, sunken water.

For a long time after Chris died, a single dream troubled me. With Jenny asleep in my arms, so warm and safe, I didn't want to remember it. But my mother's call, and the thought of Luke's parents rolling down that single, long hill into town to die, and the unforgiving flatness of the lake before me all called it forth, stronger than Jenny's charm.

It was always the same dream. I stood surrounded by black land rippling in plow waves away from me under a motionless sky. I stood alone. All around me, wherever I looked, the land stretched away to the line where it met the arch of the sky. It seemed to be breathing under my feet, seemed to swell and subside. I rose and fell slightly, and I could almost hear it. I had to struggle to keep my balance. I tipped and swayed.

Then, far away, as if it began under the horizon, something moved. At first, every time in the dream even though I dimly knew I had dreamed it before, I stared at the movement, puzzled. It looked as if the horizon had been raised, as if the line that marked it had risen just a little into the sky. But it seemed to go on rising, higher and higher, the black land going gradually up, the blue of the sky giving way before it.

I realized that the land was bulging, that the bulge was moving toward me, not getting higher, but nearer—and then I realized with growing terror that it was a wave, a swell, that the land had gained fluidity, and that something had disturbed it, and coming toward me from beyond the horizon was a literal groundswell. Across the distance between me and the horizon it came and came, until it rose high above me, blocking out the sky, an immense black wave with clods of dirt curling at its top and rolling down, and it made a sound like an entire forest moving in the wind. I watched it, horrified, my feet planted firmly in the soil as if they had grown roots, and then I felt it lift me, felt myself rise up on it, and suddenly I realized my younger brother was beside me, that I'd never been alone until this moment—when I realized that all along Chris had been beside me watching it, too, but that in this instant of knowing he was here we would be forever parted. I reached for him, crying out, but I couldn't touch him though he reached for me, too. We reached for each other across the broad back of the land rising up around us, reached as it carried us apart.

I rose up on the groundswell, light, buoyed by it, as if the roots that had anchored me before it now floated me high above its surface, carrying me upward into the blue, light sky. But Chris didn't float like I did, and even as I reached for him, as my cry turned to a scream, I saw it engulf him, saw him disappear into it as if he were a knife piercing some soft flesh, a knife sucked into a body that invited it. I shot headfirst toward the sky through the clods breaking all around me, shot through screaming for Chris, and I saw far below me his white, frightened face and his arm still reaching, and I tried to dive back into the land, tried to turn and shoot beneath the wave toward him to save him with my own lightness, bear him up, but I couldn't pierce the wave, couldn't penetrate it, couldn't turn and force my hands and head beneath it. It was as if my rooted feet forced me upright, like one of those punching clowns that always rebounds.

At the last moment of the dream I am standing in the sky, on the curling top of the clotted wave, and around me is nothing but blueness, and air so thin I can hardly breathe, and I am expending all of its rarity in screaming for Chris, who is gone, who is so far beneath me and under so much weight that nothing will ever touch him, no hand will ever reach him. And I, at the top of the wave, am part of that weight, so that I feel, though I weigh nothing, that I am driving him down, burying him, riding the wave, riding the land that devoured him. And everything is flat again, the horizon again a straight line where black meets blue without motion. And I am awake, and Chris is gone, and I am gasping for breath and struggling to shut the door to the past, where I did not save him either.

Elizabeth Gruber

≈

I WANT JEFF HOME. For just a little while. I want something besides Leo's silence. Leo will be all right. I won't let him retreat to the kind of silence he did that other time. And he won't let himself. But still it would be good to have Jeff here, to talk of other things. Perhaps he'll bring Becca and Jenny. It's been so long since I've seen them. Not since Jenny was born, when I went up to visit. Seeing Jenny would do Leo so much good. It isn't right that he's never seen his granddaughter. It would take his mind off those dead and dying cattle.

I don't believe it was an accident. Maybe that's all the more reason to remind myself it might have been. But even reminding myself, I don't believe it. I should feel for their deaths, especially LouAnn's. But even his, because whatever you say about him, and who knows what the truth is, he was a human being. But I don't feel anything. And I don't feel anything about not feeling anything.

We'd just come out of church. We'd heard the fire sirens, and the volunteer firemen had left the service. But we had no idea what really happened. The service went on, the songs and sermon. Only later, when the doors had opened, and we were standing on the church steps, all of a sudden everyone knew it wasn't a fire.

But no one seemed to know what it was. Leo and I walked out of church together, and he was standing beside me. Then he wasn't. I felt his absence, a hollow space in the air next to me. I never saw him leave. I just realized he was no longer there.

I had this strange moment. Because I looked for him, wondering where he'd gone. And I had this strange moment, thinking he had to be close, and when I saw him, it seemed he'd shrunk. He'd become little, near a little car.

He was actually on the street. He'd realized what had happened. And he left, without a word to me. It must have made more sense to me that he could shrink than that he could be that far away that fast without a word. I looked up and he was small, and I saw the sun glint off the door of the car as he got into it.

I lifted my hand to wave, to stop him. But I brought it only to my throat. No one said anything to me. They went on talking, wondering what had happened. I stood there alone.

Later I went down. I walked from the church. Everybody in town was either there or going there. People offered me rides. But I said no. It was only six blocks, but if it had been three miles I would have said no. I wanted it to take forever. I wanted to walk toward it and toward it but never reach it.

By the time I got there, he was already starting to take the cattle out. Still in his Sunday clothes and shoes. We had to throw them away later. I don't know why it's different depending on the way you're dressed. I've lived on a farm all my life. Blood and butchering don't bother me. But it was wrong to see him standing in the door of that semitrailer with a suit on. And blood all over it. And on his face.

They were hauling the cattle out one by one with a winch attached to a pickup. Men were helping him. They'd attach a cable to one of the dead steers. Then they'd hold the feet up, sliding it on its back with the winch pulling it, until it slid through the door of the semi. The shadow of the cable made a wide loop on the ground. Then suddenly it went slack, and the cable met its shadow as the steer tipped and fell. The steers made heavy, dead sounds when they hit the pavement. Dust flew from them. Sometimes their necks bent backwards under their bodies. All their weight would come down on their necks. But the man in the pickup just pulled them away. They scraped across the pavement, the cable stretching their necks. They were dead. It didn't matter how they fell.

But it did.

Then they found some alive yet. But not going to live. Leo came to the door of the trailer and called for someone to bring a gun. He saw me then. He just looked at me. He didn't say anything, didn't nod his head or anything. But I knew he wanted me to leave.

Men and their griefs. I've had a good marriage. Even with that one huge loss, I'd do it again. But sometimes it seems to me, like it did then, that marriage is one long learning of what you can't do for another person. He looked at me, and I knew he wouldn't share this with me. He couldn't. I knew the look he gave me. It shut me out like it had that other time. Not unkindness or cruelty. Just privacy.

I don't know why it's a man's job and not a woman's, when an animal is dying, to finish it. But it is. I don't know what he felt, walking among those animals, putting that gun to their skulls. Maybe that's part of marriage, too— learning what you'll never learn.

I went home and waited. When he finally came later that afternoon, his shoes and clothes were stiff. Solid with dried blood. He took them off in the mudroom and threw them in the garbage. He walked naked through the house to the shower. He looked at me as he went by, but he never said a word. He had the same look that he'd had before.

Blood had soaked right through his clothes. He looked like he'd been swimming in it. Naked and dull brown he walked through the house. Darker streaks of brown patterned his back. All the blood had dried. His bare feet left no marks on the floor. I listened to the shower start and run.

For two days he hardly talked. He got up, worked, ate, worked again. Worked all the time. He was like a body moving around near me in all the usual places, but a body with no mind. A body with habits that made it rise, work, eat, sleep. How long this time, I wondered. What will I have to break this time?

But it was only two days. He's begun talking again, noticing things. Just a little. But enough that I know he'll come back. If Jeff were here—just him being here would be good. Leo might never say it, but it would be good for him as well as me.

Two-Speed Crandall and Leo never got along. Leo's

told me about Two-Speed's cattle prod, but it was more than just that. It was all the other stories. After Chris died, Leo would get so angry after they loaded cattle that he'd lie awake at night. Maybe he just had to direct his fury somewhere, and Two-Speed was there for it. But it made him feel helpless, too. Magnified his helplessness. Or exposed it.

Maybe it was the same this last time, in the barn, when they loaded. It's hard to believe even Two-Speed Crandall would do this just because he had an argument with Leo. But I can't help but think he killed those cattle on purpose. I know I shouldn't think of only the cattle when two people are dead, and it might be suicide and murder, and what are the cattle compared to that?

But those cattle, their stretched necks, and Leo walking among them with a rifle, putting the barrel to their heads.

Simon Lane Crandall. How many times did he come out here? Hardly ever. Maybe once or twice a year. A nothing man to us. Not family, not friend, not even neighbor. Just someone we heard things about, hired by people we hired.

Yet I think of him all the time now—Simon Lane Crandall and what he did. Weeding my garden, driving tractor—he's on my mind. Why should he have my attention this way? Why should someone who had no claim on us when he was living make a claim when he's dead? It seems like cowardice to me, to come into our lives now, when we have no way to make him leave.

Jeff Gruber

≈

THE DREAMS STOPPED WHEN Jenny was born and became only the memory of a dream. I became too alert to Jenny's presence. Waking to her replaced the dreaming. Becca may be right; a child makes everything now—or ought to. I even almost forgot the memory, until my mother's call brought it back in all its force, almost with the strength of the dream itself.

I never told Becca the dream. The only one who knows it is Ellen, Luke's wife. It was before Luke or I were married, though I was seeing Becca, and Luke was serious about Ellen. The first time I met Ellen I was attracted to her. I liked the way she looked at me without averting her eyes, liked her quiet. Luke always questioned everything, but Ellen seemed to merely accept what lay before her. It was this acceptance of hers that led me, I suppose, to tell her about the dreams, a sense I had that she'd listen and not question, or try to explain, or even try to help, but merely hear the dream as something real, not something to be questioned or explained any more than you'd question a tree, explain a meadowlark singing on a fencepost.

We were all back for a weekend from college, and Luke

brought her out to visit. We went to the river together. Snow had fallen the night before, and the river was covered with it. The three of us walked on the river, on the new snow, the ice thick beneath our boots. Ellen walked between us, and snow came down, and the river stretched around its bends, the trees on its banks bowed down with their burden of snow, and we hardly said a word to each other, just walked and walked, listening to the whisper of snow and the startling crack of ice that sometimes came, though we were never in danger, the winter a cold one and the ice almost two feet thick.

Then Luke saw a deer trail leading down one bank of the river, across the ice, and up the other bank, the tracks still sharp in the new snow, and he thought we should follow, see if we could surprise the deer, but Ellen and I said no, let's just stay on the river, just walk it. But Luke wanted to follow the deer, and we finally told him to go. The tracks went into a curve, and he could follow for a ways, and then meet us on the other side of the bend. So he took off, climbed up the bank, and disappeared into the white, snow-laden trees, and Ellen and I were left alone on the muffled ice—and, with Luke gone, we began to talk.

"Luke says you won't come back here?" she asked.

"No," I said. "I don't plan to."

An owl swept over us. This part of the river was full of owls, and they appeared on silent wings, startling, like shadows solidified in the air. We both gasped, then watched as it floated over the ice, rose above the trees at the bend, and disappeared into the snowfall.

"It's a beautiful place," Ellen said, after the owl had gone.

"It is," I said.

"Let's sit down for a while over there." She pointed to a snag along the bank, protruding through the ice, covered in snow. We made our way toward it, brushed snow off the thick trunk, and sat down.

"So, what happened?" she asked.

"Happened to what?"

"That you don't plan to come back here anymore?"

"Nothing happened. For a long time I thought I'd like to farm. But I got interested in other things. And I'm not sure I want to work as hard as my dad. All he does is work."

We were sitting half-facing each other. Her eyes, dark brown, met mine. Her breath came out in white puffs, her cheeks flushed with cold. Her lips curved in a small smile. "The way you say that," she said, "it sounds like you blame him."

She surprised me. Snow lay white in her dark hair. A single flake came down, rested on her eyelashes.

I looked away from her. "I suppose I do," I said. "I guess I lied. Something did happen." Then I told her everything about Chris's death, and I ended up telling her about the dream that I'd never told to anyone, the wave of soil that washed out of my sleep. She let me talk without interrupting—just listened, with complete attention, while the snow fell down around us. When I finished she turned to me, looked into my eyes, and reached out and touched my shoulder. She let her hand rest there, wrapped in a mitten.

Just that. Nothing more.

We were alone, only she and I, in the snow-muffled

world. For a moment it was so silent I heard as well as saw her breathing.

We both began to shiver.

"We should be moving," I said. "We've been sitting still too long."

"I suppose we should."

But neither of us moved. I reached up, put my hand on hers. We were inches apart, our breath mingling in a single cloud. I felt her shivering through my glove. "I suppose Luke's back on the river by now," she said.

"Probably."

We rose then, walked out onto the ice. Ellen took my elbow in her mittened hand, pressed against me. Another owl, or perhaps the same one, floated toward us, appearing out of the snowstream, its shadow, muted in the diffracted light, slipping below it over the ice, bird and shadow equally soundless.

Dr. Piersoll

≈

WHEN TWO-SPEED CRANDALL was alive he gave this town more to talk about, and kept more people guessing, than anyone else ever did, and his death's changed none of that. Every town, I suppose, has its memorable deaths. I can think way back to when Chris Gruber rolled that tractor—pure tragedy there, and I'm not sure that family's ever recovered—or when BigJim Anderson's son ran his car off the river embankment and drowned in twenty feet of water. Town consensus came down on the side of accident that time, though some people sober and privately, or drunk and publicly, still swear the reverse, though neither to BigJim Anderson's face. Or even, more recently, though it's not a death, the whole odd business with Pop Bottle Pete and his toes. But this thing with Two-Speed Crandall is bigger than any of them.

I can't claim to know what happened, or why. I won't even say there is a why. The police, so far, are allowing accident. I didn't know the family well. Two-Speed himself I never saw—too tough to be sick or too stubborn to admit it. And LouAnn and the boys saw me only when they had to: for the births of the boys and an occasional illness.

But I know the stories. Two-Speed Crandall was barely a part of this community, yet no one was the source of more stories. I've heard them all, second- or third- or fifteenth-hand, from patients and friends and Lions Club members. You wouldn't even have to pay attention in this town and you'd hear about Two-Speed Crandall.

His family consisted of LouAnn and their three sons, Matthew, Mark, and Luke—names, I've thought since I heard them pronounced in the hospital, poignant enough to be painful. They spoke, certainly, of LouAnn's and not Two-Speed's dreams for their children, and they were as un-prophetic as names could be, since the boys had neither literary nor religious leanings. Matthew and Mark cele-brated their sixteenth birthdays by staying away from school and never returning. Luke, on the other hand, did finish school, and I always got the impression, when he was in here with his mother, that he was closer to her than the other boys were.

It's hard to know. Some parents with sick children, I can see how they've put their whole lives into their kids. They hover and worry, hurt more than the kids. Others, I can see just the opposite, how the child seems to be a nuisance more than anything else, and the sickness an irritation to the par-ent. There've been times, dealing with a sick child, I've wished I could inoculate the parent instead, against selfish-ness and stupidity and regret.

But LouAnn Crandall—she was hard to read. She seemed distracted more than anything—not without love or concern, but more like she couldn't completely focus on them. If she seemed closer to Luke, maybe it's just that she was more able to focus on him than on Matt or Mark. Maybe her focus helped him focus. Whatever it was, he finished high school and went to college. Teachers told me he was terribly bright, when he wanted to be. He married Ellen Easton, a girl from Clear River. I like her a lot. She was in here a while back for a pregnancy test. I doubt I'm breaking any confidentiality in this town if I say they're going to have a baby.

It's hard to talk about Two-Speed Crandall and his family in any definite way. As soon as I think I'm talking about what I know, and then I think a little deeper, I realize I'm talking about what I've heard. Years ago, for instance, when the barn burned down at the abandoned Millhauser place and lit up the sky, by the next morning everyone knew that Matt and Mark Crandall had set the fire. There was never any proof. No evidence at all, and no one was ever prosecuted. Still, they did set the fire.

No one seems to know anything about LouAnn. She was quiet and constrained in my office during her pregnancies, even then seeming distracted. She always answered my questions with a yes or a no, and asked none herself. She submitted to the examinations and walked from the room without comment. I always got the sense that she was on her way to someplace else and accidentally came through my door, and being there, gave in to what followed, until she could find her way out. She delivered her three children with a silence that bordered on martyrdom, as if redemption—from what, I don't know—could be gained if only she didn't complain or make a show of pain. It may have been just more of her distraction, that even the pain of labor couldn't get her to focus. She's the only woman I've ever wanted to encourage to scream in the labor room. There were times I thought that if she didn't, I would. She made me so tense with her silence I had to remind myself to be gentle with the baby.

If no one knew a thing about LouAnn, though, everyone knew something about Two-Speed—or thought they did—though most of it was distorted and half-true. He was a character. The one thing in which he could be absolutely trusted was in handling a semitruck. His greatest source of pride was his Class A driver's license. If anything at all was certain about him, it was that somewhere on the downward slope to drunkenness in the municipal bar, he would produce this license. The certainty was so great, but the exact point so varied, that men made bets on the number of drinks it would take for the license to appear. This gambling turned out to be truly random. The license's appearance seemed, even to those who studied Two-Speed with the care that other men study a horse-racing program—and there were those men in town—to be dependent not on the alcohol in his system but on the waverings of his heart and mind, waverings too complicated for pattern or prediction.

Two-Speed would slap the license down on the scarred surface of the bar table and force his companions of the evening—men who barely tolerated him during the day—to stoop over it while he pointed out the A. Then, flipping the card over, he would read aloud the description on the back: "Classes: A: Tractor/trailer combination." He would then challenge anyone within earshot to produce such a license, launch into a description of the testing, detailing its difficulties, and end by claiming that he had never failed to pass it, even the first time.

No one doubted that. Whether or not he lied about other things, and most people assumed that he did, Two-Speed could be trusted in anything to do with a semi—so much so that he often turned down jobs, claiming with complete forthrightness that he wasn't sober enough. He had no time for drunk drivers. He walked the half mile from his house at the edge of town to the bar on Main Street to ensure that when drunk, as he knew he would be later, he wouldn't be tempted to drive home. He insulted those who staggered up from the table pulling their keys from their pockets, calling them damn fools and menaces to society, and went so far as to stand behind their vehicles, cursing them, daring them to back over him, the red light from their brakes glowing over his thin limbs.

His stubbornness was so great that he would indeed have let himself be run over. Perhaps the most famous story of all those told about him—and it ought to be clear again that I'm telling not what I've seen but what I've heard—is one that happened not long ago, just last winter, when Hank Tyrrell challenged Two-Speed by slowly backing up until his bumper touched Two-Speed's knees. Two-Speed remained, swaying and cursing, without moving his feet.

Hank backed further, drunk enough to think he could push Two-Speed out of the way and ornery enough to think he could put an end to Two-Speed's nuisance. Two-Speed's knees crumpled. He fell to the pavement, down into the red, glowing cloud of exhaust steam, and remained there, damning Hank with all the obscenities in his repertoire, which was more varied and rich than anyone else's in town. Still Hank backed up, in spite of the protestations of onlookers. Two-Speed began to disappear under the pickup until some say his clothing caught on a rusted piece of metal, others that he grabbed the bumper and held on with all his drunken strength. In either case he began to be dragged backwards across the pavement, his head hanging limply, scraping along.

Never, though, did he shout for Hank to stop, but continued to scream like a crow that has learned to curse, his voice rising up from the exhaust calling Hank to judgment for the menace he was to the road, to the drivers who took their responsibilities seriously. Hank backed clear into the street, reassured, though he couldn't see Two-Speed, by the health and vigor of his voice. He then put the pickup into drive and began to leave the scene, thinking, naturally enough, that if Two-Speed had survived the backing-up he was out of danger and that he, Hank, had outdone Two-Speed's stubbornness, and outdone it with style.

He made it half a block down the street to the stop sign at the highway before he became puzzled by Two-Speed's voice following him and by the spectators running along the sidewalk waving their arms. When he got out of his pickup to look, he and the men who came panting up found Two-Speed's head sticking out from under the bumper, still cursing, and lying in blood that was beginning to pool from the great gash scraped in his scalp. Looking down the street they could see a trail of that same blood steaming slightly in the winter air. Two-Speed did nothing to extricate himself from under the pickup. Instead, looking up into Hank Tyrrell's horrified face bending over him, he accused Hank of being so drunk he would drag a man under his pickup and down the highway. "Proof!" he screamed. "Proof that you're too damn drunk to drive, Hank Tyrrell, just like I said, and you got no right to be on the road in the condition you're in! There might be a woman on her way to the hospital right now, you know! On her way to the hospital to give birth to a baby! And you'd come swerving into her lane the way you are, and the last thing she'd ever see would be your headlights in the wrong lane, you damn stupid drunk driver!"

It was all too much for Hank. For the first time in his life he admitted he was too drunk to drive. For the first time in his life he called his wife and had her retrieve him from the bar, waiting patiently outside in the sharp wind and snow for her to arrive, then climbing mutely into the passenger seat while his drunken friends, delighted, cheered at this indignity.

When they finally managed to get Two-Speed out from under the pickup and standing, they discovered a great patch of skull, white but flowing with blood, showing through the matted hair at the back of his head. They told Two-Speed they'd call me, wake me up to look at it, but he declined offers of aid, shook off the hands held out to him, pulled a dirty stocking cap out of his pocket, shoved it down over his head and walked, dignified but drunk, through the cold, wavering light of the street lamps, home.

But I've always wondered about that night. If the descriptions of the amount of blood he lost are not too much exaggerated, I'm amazed that he got home at all. I'm surprised we didn't find his frozen corpse the next morning

shaking underneath her halter top. Bu[...]
think he's going to, we're going to, help [...]
darkness, take her to a safe place. It cou[...]
open the door and, stretched out across[...]
down through that halter top. Does she[...]
go and invite it, or is she so innocent she[...]
or so tough she doesn't care, or so sure[...]
matter? It's up to us, because all he says i[...]
one, I could smell the heat coming out[...]
an engine manifold I tell ya, and she [...]
and I damn near caught my nose in tha[...]
er singed, whoo-ee! Thought I was gon[...]
next day, and she asks me, did I lose s[...]
was looking, and I say right back, no, I [...]
my pocket, you've been a help alread[...]
without ya, nosiree!

It may all be a lie or what-might-h[...]
think that it didn't happen, and the mo[...]
it seems that it didn't, so she can still b[...]
She sets, as he says, her sweet little ass[...]
side us and asks if we're going where sh[...]
am, honey, and other places, too. So c[...]
or pretend that you're lost, or tell her y[...]
bles until she turns and puts her hand[...]
points to a motel. Have it as you will[...]
Crandall leads you on, hinting at force[...]
getting less and less specific as the wh[...]
throat, until finally he's just staring ove[...]
black vinyl of the booth across from h[...]
and saying, Man, it was something els[...]

somewhere along the way. It was the middle of winter, below zero, and a hard wind that night, a nasty, cutting windchill, with snow obscuring visibility. All that would be hard on a sober man, but he was drunk, and the alcohol would have increased his heat loss badly. One stumble and fall, and I could imagine him not getting up.

Nevertheless, he did make it home, with more luck than sense. And that night, for what it's worth, I did deliver a baby, Marilyn Muller's, a young farm woman who had come in on the same narrow county road that Hank Tyrrell lived on, and whom, for all I know, Hank's wife, steadily clinging to her side of the road, may have dimmed her lights for and safely passed.

Since this accident I've been thinking a lot, so much so that I missed four pigeons in a row at the skeet range the other night and had to suffer the jokes that I still get about being from the city. I powdered the next ten to gain the right to joke back about country hicks who never quite know where to point their guns. We had a good time. But maybe that's part of why I'm thinking so much. I don't know that anyone ever actually joked with Two-Speed. At least no sober person did, and even the half-drunk ones went into that territory with anxiety, never sure when Two-Speed might take a joke wrong. He didn't seem to care about anything or anybody, and yet had the strangest sensitivity to being wronged. He earned a kind of grudging respect in the bar for his willingness to fly into a fighting rage over anything and with anybody. Men who in the daylight would struggle for words to bridge the gap they perceived between themselves and

Two-Speed, would sit at his table in the b
story, claiming the next day that they
anyway.

I wonder now why the stories, and no
cepted. The stories were retold and r
reached all levels of people in town, do
boys gathered in groups on the playgr
pretty stories—the Indian whose nose h
in Sioux Falls; the motorcyclist he'd fo
ramp outside of St. Paul; the young g
hitchhiking, and the fun he had with her
hearing him tell them, with a few drin
and the way he must have told them,
funny stories, too.

Without ever being one of the first l
about how they were heard. Consider n
little light still in the sky, and up ahead
road with an arm out like half a crucifixi
accelerator. The diesel flutters against i
ing, and the cattle shift and slide but a
they can't fall. We move forward on his v
anything we want, anybody we don't ev
an old girlfriend or teacher, a movie ac
we subscribe to Freud. She can be a
story's just vague enough, and we're jus
the people around us are laughing just l

He could stop right beside her, bu
ahead of her so that as he talks, sucki
sentences, we can see her in the mirro
cab, the red running lights playing

So the stories that spin out of the bar and swirl through town are all different, and for several weeks they intersect and cut through each other until finally a standard version is formed. Discount it, believe it, invent it differently. Two-Speed Crandall is as untrustworthy a storyteller as you can hope to find. Or perhaps he's not, but you have every reason to believe he is, and this is even better, because then he just might be telling the truth, the liar.

Have it as you will, your dreams and your longings. Or don't have it if you don't want it. Don't think, if you don't want to, that it could be your own daughter climbing into the cab of a semi toward a stranger. No need to rise from your booth and walk to where Two-Speed is spouting words, to jerk him from his seat and say: What did you do, dammit? You talking rape? Is that what you're saying? No need to turn the whole bar quiet like that, no need to make anyone think of the girl, to see the story from her angle, the dreams she may wake from, the memories she may carry.

She may exist only in Two-Speed's story—not even in his mind but only in the words that at the moment emerge from his mouth. You can go home through those streets, as quiet as any in the world, and waver before your house and bend back your head until you see the stars whirling. And then you can catch yourself and step forward through your door and realize how different you are from Two-Speed Crandall, who is finally worth nothing but a laugh, and who has furnished you with nothing but—you can almost be convinced—a lie.

Jeff Gruber

≈

I WAS FIFTEEN, AND CHRIS WAS NINE, and it was one of those summers when things never stop growing. The rains came when they should, and the sun beat down, and the corn and soybeans grew as if the soil contained a pressure forcing them up. The alfalfa gave us four good cuttings that year, the corn went one hundred and twenty bushels, the soybeans eighty. I'd walk out the door in the mornings to feed the cattle and see the fields steaming in the early sun, the smell of pollen and milky juice so thick it seemed more syrup than smell.

That particular morning I felt the pleasure of the land so acutely that my chest hurt. I had cut the road ditch two days earlier, the sickle chattering as the bromegrass fell in a shuddering wave over the bar. Now we had to rake it into piles and pick it up. We used an old, rusty dump rake that had originally been pulled by horses for this job. It had a hundred curved teeth that gathered the cut grass out of the stubble and then, when the rider kicked a lever, lifted up and left the hay lying in a pile.

Part of our land bordered a dredge ditch, a V-shaped gash thirty feet deep, cut into the earth by power shovels after World War I. These ditches allowed the land to be tiled and drained, so that what was at one time a country of sloughs and ponds and marsh grass and shallow lakes, a land I imagined to be filled with the sound of waterfowl and frogs, heavy with insects, the night air flickering with bats, was now covered in the summer with millions of straight rows of corn and soybeans marching like stationary lines of soldiers across the rich remains of old swamps, the water funneled away through the underground tiles and into the dredge ditches that led to creeks and eventually the river.

At night sometimes when I was younger I would waken and think I heard through the open window of my upstairs bedroom water trickling away eternally, unmuffled by the earth, flowing through those tiles in the darkness as if the land were a sponge being squeezed. Underneath the sound of the shrilling crickets' cadence that came from all around me as I lay in bed, the covers thrown back from the heat and humidity, I heard, or imagined I heard, the blood of the land moving along man-made veins toward the river that gleamed dark and oily in its wide valley.

It seemed to me, too, that I could flow like water out of my bed, slide and drip down off the porch roof outside my window, make my way into those mossy tiles, and be at the sea. Falling back to sleep, I sometimes had a vision of that land transformed and thought that if I went to the window I would find it as it had been before the sod was turned, long grasses waving under an open sky, and water in sloughs lapping muddy shores, and thousands of ducks asleep. But I could never rouse myself—this vision always came too close to unconsciousness—and I couldn't force myself to the window to look. In the morning, seeing the corn standing, I would wonder if there had been another land imposed upon it during the night, if the ghost of old waters could perhaps still be here not just as dream inside my head but something more.

I'm more familiar with ghosts now, and of how we let them haunt us, but I still don't know whether their haunting is something we invent, or they do.

Chris was old enough to drive a tractor. He was. Becca is right about that. I was driving them when I was seven, steering the H around the yard, and by nine I was pulling wagons and equipment, even doing field work. At the time I thought nothing of it when my father put Chris on the little Oliver to pull the dump rake.

Normally I'd drive and Dad'd sit on the steel seat of the rake. When the rake filled, he'd kick the foot-catch hard and hold it until the wheels engaged to bring the rake off the ground and dump the hay. The person driving had only to keep going, halfway down the road ditch, the tractor tipped at an angle that seemed perilous when I first did it, but that I soon learned was far from enough to overcome the tractor's center of gravity.

Chris was excited and scared when Dad told him. I remember the tight light in his eyes, the gleam of muscle in his jaw beneath the still-soft skin. Don't worry, I told him. Dad's got things to do, and the grass needs raking. It's just driving tractor, just going in a straight line. Let me do the work on the rake.

Sure, he said. I can do it, Jeff. I've driven the Oliver lots of times.

Right, I said. So let's get to it.

We hooked the tractor up, and I drove it to the driveway with Chris standing behind me on the hitch. The dump rake clanged, its steel wheels bouncing on the gravel. The smell of the tractor's exhaust mingled with the dust and the creamy smell of tasseling corn. I drove the tractor halfway into the ditch. Chris's hands were tight on the wheel when he climbed onto the seat.

It's like a circus ride, I said. Kind of scary, but no problem. Just keep it straight. Third gear, OK?

He nodded. OK.

I grabbed his head and squeezed it between my rib cage and elbow, in the headlock of a professional wrestler. We laughed, and I hopped to the ground, the dry hay crackling under my feet, dandelion tufts exploding and rising in the air. I climbed onto the dump-rake seat. Chris's round face stared back at me. I circled my finger in the air. Let's go, I shouted. He turned around, put the tractor into gear, and started. I jerked on the seat, regained my balance, released the lever that held the rake up, and dropped it into the stubble.

It whispered along, gathering the grass. Chris opened the throttle on the tractor, and it belched noise; I could hear the rake's metal tines sing in different pitches, and the steel wheels faintly hum, and the grass rustle up from the ground into the curved space of the teeth. When it filled, I kicked in the foot-catch, and it rose up, reached the top of its arc, then clanged back down, leaving behind a windrow of grass we could pick up later.

Swallows gathered around us, attracted by the insects, and flew their orange and purple arcs around the tractor, rising and dipping, chattering. We went up the driveway. Chris's shoulders gradually relaxed as he grew accustomed to the tilt of the tractor. At the end of the driveway he looked back for directions, and I signaled him to turn left, staying in the ditch, so we could rake the grass along the county road. The ditch there was a little steeper, but soon Chris relaxed again, and finally drove with one hand on the steering wheel, the other on the fender of the Oliver.

Then he began to sing.

His high, little-boy voice rose over the tractor's roar, only the melody distinguishable, off-key—first "Yankee Doodle," and then "Holy, Holy, Holy." I laughed at his lack of inhibition. We had a half mile of road to rake before we reached our property line, and the work fell into a rhythm as I kicked the catch to the random beat of Chris's singing and the swoops and chirps of the swallows.

When we reached the uncut grass of Peter Olaffsen's ditch, Chris kicked in the clutch and looked back to me for directions. Pull up out of the ditch, I yelled. When I saw that he couldn't hear me, I jerked my finger across my throat. He cut the engine, and silence, deeper for being full of sound, a world hushed, poured out of the surrounding cornfields—the rustle of sharp-edged leaves, air moving, water suspiring. Semi tires whined on the highway a mile away.

Pull out of the ditch and cross the road, I told Chris. Watch for any cars. The dredge ditch is on the other side, but don't let that bother you. Angle down into it. Then just run along like you were. Stay up along the road, where the grass is cut. It's a little spooky, having all that ditch below you, but don't worry. Just do like you were doing, OK?

He pushed his hair back from his forehead and rubbed his nose. OK, he said.

Let's go then.

The back of his head bobbed as he stooped over the ignition, and then he kicked the starter with his foot, holding onto the steering wheel to get leverage and straightening his whole body. I felt an almost paternal pride, seeing how much of himself he put into those things that I'd learned to do without thinking or effort. The tractor blatted into life. Chris looked back at me. I gave him the thumbs-up sign to cross the road, and he steered the tractor out of the ditch onto the gravel and over to the other side.

He angled the machine expertly down, the dredge ditch yawning beside us now, full of uncut wild grass, weeds, and flowers. In the bottom a thin stream of water flowed, only a few inches deep and perhaps four or five feet wide. From the dump-rake seat I could see it glittering below us, moving slowly. Frogs and turtles lived in it, and minnows, and sometimes carp made their way up from the river to feed on the effluvium of the fields in the shadow of concrete bridges.

The road ditch itself was no steeper than the other, but it faded into the dredge ditch, leveling out slightly and then angling sharply down. Chris looked back, worried, and I reassured him with my face, shrugged, and grinned. We headed west, the tractor crawling along like an insect, its lugged tires gripping the grasses, the rake gathering and releasing the hay. We passed the driveway to our place and continued west another quarter mile to the end of our land. Chris relaxed again as he grew more confident in the tractor's ability to keep the slope.

The dredge ditch turned at right angles away from the road at the edge of our land, forming a border between our land and our neighbor's. It went south, splitting the section. For some reason I'll never know, Chris grew confused when we reached the turn in the ditch. He might have thought he could turn around on the slight leveling where the road ditch blended into the dredge ditch. I don't know. Instead of stopping or turning to the road, he turned toward the ditch. I was dumping the last load of hay when he started the turn, looking back at the steel tines lifting from the ground and shaking free the tangled hay. I had grabbed the lever that held the tines up and was catching it in its hook when I realized Chris's mistake. I looked up and saw the tractor turning toward the ditch, Chris with both hands on the wheel, his back rigid, staring at the front end swinging toward the space opening up before it.

Before alarm hit me, I thought merely: What's he doing? I gave myself that time to wonder. And in that time the wheels of the tractor crushed that many more feet of grass, dropped that much closer to the deepening slope.

Stop! I yelled. Chris! Stop!

He could have. There was plenty of time. But he didn't hear me. I screamed again for him to stop, but still he turned the wheels toward the ditch.

I can't explain any of it. I don't know what he was thinking. I don't know why I didn't react sooner, why I didn't immediately go after him. He turned sharply into the ditch. He must have thought he could still make the turn on the level area before the dredge ditch slope dropped.

Sto-o-o-o-p! I screamed.

Even then I didn't move. I saw the left rear wheel of the tractor, jackknifed now nearly against the hitch of the dump rake, swing its lugs up and over as it turned, saw the grass in front of it bow and shiver and disappear, shaking off dust and light. I sat there and watched all this happen, and only then did I finally leap from my seat. I stepped onto the hitch of the rake, to run across it to Chris as if across an iron scaffolding or bridge, and I felt for an eternal moment that I was high up on a narrow walk with the grass reaching up to brush my boots from thousands of feet below.

I took one more step and lunged for Chris, trying to grab the seat of the tractor, but as I stepped, the ditch slope took the tractor, and it slipped sideways a foot or more and began to roll. My foot missed the hitch, and I flailed at empty air, and fell into the grass; I saw the dump rake rise into the air over me, swing up and up, rusty and grotesque and huge as if it were gathering the entire sky into its pointed iron prongs.

It swung right over me in an immense arc from horizon to horizon, raking the heavens. The world crashed.

I rolled, without knowing what I was doing, down the dredge ditch after it. I tried to gain my feet but only fell and rolled again, through thistles and wild roses, which I didn't feel, toward what I couldn't bear to see, but did see in flashes as I rolled—the tractor upside down in the bottom of the ditch, and Chris under it.

He must have held on with all his strength, to stay in the seat as the thing went upside down, clutching the steering wheel, bracing against gravity, driving the thing even with the wheels turning in the air and the engine shutting off.

He could have jumped. If only he'd let go.

I couldn't lift it off him.

I couldn't.

If I'd jumped for him sooner.

He wasn't crushed. Just held.

Five inches of water. Held by that machine in five inches of water.

"Is she sleeping?"

Becca had come out of the kitchen without my knowing it. I was glad to let the memory go, to look down at Jenny, so still in my arms, and say, "Yes."

"Do you want to lay her down?"

"No. I'll hold her."

Becca came and stood behind me. She touched the top of Jenny's head, then my shoulder.

"Those ships out there," I said. "Do you think they're ever going to move?"

"I'm sorry," she said. "About what I said before."

"No, you're right."

She bent and rested her cheek on my shoulder, her hair falling onto my chest, and I felt her breath, warm on my neck. "You going back, then?"

"Yeah. But I won't promise anything."

≈ 75 ≈

Our voices were quiet. Jenny didn't stir.

Becca kissed my neck, lightly.

"He never stopped working, Becca. Just kept on working. Things kept growing, and he kept on working."

"What should he have done, though? The world didn't end."

"Didn't it?"

She didn't respond. I felt her sadness through her breathing, through the limp way her body lay against me. She knew I didn't want an answer, and I felt a small gratefulness that she didn't give one.

For three years after Chris's death I went on working with my father. His capacity for work grated on me. Nothing seemed to have changed for him. The old chores still defined him—plowing, discing, harrowing, planting, cultivating, harvesting, feeding the cattle. During the day I worked with him, and during the night the dream of the land rising up to engulf Chris came to me, but I never told anyone about it. I won two state wrestling championships, lifting weights in the locker room with a fury that made me want to bend the bars—but no matter how much I lifted, it was never enough, though my coach held me up as an example of competitive fire for the other wrestlers.

The spring that I graduated from high school, I was in the bare fields picking up rocks with my father. The rocks had been buried by glaciers after the last Ice Age. The wall of ice had come down, a mile thick, scraping out the beds of lakes and leaving, when it retreated, these rocks that rose through the ground year after year, floating upward through the workings of frost, so that every spring we walked the fields with a tractor hooked to a bale rack, and filled the rack with rocks that had, it seemed to me, the smell of mammoth in them.

I loved the story of the glaciers and had told it to Chris, how the ice had lain a mile thick on the land and then melted and retreated. One of the few things that made the job of picking rocks bearable was Chris's jabbering about whether or not a particular rock had been stepped on by a mastodon or mammoth. He would bring them to me or our father to smell, and he would find spots in them that, he claimed, were fossilized mammoth spoor.

After his death, Dad and I did the job in silence. We never talked about Chris. We never spoke of the glacier again. We picked up rocks and dumped them onto the wooden rack, and they thudded, lifeless, the job merely something that had to be done.

I was eighteen and still not sure what I was going to do with my life. I had enrolled in college, but thought that perhaps when I graduated I'd come back and farm. I carried a rock to the bale rack and laid it there, removed my leather gloves, and leaned against the rack to rest. I looked up and saw Dad walking away from me, his eyes on a large rock lying in the black earth several yards in front of him. His shoulders were stooped, as if the rock were drawing him to it, as if he couldn't escape its pull. It seemed to me that the gravity of that single rock was stronger than the death of his son. All he did was work and work and work, walk over this land and respond to its seasons and demands, and it never stopped demanding; twenty-five thousand years later we were still picking up after a moving wall of ice, and the land would never release him from its grip of winter, give him time to feel. If he even wanted to feel. If he even cared. A rock was nothing. A trailer full of rocks was a pile of nothing, but it seemed to mean more to him than the absence of his son.

I wanted to scream, wanted to scream at my father that Chris was dead, and what were we doing out here pretending that he wasn't. But for three years we hadn't spoken of what had happened, and words congealed in my mind like rocks in grinding ice, and I couldn't release them. My father had his back to me, his shirt dark with sweat. His vertebrae strained against the thin cloth as he stooped to pick up the rock that had drawn him. I turned away from the sight of it and slammed my open palm against the rough wood of the bale rack. Even as I was doing it I saw a long, jagged splinter sticking up right where my hand was going. I watched my hand go toward it dispassionately, with mild interest, as if watching something far away. The splinter met my palm and suddenly, as if it disappeared and then reappeared, was sticking through the back of my hand, and my palm was flat on the rack.

I stared at the jagged wood protruding through my skin from out of my hand, red with blood, gleaming in the spring sun. That's all—I looked, and then I looked away, at the flat black field in which we stood, at the horizon. I looked around and felt the splinter begin to throb, felt blood drip off my hand, and I swore I wouldn't stay here, trapped like my father by this soil.

I swore it, but I wanted to weep at the loss, knowing how

much I loved the land, and the work, and the life, all of it, how much I was turning against.

I heard Dad's feet behind me, walking slowly, weighted down. I jerked my hand up from the rack, holding in my cry, then broke the splinter off and threw it over the rack and quickly put my gloves back on. The black soil had absorbed my blood, and nothing was visible, but the rack was stained red. I put my gloved hand over the blood and pretended to be looking off at the sky.

Next to me my father grunted and heaved an enormous rock onto the rack. The whole rack clattered and shook. I saw his corded forearms, the swell of his biceps, smelled his sweat.

Heck of a job, isn't it? he said.

I didn't reply. He wiped his brow with the back of his glove. How you doing? he asked.

I wanted to say: God, Dad, I'm hurt. I'm really hurt.

I felt the blood dripping down my hand and pooling in the fingers of the glove.

I'm fine, I said. I waited for him to turn away, then reached down, scooped up some soil, and smeared it over the bloodstain. I walked away, to a rock larger than the one my father had lifted. This is the last time I ever do this, I said to myself. And with every rock I lifted for the rest of the afternoon I repeated the promise.

Elizabeth Gruber

≈

TIME CAN LOSE ALL STRUCTURE. It can turn to mush, and it did after that tractor and dump rake rolled. I don't know how many weeks passed, or months, or years, or maybe it was decades or centuries, before I came up out of whatever time had become and realized the silence. I realized I'd been talking, I'd been asking questions, but no answers were returned. And no questions either. As if my voice were sucked out of me to an echoless place, before I heard it myself.

I listened to this silence and saw it came from Leo. I saw how he moved within it. Just like for the two days after this semi accident, he moved as if his life had become all habit. I didn't care at first. Losing a child is the worst thing in the world. Chris. My baby. If it's made even worse by someone else's silence, or someone else's guilt and blame, it doesn't matter. It's already as bad as it can be.

But the first day I tasted food again, I cared. I'd made a hotdish, and it tasted bland. I was surprised to notice; I hadn't for so long. Then I felt guilty for noticing—that the taste of food should matter. And I felt scared. To think that simple things like that might again make up my life.

I stared at my food for a while and silently said: I'll never forget. I'll never, ever forget. And I'll never stop missing you, baby. I'll never stop grieving. Then I pushed my chair back and got the salt and pepper from the ledge above the stove. When I turned back to the table, I saw Leo eating. He was lifting the food to his mouth as if he were shoveling it, just something he had to do. I sprinkled salt on my food in a silence so great I heard the tiny crystals strike the edge of the plate, and ring.

The world is irresistible. It began to come back to me, no matter how hard I tried to hold it off, no matter how much it frightened me. First the taste of food, then other things: sunsets behind the grove, shadows, the song of a meadowlark, the sound of church bells carrying across the fields. But also, I noticed that Leo didn't notice. I grew jealous and angry. Jealous of his grief. To think that he felt more deeply than me, grieved more deeply. To think that he missed Chris more.

But we never talked about it. He wouldn't. I realized that's what I'd been trying to do during that strange time when there was no time, after Chris's death. We talked, but not about that. His silence was not a steady thing. If it had been steady and brooding, I might have borne it. I might have felt such a thing too profound to break or enter. But instead he pretended there was no silence. He talked of things as if Chris had never died—crops and weather and people— as if they were unchanged in his mind, as if they mattered in the old, habitual way.

Then slowly I began to realize it was just the opposite— that none of it mattered to him. The world hadn't come back to him. He was able to resist it. His habits and his work allowed him to resist it in a way that I couldn't. I became jealous of his joylessness. I knew where it came from. I knew that he blamed himself, that it was guilt and not just grief that held the world away from him. But it angered me, and his silence angered me, and the way he seemed to feel nothing, and seemed to feel everything.

Then one day I swore. I never swear. But I did. There had been flights of geese flying south. The evening before I'd heard their dropping calls. The sound paralyzed me with so much longing and so much loss, I couldn't cry or move or speak. I stood in the center of the lawn and couldn't raise my eyes to look. When the world comes back, it can hurt and hurt and hurt you. It slammed a memory into my heart, of standing with Chris and watching geese together.

I listened until the sound faded altogether, and then looked up at the empty curve of the sky. I realized that until that moment, in spite of all my grief and all my weeping, I'd not felt the magnitude of his absence. I'd never again watch his face turned to the sky.

I heard footsteps behind me and saw Leo walking across the gravel toward me. His head was down, watching his boots. His heels sprayed small stones. He hadn't even heard the geese. He didn't need to look up to know where he was going. And somehow, in spite of my own hurt, I felt sorry for him.

The next day he was in the fields, and I was alone in the house, and I remembered how he'd looked, walking without noticing anything, going about his work. I heard myself say,

"Goddamn" so loud that it rang in the pans in the sink. It startled me, but when I realized I'd said it, I said, more quietly: "Yes. Goddamn anyway."

I went outside and got in the pickup. I turned it down the field road, to where Leo was spring plowing. When I came to the end of the field road, I could see the smoke from the tractor smudging the sky behind a little rise far up the field. I drove over the unplowed cornstalks toward it. I came over the rise and drove down toward him, seeing the land ride up and turn on the plowshares, so black and shiny it reflected the sun. I gunned the pickup down the rise, cornstalks scraping and whipping under it, banging on the oil pan. The smell of corn dust rose around me. Leo was watching the furrow and didn't see me until I was nearly alongside him. His face stared through the tractor cab at me.

He stopped the tractor, but I pulled in front of it anyway and stopped, and killed the pickup engine. I got out. He was already climbing out of the cab, turning to back down the ladder, his face twisted to see me. The diesel engine throbbed and rattled.

He stepped to the ground and came toward me. "What's wrong?" he shouted over the engine.

"Everything!" I shouted back. "Goddammit, every-thing's wrong!"

He stopped walking toward me and stared, his mouth open.

"Shut off the engine," I shouted at him. "Shut off the damn engine."

He came toward me, his arms open to hold me. "Elizabeth?" he said, his face worried. I twisted away from him, shaking my head. "No!" I shouted. "I won't talk with the tractor running! Shut it off!"

But still he came toward me, concerned for me. But I was all right. I was all right. I was sure of that. Standing under that empty sky the previous night, with the sound of Chris's absence still hollow in my ears, and the air beside me cold with it, and the realization that all my life the world would find ways to strike me with it, to hurt me out of memory, I'd known that I was all right, that that was the way it had to be and should be. And then I'd known that Leo was the one who needed help, to bring his face back up, away from his boots, to where it could be struck by the world, and his hurt both forgotten and renewed.

I turned and ran from the concern in his face, knowing that if he managed to take me in his arms, if he were allowed to think that he was comforting me—though always before I thought that's what I wanted—he'd never have a chance. And I knew the strength in his arms, how if he reached me I'd never escape that strength and gentleness, and he'd press me into him and suffocate himself, and I would let him, wanting it.

I ran to the pickup and opened the door. I didn't know what I was going to do. I think I thought I was going to climb in and lock him out and talk to him through the window. But when I opened the door I saw a metal pipe sticking out from under the seat. I snatched it up and turned back around, gripping it in both hands. "No!" I shouted. He was about to grasp me, and I was cornered within the open door. He stopped when I lifted the pipe. I don't know if I would have hit him. I don't know. He stopped.

"Shut off the tractor," I shouted. "Shut if off, Leo."

I hated the running engine. I hated its steady rumbling, hated its making us shout, hated the way it waited for him to climb back into the cab and continue down the furrow, his eyes on the folding land.

"Elizabeth!" he said. "Just tell me . . ."

He dropped his hands, and I ducked around the door before he could catch me, and ran to the tractor. He needed to shut it off. Not me. He had to be the one. The pipe was heavy in my hand, swinging in my hand as I ran. I let it swing up, and suddenly two lights were coming together, startling me, the silver light off the galvanized pipe and the white, reflected light out of the tractor's headlight. It seemed to me as I ran that they were suddenly darting toward each other, and then light was shattering and going everywhere, and the metal of the tractor was ringing over its steady turning and drumming.

"Shut it off! Shut if off, Leo!" I screamed. "Shut it off now!" I swung the pipe again. The first time it had seemed to do it by itself, but now I knew, and I swung it hard and deliberately, full of anger and full of grief. The second headlight on that side smashed and exploded, shards spraying and glittering in the furrow. I let myself cry. "Shut it off," I wept, but not loud enough for him to hear anymore, just saying it, weeping and saying it, and stepping back to the rear fender of the tractor and smashing the orange taillight there, seeing it hang by its wires over the fender, the pipe vibrating in my hand, stinging, and paint flaking on the tractor where it was struck.

I lost Leo. I beat on the tractor, wanting to silence it. The pipe seemed featherlight in my hands, whistling as I swung it, light as a music baton. Too light for what I wanted. Needed. I saw a rock at my feet, turned up by the plow, gray and rough, large as a lampshade. I threw the pipe down and picked it up, and it seemed to bolt out of the ground into my hands and over my head.

I struck the tractor with it, the fender banging. Then I struck the hydraulic couplings, saw them bend, and oil sprayed from the hoses. I smashed the cover over the PTO shaft, then banged the rock on the hitch. I moved back to the plow, raising the rock over my head and smashing it down, again and again, and it felt so good, against the square steel beam of the plow, smashing and crying out words, but I don't know what they were, and seeing the paint discolor and flake, and the heavy thuds of the rock coming into my shoulders.

Then I heard my name spoken twice, quietly and clearly, the way he used to speak it, like two names: "Liz Beth," he said. "Liz Beth."

I don't know when he had shut off the tractor. His voice came from behind me as I was lifting the rock to strike again, and it seemed like the only sound in the world. I felt his hands grab my wrists. I knew I had broken through, that I was to him what the geese had been to me the night before—something he couldn't help but notice. I let my own strength, then, be stopped by his, and felt the weight of the rock above my head pushing down, too heavy for me to lift. His hands moved up my wrists and took it. I turned around. His face looked into mine, large and grave eyed and creased with dirt. He let the rock drop slowly in his hands, then swung it sideways and let it fall.

In the silence my eyes grew wide and startled as I realized what I'd been doing.

"You can't hurt a plow, Liz Beth," he said. "Not a plow. Just can't be done."

I looked at the steel beam I'd been pounding. My arms trembled from exhaustion. The beam had a few scratches in the paint. That's all.

"The tractor, though?" I asked, looking back up into his face.

"You did OK there," he said. His mouth twitched.

"Good," I said. "All right, then."

We nodded, both together.

Then we were laughing. I hated it, because it felt good, to laugh, and to hear him laugh; it felt terrible because it felt good. I wanted to stop but couldn't, and I never wanted to stop. He couldn't stop either. Then the good and the terrible changed and got mixed up, and somehow we were crying, and then laughing again, and crying.

Finally we stopped, out of breath and looking at each other. He took his cap off and ran his hand back over his head. He'd just started to bald then, and the sun shone on the smooth skin. Still holding his cap he reached out and took me into his arms, drew me into his smell of land and sweat and machine oil, all hot from the sun and his body. I pressed him into whatever he smelled in me.

I didn't tell him what I'd done. I didn't tell him that I was that part of his world that was irresistible, that it had to be something, and that it was me.

I just said, into his shoulder: "Damn, Leo. Damn, I miss him."

"I know," he said. "I know."

"I'll bear your grief," I said. "I'll live with that. But I won't bear your guilt."

He drew a deep breath that I felt in my chest through his. It trembled in both of us. "I feel guilty," he finally said, quietly.

"You're not."

"I know, Liz Beth. I just feel that way."

I squeezed him tight. "Goddamn," I said. "Goddamn anyway."

"You don't swear, Liz Beth," he said.

"I'm not."

I felt a breeze in my hair. I felt his arms hold me tight. "No," he said. "I guess you're not."

Jeff Gruber

≈

TWELVE MILES FROM CLOTEN on my way back from
Duluth I stopped my car at a wayside rest on top of the
bluffs above the river and looked down at the valley. The
river was a snatch of silver far away where it rounded a bend.
Though it was late spring the day had an edge of cold to it.
The wind touching my cheek could have been a breeze from
the beginnings of the world—or not the world entirely, but
this world, this valley, which had been birthed in ice. I
thought of Angel Finn's gaunt face, barely visible, his voice
barely audible over the sound of flowing water as he told
Luke and me, all of us sitting in his boat at night, of the old
river that had once roared through this valley, full of melted
glacial water, larger than any river the world had ever
known.

I shut my eyes and felt time in suspension. I remembered Jenny and Becca back in Duluth. Jenny had waved
good-bye to me happily, without any sense of what a good-
bye meant. A cool breeze rose and rushed past me into the
valley. I opened my eyes and watched where it bent the tree-
tops down, turned leaves over, pale and shining. The movement in the trees reached the distant water, leaped over it,

and spun away across the bed of the ancient river. Near me, brown, dried leaves left over from winter skittered down the pavement, scratching something guttural yet musical out of their fine, brittle edges.

I remembered Luke standing on the bank of the river, the water fifteen feet below him, its slow surface rippling around a cottonwood snag, the roots of the tree rising from the water like a huge, deformed hand. Luke wore polarized sunglasses, and in his hand he held a recurve bow with a tin can taped to it. Nylon string was wound around the can. The string was fastened to a heavy, barbed arrow.

"There's one," he said.

I looked and saw a shadow beneath the surface, rising slowly out of the murky water until it took on the wavering shape of a carp. Luke drew back the bow, talking as he drew. "Big old pig," he said. "Come on up."

He released. The arrow lanced into the water, cord whipping off the can and trailing it. With a single lunge of its tail the fish disappeared back into the dark depths.

"Missed," Luke said.

He began to wrap the cord around the can, retrieving the arrow. "I'm giving up on Dad," he said. "I'm sick of being a rock for him."

Out of nowhere. He was shooting carp and winding the cord back in, and then he said that, and though I knew all the stories about Two-Speed, this was the first time Luke had ever said anything about him. I'd never talked about my father, either. Luke's words confused me, and I tried to make some connection to the missed shot, the river, the fish. Beyond my own polarized glasses, the river was gray green.

I stared at it. A little whirlpool eddied against the bank, floated away, dissipated.

"What do you mean?" I asked casually, pretending nothing important had just been said, no new boundary crossed.

"You ever watch the Road Runner?"

"Sure. Used to."

"Bullshit. You still do, I bet."

"All right. Sometimes. If I'm in the house between chores."

"Right. You know how the coyote'll be standing on a cliff, and the cliff breaks off and he starts to fall? But he's always thinking, so he throws off a rock, higher up, and climbs onto it. Then he throws off another and climbs onto it. Then another. And another. Till he's climbing so fast he thinks he's not even falling anymore. He thinks he's got it licked. Thinks he's going up instead of down.

"But he's going down all right. The whole time. Falling down a big, empty hole. And just when he grins and wipes his brow, Bam! he hits. Been screwed all along. Just throwing off rocks so he won't have to notice."

Luke picked up the arrow and nocked it on his bowstring. His eyes went back to the water. "There's another one," he said. "Farther out. Take it."

But I didn't raise my bow. "I don't get it," I said, watching the fish below the surface, wavering.

"The world's nothing but a big, empty hole for Dad. That's the way I figure it." His face turned toward me, but I couldn't see his eyes. "Been falling all his life. Mom, Matt, Mark, me—we're just rocks he's picked up so he'll have something to throw off when he needs to do some climbing.

Mom, she won't see it. And Matt and Mark, I don't know. But hell, the rocks fall too. Wile E. takes them down with him. Then he hits. And there's a shadow. You ever notice that, on those cartoons? A shadow, and he looks up, and Bam! Bam! Bam! again. All the rocks he threw off smash him."

I felt his eyes on me but didn't look at him. The carp's yellow mouth reached the surface of the river and made soft, sucking sounds.

"I'm not going down that hole anymore," he finally said. He looked back to the river. "Whatever it takes. Hell, I'm even thinking of going to college, man."

I stared at him.

"You gonna shoot, or should I take it?"

He began to raise the bow in his skinny arm.

I shook my head, drew back my bow and aimed below the feeding fish, not where it appeared in the refraction of the water, but where it actually was. I held the draw a moment, then released. String spun, uncoiling in the light.

Sitting there above the valley, I thought that Luke was more prescient than he knew. His father surely did fall down a big, empty hole, taking LouAnn with him. I wondered if Luke had escaped, as he'd claimed he would back then. He was back in Cloten; you'd hardly call that an escape. On the other hand, I wasn't living in Cloten, and—as Becca would point out—I hadn't exactly escaped either. Luke would no doubt say there's some bullshit somewhere here. Another wind swirled the trees in the valley. The river glinted silver at the bend.

My mind returned to Two-Speed. I'd known him before I'd known Luke—though not really known him. He hauled cattle for Dad. I wondered if, the night before he crashed his semi, he and my father had gone through their usual confrontation in the barn.

The semis often came at night. I would wake to their lights spreading shadows in my room as they came down the driveway, shadows like a net cast through the branches of the elm in the front yard. The shadows moved along the walls as the angle of the light changed, passed up and over the dresser, bending, dropped to the floor, slid along it, reached my bed, moved over my face. It was like waking underwater to light shuffled by waves.

The diesels throbbed through the window, and I'd throw back the covers, my heart quick. Chris went on sleeping in his bed, the shadows moving over him. I strode across the cool floor and looked over the porch roof. Down the driveway, their running lights framing them, came the big trucks. They pulled into the yard, and the drivers got out. I threw open the window. The cool night air caught my naked chest. Out in the yard, under the turning of the engines, the men were muttering, pointing and gesturing, their shadows, stretching down the yellow-lit lawn, moving strangely in the branches of the grove a hundred yards away.

The screen door skreeked open and then clapped shut, and my father came out from under the porch roof, putting on his cap. I breathed one more gulp of air—the diesel smell and old manure of the trucks—then reached for my clothes heaped on a chair and climbed into them, not even bothering to find a light.

Jeff? Chris mumbled, his round face gazing at me.

The semis are here, Bud.

Can I come?

Not yet.

When?

Sometime. When you're older. Go back to sleep.

I went to him, rumpled his hair lightly, then went out the door. He was too tired to complain, and his bed was too warm. I took the steps two at a time. At the fifth step from the bottom I grasped the banister overhang and swung myself through the air—arching backwards so my chin missed the top of the door jamb—and landed on my feet in the living room. I went to the mudroom, shrugged into coveralls, put on socks and boots, and went outside.

The first semi was just beginning to back up. I could tell Two-Speed wasn't driving that one. The trailer had to be guided between two grain bins, had to swerve to miss a tree, then straighten out to meet the chute that was placed straight out the barn door. The driver was already off-course, and behind him, in the yellow light of the yard pole, my father was waving and gesturing while the driver, keeping him in the mirrors, tried to follow his directions. Three or four times he went forward and back before he managed to make it around the tree, the brakes expelling air in explosive bursts.

I looked around for a while before I found Two-Speed, leaning against his semi, the studied uninterest on his face illuminated by his cigarette's glow. I stood in the dark near the grain bins where I didn't think he could see me and watched the shadows deepen and recede on his face as he pulled on the cigarette, saw the pockets of his eyes turn hollow. His cattle prod dangled from his belt, clicking against the semi door whenever he moved.

Then it was his turn to back his semi up. He would drop his cigarette, stub it out with his toe, and climb into the cab. When he put the transmission into reverse and released the clutch with a belch of diesel smoke, he never stopped, never slowed down, never readjusted. He simply started, and once started, never had to make corrections, as if the huge semi were following a track, one that existed nowhere but in Two-Speed's mind but was nevertheless as inevitable as steel rails. I watched, entranced. There was something inexorable and beautiful about it, the contained and churning engine, the diesel smoke, the massive, rectangular rig rolling backwards, twisting without pause, reasserting its course, stroked by tree branches as it moved under them, everything throbbing, until the trailer, as wary and gentle as a dog meeting another, eased up to the chute and stopped with a sigh of air brakes, just touching the wood.

It mesmerized me. The semi glowed in the orange and red of its running lights, and I was young, and it was night. It was like waking from sleep to a bigger dream. Then Two-Speed climbed out of the cab, his pants tucked into his boots, gaunt and stringy as a heron, with the same enigmatic glitter in his eyes, the same careful delicacy about his walk. He'd step to the back of the trailer, and if he were more than an inch away from the chute he'd grunt and spit, disgusted with himself.

I knew what was coming, and I trembled, half in anticipation, half in fear. As we began to load cattle, in the low space of the barn, in the acrid smell of scoury shit and animal fear and sweat, forcing the cattle up the chute, always one would turn away from the chute and try to twist back against the force of the other cattle crowding it. Then Two-Speed would shout, and I'd look up and see him pull the cattle prod from his coverall pocket, sweep it up like a wand, like a sorcerer's stick. Through the mist and steam I'd see the wild eyes of the steer rolling in their sockets, patches of sweat dark in its matted hair, its neck twisted back as it tried to turn. The wooden chute creaked and groaned with the pressure of the animals pushing against it.

Two-Speed swore, the cigarette bobbing in his mouth, and then he brought the prod up and over the side of the chute, quick and skinny and heron-like. He brought it up and over and then down hard, and the blunt, gray prongs caught the returning steer in the middle of its forehead. A sharp z-zz-z-z-zz-t rasped across the barn, and if I was close enough I could see the blue spark before the prongs were buried in the animal's hair. The steer grunted and leaped. It swung its head, trying to escape, but Two-Speed remained, relentless, following its every move, forcing it to turn. It lunged, snorted, dodged. The prod remained. Slipping on the chute floor, perhaps falling to its knees, the steer made wet, low noises in its throat. Two-Speed waited for it to rise, then buried the prongs again, now in the animal's flank. Hard hoof against wood, booming inside the barn, the steer's legs pounded a rhythm, seeking the false safety of the truck.

Something changed in Two-Speed's face then, some-thing even I, young as I was, could see through the thick air of the barn. C'mon, you sonsabitches, c'mon, he muttered. Something gripped him, some inability to stop himself, and though the animals were again moving well he'd hang over the chute and bury the prod in the flank of the next animal, *zzzzzz-z-z-zz-t*, and hold it there as long as his arm could reach.

One steer, perhaps two, perhaps even three, and I'd feel in my solar plexus a great, tight excitement, waiting for what would happen. I'd hold my breath, waiting. Rage seemed to have overtaken Two-Speed, until he had no control, as if he'd gone into his own warped and driven world, as the prod played its vicious, its random, its senseless melody over the backs of the cattle, like a terrible, alien insect.

Then I'd hear my father's voice: "Dammit, Two-Speed. Lay off the electricity!"

This was one of the few times I ever heard my father swear. The words—calm with their own rage, command-ing—descended into the confusion like a cold, clarifying liquid. In midair the prod stopped, Two-Speed jerking it back as if he'd been slapped, and he snapped his head in my father's direction, and across the backs of the milling steers the two men's eyes met and locked.

They always stared at each other, some challenge I only half-understood running between them. But Two-Speed al-ways wrenched his thin face around finally, breaking the stare to jam the cattle prod into his back pocket, where it pro-truded, stiff and ungainly, making him look even more like an unkempt wading bird in the dim, manurey air of the barn.

On Two-Speed's face was a look more violent and twisted than anything I'd ever seen, but also more frightened. I could never sleep afterwards. I'd lie in bed, listening to Chris's light breathing, and wonder what could turn a man's face that way, and what about my father could bring it out of Two-Speed, and then contain it, as if my father were a wall that Two-Speed hated and yet could never think of scaling or battering down.

I couldn't understand it then, and it still makes little sense to me. Mom thinks it was enough, whatever it was, to make Two-Speed run his semi down that hill and kill himself, his wife, and Dad's cattle. The old river valley stretched out before me, and I stared into it, and couldn't bring myself to believe it. I picked up a dead leaf, crushed it in my hand, let its shattered pieces, like brown snow, drift away in the wind. I remembered that hot, cicada-laden afternoon that had begun my friendship with Luke, when I had seen that cattle prod used for different purposes.

Pop Bottle Pete

≈

WINTER IS COLD. NOT SUMMER. Summer is when I find the bottles. And rocks. Rocks are like bottles. People give me dollars to throw rocks away. And cents to pick bottles up. Rocks don't like light. When I dig them out, they heavy themselves up. I put them where bales go. Then I take them off and put them with each other. In piles. They have winter in them. Even in summer. They scratch me and they're cold. Because they want to stay in the ground.

People don't like rocks. So they give me dollars. I can pick up the most ones that want to stay in the ground. I talk to them. Quiet, so people won't think. I say, rock, I'm your friend. I'll put you with some rock friends. You'll be a mountain. To the sky. They still don't want to go, but they heavy themselves down some then. And I can pick them up. Some of the piles I make are mountains.

Bottles and rocks are always cool. They have winter in them always. Even in summer. In winter I don't look. Mom says I'd freeze. So the bottles lay in the snow all winter. Snow is water. But it's too hard to drink. Like ice. Bottles are like ice. Ice is like rocks.

In summer the house is cool. In winter it's hot. What's

inside is always different than what's outside. Hot makes me sweat. At night if I sweat I make the sheets wet. Then I have to get up. Because the sheets are wet.

I go outside. Mom caught me once and said not to do that. If people see you, she said, they'll think. So I'm quiet now. I get up because the hot in the house makes me sweat. And the sheets are wet. And my pajamas, too. I take them off because they're wet.

I go outside. I learned how to make the door open without it noisy. One day. I opened and shut it. I opened and shut it. Until Mom said, Peter, what are you doing? But I learned how it's not noisy.

The wind goes wa-a-a-a. It goes wa-a-a-a and wa-a-a-a-a. It goes against me. My feet go in the snow and they get cold. I leave the hot in my feet in the snow where they go in.

No one sees me. No one thinks. The dark goes in and makes me dark. The cold goes in and makes me cold. So no one sees. And thinks.

Except sometimes he did. See. Simon. But he didn't think. Because if he did, Mom would know. She knows when people think. The first time he saw me he stopped and looked. He was on the sidewalk. The dark was in me a long ways, and he had to look and look. He walked across the lawn. Our lawn. He shouldn't have done that, but he did. Not straight. His feet went back and forth, not straight, in the snow.

He stood by me. I didn't move. Maybe he didn't see me yet. That's the idea, Peter, he said. Your old lady got you stuffed up, right? Shityeah. So you gotta cool off, right?

Shityeah, I said.

He made his teeth big and smiley then. Whoa, Peter, he said.

Shityeah, I said again.

He laughed. Me too, then.

Peter, he said. I gotta take you trucking. We'd have a helluva time, huh?

A helluva time, I said.

You bet, he said. All the Coke we could drink. And maybe something else, huh? And you get the bottles.

And a Walkman? I said.

Fucking right, he said.

The wind went wa-a-a-a-a behind the house. It went against me. I sheeby-jeebed.

Hey, he said. His teeth were like snows. His breath smelled sweet and funny. It's mighty cold out here. Don't let that little guy freeze off.

I looked down where he pointed. No, I said. It's not like an icicle. Cold makes it thaw.

He laughed so hard I thought Mom would wake up and come. He grabbed on my arm so he wouldn't fall. He laughed his sweet out. Not an icicle, he said. Cold makes it thaw. It sure does, Peter. You sure got that right. Bet your old lady don't know that though, huh?

I made my shoulders go up and down. Mom says I got to be sure no one sees, I said. Cause they'll think.

He laughed even louder then. They'll think? he said. Whoo-ee. They sure would think. You get nowhere if you let em think.

Yeah, I said. Nowhere.

When he got done laughing, he said, Peter, this town needs more people like you.

Fucking right, I said.

He almost fell down. He laughed so hard he moved back and forth, and then his hand, where it was on my arm, grabbed hard. His hand had too much hot in it. I let my cold go into it.

Fucking right is right, he said. Oh Peter, I had a bit much tonight.

His hot hand held my shoulder hard.

Gotta go, Peter, he said. Damn, though. Let's do this again. Don't let your old lady stuff you up. Come out again, all right? We'll talk more.

Fucking right, I said.

Don't freeze, though, he said. You stay out in this too long you could freeze.

His hand went wave wave in the air. He walked across the snow. His hand made a light across the street go onoff-onoff. Then his knees went too much bend. His hand went down. Like to grab something in the snow. Then he got to the sidewalk and the dark went in him.

The wind went wa-a-a-a against me. I sheeby-jeebed all over.

I could freeze, I said. Shityeah. I could freeze.

Ellen Easton Crandall

≈

I WORRY ABOUT THE BABY. It's tiny yet, inside me. I don't even know it's there, not as a thing. It's my own body that tells me—the different heat, the sponginess of my flesh, a tenderness. As if, carrying something easily hurt, I'm touched by the world more insistently—probed—and asked: Who are you? And my body responds: A carrier. For now. A sheath, a pod.

It's got to be so small yet. No kicks, no movement, nothing to tell me it's there. But I know. The test merely confirmed it. But knowing just makes me feel my whole body is a larger secret, a secret I don't really know and can't tell, not even to myself.

How far can shock waves carry? How deep can they go? I was in church when it happened. We were singing "How Great Thou Art." I felt as if my body were singing. I was singing with everyone else, but I felt as if my body were singing in secret, by itself. Then sings my soul. Then sings my body. And deep inside, I thought, sings the baby. All around me the sound went up, and I was with it and apart from it, singing and silent both.

Then like a wave rushing at me, I felt it. It came like

something built of water. It lifted me, swept me, curled me, crashed me.

I dropped my hymnal. I saw it fall from my hands like a heavy, lifeless bird, its pages fluttering. It seemed like I watched it fall forever. Fall and fall. I couldn't breathe, and I was being swept and floated, and the pages of the hymnal curled in the wind they made. A thousand useless wings.

It hit the seat in front of me and lay there. Opened up. The sound of its hitting came to me like echoes underwater. It freed my breathing, and I gasped. I clutched the seat in front of me to keep from falling. My knees bent, but not because I bent them, and I sat down.

Around me the hymn went on. Around me nothing changed. I felt a hand on my shoulder. I heard a voice: "Are you all right?" I nodded, but I couldn't look up. "Are you sure?"

I forced myself to see. Faces looked at me, helpless and concerned. As if I were the one who needed help. But I couldn't tell them. I didn't know what had happened. Just that it had. "I'm fine," I said. "Just faint. Please. I'm fine."

I wrapped my hands around my womb. How couldn't they know? I felt the wave recede. My body no longer sang. I knew, but didn't know, what had happened. Something. I knew, but not what.

I bent over and wrapped my hands around my womb, to protect the child. As if flesh could do anything at all. As if flesh had boundaries and power.

When the song ended and people sat, the woman in front of me picked up the hymnal. She straightened its bent pages and closed it. She turned around and handed it to me and smiled. I raised my hand to take it, a hard and heavy thing. A block, a brick of paper. I put it beside me and wrapped myself again. I waited. Then the sirens went off. The volunteer firemen rushed from church. I hugged myself and waited. To find out what I knew.

Jeff Gruber

≈

A YEAR AFTER CHRIS'S DEATH, when I was sixteen years old, I became friends with Luke. I can pinpoint the day and hour. It was late summer, barely over a week before school would start again. I'd just finished hauling a load of soybeans into the elevator. I drove slowly back through town, the empty truck creaking around me, the high scream of cicadas pouring out of the trees into my open windows. Then I heard a dog yelping—bright clots of sound that rose over the rhythmic swelling and fading chant of the cicadas.

The sound got louder as the truck moved toward it. I tried to ignore it, but the dog was in pain, and no one seemed to be hearing or helping it. I jerked the wheel of the truck over and braked at the curb. For a moment I clutched the wheel, staring through the windshield. The dog yelped again. I snapped the ignition off and swung open the door. When I stepped from the truck the heat from the pavement bore right through the soles of my boots.

I held onto the door, trying to decide whether this was my business or not. Again the dog screamed. I hit the hot fender with my fist and ran across the street onto Eddie Jorgensen's lawn. A sprinkler arched a rainbow of mist and I swerved to avoid it. When I came around the corner of the house into the Jorgensen's yard, the yelps jumped in intensity. But I felt strange running through people's yards, and I slowed down. I looked into the windows of the house to see if anyone was watching me but could see only a few feet beyond the glass.

The dog yelped again. I nearly stumbled, then heard voices, an adolescent's first, pleading, "Stop. Leave him alone," and then an older man's, low and menacing, "Let go of him. I'll kill the little bastard. Let go."

I jumped a flower bed, felt blossoms catch on the toe of my boot and rip off. Through a gap in the hedge I glimpsed a man and a boy with their backs to me, the boy kneeling with his arms protecting a dog, and the man, long hair falling down the sides of his face, standing over them. I realized that I was looking into Two-Speed Crandall's yard. It made me hesitate. Friends of mine who lived in town had told me stories of wandering onto Two-Speed's lawn and being chased away with curses and threats of grave bodily injury, and there were all the other stories too, usually laughed at and disbelieved, but scary nonetheless.

And Two-Speed impressed me, had since I'd first walked out in the dark, as a grade-schooler, to help load cattle. It wasn't just that he'd mastered the art of the big rigs, and the big rigs took him places. It was that nothing else seemed to matter to him. The cigarette bobbing from his lips as if he didn't even know it was there; the staccato bark of his laugh, changing quickly to a high-pitched, raw, and birdlike screech, on the edge of hysterics, when he thought something was really funny; even the violent abandon of the cattle prod—to me they all marked him, when I was younger, as a man without bounds.

The first time I'd helped load cattle I'd gone to bed and lain awake reliving the scene in the barn. I was ten years old. The next morning my father had caught me pushing a blunt, forked stick and making sizzling sounds against the heads of the cattle eating from the bunks. When I saw him staring at me, his eyes steady as stone, I knew I'd done something wrong, though I'd only been playing. I dropped the stick into the bunk, while the cattle reached their massive heads around my feet, licking up the silage we were dumping there. The cattle's teeth ground steadily around me. Their hooves sucked in and out of the cattle yard mud, and their stomachs churned and rumbled, the mineral-oil smell of their hides mingling with the fermented, sweet-sour smell of the silage.

"We don't do that, son," my father said.

He walked between the two rows of heads toward me, his eyes never leaving mine. I felt pinned by them, rooted. He reached me, bent down, picked up the stick, and threw it, sidearm, over the cattle yard and into the grove. I watched it twist away against the blue of the sky. My father's hand touched my shoulder briefly, and he went on down the bunks, the cattle not even bothering to pull their heads away from him.

I'd never again even considered playing at shocking the cattle. Still, whenever we sold cattle, I was secretly excited when Two-Speed was one of the drivers, barging onto our place with his reckless laughter and language, and the obscene jokes he told to the other drivers within my hearing—

jokes my father wouldn't even smile at—and his absolute control of his rig, into which he'd casually climb, as if it were nothing, and put it into gear, and go, just go and be gone, away.

By the time I was sixteen, much of this boyhood fascination had passed, but even so I paused outside Two-Speed's lawn, uncertain, half-hidden by Eddie Jorgensen's hedge. This was the Crandall's; their business was their own. I recognized the kneeling boy, Luke Crandall. I knew him, but not well. He was a year younger than me and a member of the wrestling team—skinny, a bit awkward. He wrestled without control, either overwhelming his opponent with constant, unorthodox, and furious moves, or else losing his balance and getting pinned. I'd worked with him a few times, trying to give him more control, but my attempts were met with sullen quiet, and I quit having much to do with him. Winning and losing seemed the same to him; he showed indifference to both, and I wondered why he even went out for the team and bothered trying to cut weight for meets.

The cicadas pitched their screams in the heat as I stood outside Two-Speed's lawn, wondering what to do. "I'll teach the little bastard to piss on my hubcaps," Matt Crandall, Luke's older brother—growled. "Let go or you'll get it yourself."

The dog whined. I could see its slim muzzle around Luke's arms. I was about to turn and sneak away when Luke opened his arms slightly. "Run, Lummox," he said. "Run." But the dog only whined and remained. Luke wrapped his arms around the animal again.

"Have it your way," Matt said. He bent down and pushed something that looked like a stick in a short, vicious movement toward Luke. "No, Matt," Luke said. "Don't." And then his speech disintegrated, and his arms shot out, and he fell backwards onto the lawn.

For a moment the world was emptied of anything but the cicadas' shrill cadence. I recognized the stick as Two-Speed's cattle prod, the prod I'd seen arcing and sizzling in our barn, turning thousand-pound steers, terrifying them more than the slatted truck. Luke's face twisted and contorted as Matt held the prongs against his side.

Anger swelled like compressed air bursting inside me, but it seemed to swell outside me, too, with an almost physical pressure, so that I felt I floated in it. I walked, rocked within the cicadas' rocking chant, borne along by its buzz-saw snarl that cut a column through the air to Matt Crandall bending over Luke.

Matt lifted the prod, then bent with it again. I saw Luke's mouth, wide open, saw a strand of Matt's hair lift in the breeze and curl over his head, saw the wand with its blunt prongs float in his hand and descend. I had a moment of sickness when I thought he was going to zap Luke's groin. But the prod went past, and then, even in the bright sun, I saw the blue arc on Luke's stomach and heard the current snap.

Luke convulsed. His face crumbled like a crushed cracker. His legs jerked into the fetal position as if he were cradling the prod into his stomach. Only later did I realize I was running by then. Only later did I recall my own shout. Matt's hair swayed for a moment, then caught up with the movement of his head as he turned to find me running across the lawn. His hair swung out like a skirt in a waltz. The prod arced blue light again as he pulled it away. Luke went limp, and the dog cowered and howled, and Matt rose, turning, his face surprised, mean, distorted.

He swung the prod up and pointed it at me, but I was too close to stop. I ducked under the thrust, caught his elbow, twisted, and using his momentum, fell backwards, rolling, my other arm around his waist, slinging him over my body in a short fireman's carry, a wrestling move I'd perfected. He whumped onto the baked lawn, flat on his back. His head thudded, his breath whooshed out of him. The prod flew from his hand.

I scrambled to the prod, then knelt over Matt's dazed face. I wanted to shove the two prongs into his forehead and rake them down the length of his body. My muscles tensed, and the movement started. But it stopped as if my arms had hit the end of a chain, and I recoiled from what I was doing.

All the violence had gone from Matt Crandall's face. He stared past the prod into my eyes. In his I saw resignation. I saw him waiting.

For just a moment, with a power that stunned me, I was kneeling in that dredge ditch, screaming, pulling on Chris's legs, the water flowing sedately past me, the wind moving easily in the long grass, pulling and pulling, but Chris's legs were as unmovable as if they were anchored. I screamed at him to hold on, to not breathe. I let go of his legs and splashed to the tractor, stood in the water and strained with all my might against the machine's weight. Blood boiled inside my skull, my joints popped, my screams turned to grunts, I felt my shoulders would tear apart, but the tractor didn't rise, didn't tip. My efforts drove my feet deep into the soft mud bottom of the ditch. I threw myself flat into the water and tried to dig under Chris, flailing, bawling, scooping up gobs of thick mud with my hands and pulling at him, but nothing moved, nothing happened. The tractor still rested on his chest, and I couldn't get his head above the water. His face was covered, the water so muddy I couldn't even see it.

I half-ran, half-crawled out of the ditch, weeping and screaming, crying for help, but no one answered. I was alone and help was a half mile away. I saw the house, a white square against the blue sky and green trees of the grove, so far away, and I screamed at it, but no one answered. In the field behind the house I saw blue diesel smoke rise over the grove—Dad cultivating corn. I screamed at him, but the smoke went on rising, thinning, and the muted sound of the tractor continued.

I looked down into the ditch again, then back at the house. I didn't know what to do. I couldn't move. Then, as if it had been shot out of the sky, resignation hit me, so leaden that I collapsed in the middle of the road. I heard the tick of tiny stones as grasshoppers sprayed across the gravel, and I knew. It seemed impossible. So little, and so awful because it was so little. Five inches of water. An inch less and I might have saved him. But I couldn't and didn't.

It all came back when I looked into Matt Crandall's eyes, and I jerked away from the resignation there as if it were a deadly infection. I stumbled away from him, gasping.

I felt my boots, like clumsy, fat animals, hit the earth, but I was blind, circling, and then I found myself standing over Luke, the cattle prod hanging from my fingers. I stared down at him, groping for comprehension.

"Are you all right?" I managed to whisper.

Behind me Matt rose. I half-turned, then heard his feet shuffle away over the hard lawn. Luke and I stared at each other. He turned his face away, rolled over, and rose. His body didn't know what to do with itself. He began to walk away, then stopped, came back. He went to Lummox and bent down to examine him.

I put my hands on my knees to brace myself and stared straight down at the ground, breathing fast, feeling like I was in one of my dreams, as if the ground were rolling and heaving. I shut my eyes and floated. When I opened them, Luke's back was still toward me, his thin neck bent over the dog. An untucked corner of his ragged shirt hung limply over his hip.

I stared at his back, waiting for him to acknowledge me, acknowledge something, do or say anything. It was odd, the way he ignored me. Then the stiffness in his neck, the stillness in his posture, told me: he was ashamed. He wanted to be invisible. It embarrassed me to realize it, but it also steadied me, put me in control. The ground quit moving.

"What happened?" I asked.

Luke didn't turn around. "Matt gets mad sometimes," he said, without inflection. "Lummox pissed on his wheels. I should train him not to do that." One of his shoulder blades twitched.

"Dogs are hard to train," I said.

He almost looked back at me. I saw his thin jaw, sweat on his cheek, the faint fuzz of first whiskers.

"A Lab, huh?" I said. "You had him hunting?"

His face, what I could see of it, opened for a moment, but closed down immediately. "No," he said. "Not yet. But I'm going to."

"Yeah," I said. "Ducks and geese. He'd do real good."

He nodded. I moved toward the dog, but it whined and shied away from me. The prod still dangled from my fingertips. I looked down at the thing, then swung it up in front of me. Luke's eyes followed it.

"I'm going to break this thing," I announced. I lifted my knee to slam the prod down over it.

"No!"

Luke leaped up, his bony body erupting so quickly he startled me. He grabbed the prod and tried to jerk it away from me, but I resisted, as if it were some trophy I'd captured. But it was more than that. Breaking it seemed like the only thing that could relieve the emotions I'd been feeling since I'd first heard the dog's yelps. When Luke grabbed the prod, I tried to force it down against his resistance, and for a moment we struggled, face-to-face. I almost flung him away, then realized what I was doing. The desperation in his face confused me. We stared at each other, each of us gripping the thing with both hands.

"Don't," Luke said quietly.

I almost argued. I felt his tight muscles through the plastic and metal, quivering, like the tension on a line at a fish's first, tentative, exploratory strike.

"Hell!" I jerked my hands off the thing.

It swung down the arc of Luke's arms as if it were dead weight.

"I'll put it back," he said.

"Yeah. Whatever you want." I suddenly wanted nothing more to do with him. Something had just happened that shouldn't have, but I didn't know what.

"I gotta go," I said.

"That was a nice move," he said.

"What?"

"The fireman's."

"Yeah? I guess it works."

"I should learn it."

"Sure."

We both looked at the ground.

"I gotta go," I said. "See you around." I began to turn away.

"Wait."

His voice was too quiet. I turned back. He stood with one hand on the dog's head. The other held the prod. He lifted it vaguely, without looking up. Finally he said: "This."

He raised his eyes to mine, lifted the prod slightly, and glanced down at it. I shook my head. "What?"

"I'd rather. You know. You wouldn't."

For a moment I stared at him. "What are you . . . ?" His eyes suddenly blazed with anger and defiance.

"Oh, shit," I said, understanding. "Hell. Did something happen here? I was just looking at your dog, right? Seeing what kind of hunter he'd make."

He didn't say anything, just nodded, his eyes still hard, but mixed with doubt, and a desire to believe me.

"See you around," I said.

"Yeah. See you."

I walked back to the truck, got in, and shut the door. I stared through the windshield and began to shake. I shook and shook in the hot confines of the cab, too weak to press the clutch in, too weak to turn the key.

A week later my father and I were walking a soybean field, cutting out rogue corn, cocklebur, and buttonweed that we'd missed the first time through. The beans stood as high as our waists, and we struggled through them, the vines catching at our boots. We worked in silence, mosquitoes rising from the vegetation around us, the fields stretching away to a pale horizon broken by groves of trees. Luke was still on my mind, and the quiet of the fields and sheer drudgery of the labor urged me to speak, but because of my implied promise to Luke I edged around the truth.

As we stopped near a scattering of corn plants I asked: "Dad, why do you think people are cruel to animals?" I tried to make my voice casual, as if the question weren't important.

My father bent over and sliced a cornstalk off neatly with a cornhook. The plant stood for a moment, then fell rustling into the soybeans. He moved it with his foot until it lay between the rows, then took off his cap and wiped his brow with the sleeve of his shirt. He stuck the cap back on his head.

"What's got you thinking about that?" he finally asked.

Why'd he have to question my question? "Just thinking," I said shortly, and sliced off a cornstalk with a hard jerk of my hook.

When I looked back up he was gazing at me. "Uh-huh," he said. "Well, I don't know. Some people can't stand themselves, maybe. So they take it out on something helpless."

I wanted an argument. "That doesn't make sense."

"Sure it does. If you're feeling helpless and can't stand it, you might hurt something helpless."

That just angered me more. I shrugged and started across the field toward a patch of buttonweeds sticking above the soybeans. I was pulling one when he reached me. He stood next to me and pulled one out himself. "What happened?" he asked as I reached for another.

I jerked the buttonweed out by the roots and threw it down. "Damn," I said, expecting him to reprimand me, but he didn't.

I hesitated. "All right," I said: "I saw Matt Crandall shocking a dog with a cattle prod."

My father was silent so long that I finally turned to look at him. He stood still as a statue underneath the sky, staring into the plants at his feet.

"What'd you do?" he finally asked.

"A short fireman's," I said. "I got the prod away."

I didn't tell him what I'd seen in Matt's eyes, didn't tell him how I'd remembered the ditch.

Dad nodded. "A dog, huh?"

His pale eyes looked at me, searching. I held them for a moment, then looked away. "Yeah. Luke Crandall's."

He took off his cap, stuck it back on his head. "Christ!" he exploded.

He walked five rows over and pulled a buttonweed taller than himself. The roots came up trailing dirt. He held the plant in his hand and stared at it. Some intensity within him frightened me.

To break the silence I said, "I wanted to smash that prod, but Luke was there, and he stopped me. And it was his dog."

My father beat the dirt from the tangled roots with his cornhook. Soil clung, and as he beat the stem the chunks splatted like a small rainshower against the leaves of the field. He went on hitting the plant methodically until the roots were nothing but a stringy skeleton quivering with each blow of the hook. Finally he stopped and stared at the naked roots. "It was probably Two-Speed's prod," he said.

"What?"

"It was probably Two-Speed's prod." He said it more loudly and threw the denuded buttonweed at his feet. "Would've been hell to pay if Two-Speed'd found it broken."

He looked up from the plant at his feet. "Hell, son," he said, looking straight into my eyes. "Where do you think Matt learned that trick?"

We stood in the middle of the field, soybeans up to our waists. The green leaves moved like a sea around us. He knew it wasn't just the dog.

"You mean Two-Speed . . . ?"

"You see someone shocking a dog, you stop him," my father said. "You did good. Or cattle. You don't have to let that happen. But when all you got's what you hear . . ." He stopped, nudged a dead buttonweed with his toe, looked up, met my eyes. "Well, it isn't much, is it?"

He looked small, half-eaten up by the field. It made me feel small, made me feel we were both being submerged.

"Hell, I don't know," he said. "Who knows anything?"

Luke Crandall

≈

GRUBER CAME BACK FOR THE FUNERAL. I saw him there. Didn't talk to him much, everybody who never had much to do with Dad coming up and saying how sorry they were, but we said we'd go to the river together as long as he's here. That'll be good. Gruber's the first person I ever knew who didn't bullshit, at least not with me. That time he took on Matt, I kept waiting for the whole school to find out, figured I'd come in the door and there'd be the seniors, big shit-eating grins on their faces, waiting for me: "Sure is *sizzling* today! Hey Crandall, did you hear the *shocking* news?" and the girls pretending they don't know what's going on, or looking at me with their faces all made up to be sorry.

But I walked in the school for a week and nothing happened. Nothing. I couldn't believe it. Why the hell wouldn't he spread the word? Shit, he took on Matt. That'd be worth bragging rights. Must be biding his time, I thought. Waiting for when I'd be thinking I was safe, and then hit me with it. But still nothing happened, and then I had a worse thought, that he was feeling sorry for me, and when I thought that I couldn't even look at him when I passed him in the hall, pretended to be doing something else, because I

≈ 119 ≈

didn't want to see some puppy-dog look on his face when he saw me.

Then I thought: He isn't going to keep me from looking where I want to look. Shit. So I finally looked right at him when I went by, and I couldn't believe it, there was nothing like pity there at all. There was something, he remembered it, but that was it. No sign he ever intended to tell anyone. He actually meant what he said when he said it.

Still, that seemed like bullshit. I figured even if he wasn't going to tell anyone, he sure as hell wanted to. But as soon as I thought that, I realized I was bullshitting myself. Did I expect him to forget? Expect it to not be part of his memory, even though he's the one who came across the lawn and stopped Matt? When you start to turn what isn't bullshit into bullshit, then you've got the ultimate, something beyond category. I'd gotten myself completely screwed up with all my thinking.

Dad could always turn what was into what wasn't, and what wasn't into what should have been, and what should have been into some reason to get drunk. I'd thought all my thinking and classifying was going to keep me from turning into him, and instead it just drove me deeper into it. I tore up that classification scheme. Tore it into little bits and threw it in the garbage. All it gave me was what *was* bullshit. It didn't tell me a damn thing about what wasn't.

When wrestling season started, I asked Gruber one day, when the coach was letting us work on moves, if he could show me the fireman's carry. And I guess that started it. It wasn't the wrestling though. I never cared about wrestling the way Gruber did. The guy'd go out on that mat like it meant the world, like picking up and slamming people down was life or death. Pretty mellow and laid-back generally, but get him on that mat and watch out. I could never care that much. Could never quite figure out why he did.

Still, it started there—the way-to-go's when one of us won, the too-bads at a loss, and those bus rides after a meet, staring out the windows with nothing to think about, at the snow blowing across the fields in the night. One of those nights he was sitting in the same seat with me, and he asked me how Lummox was doing, if I'd had him hunting yet, and we got to talking about the dog, and pretty soon we were making plans to go to the river together.

After that we started spending time together. And we met Angel Finn down there one night, and he took a liking to us, and we'd sit out on his boat at night, fishing, and Angel'd talk—told us all about Lake Agassiz and the River Warren, all that water booming out of the glacier, all that size and darkness. And Gruber'd talk right up, saying things, not at all embarrassed about knowing stuff.

And it wasn't bullshit. One night, sitting on that river, on the bank, just me and Gruber, saying things once in a while, and generally saying nothing, I thought: This is the way it's supposed to be—just sitting here, talking if you want to, the water going by, and sand eroding off the banks, and trees weakening and falling. This is it: these are the questions. There's no A, B, C, D, or none or all of the above. This is how the questions feel.

It was a real feeling—like some big loosening inside me, some clamp giving way. The whole damn river became a question, and the night became a question and us sitting there, and then the strike of a beaver's tail became a question, and the fish finding their way to our lines.

It was good times. I swear, it changed my life. Gruber and I haven't seen each other for a while, but something clicks when we do. I was glad to see him at the funeral. It'll be good to go down to the river with him, pretend that things are still the same.

Jeff Gruber

≈

AS I CAME DOWN THE HILL into Cloten, everything looked as it always had. The trees hid everything except the church steeples, and it wasn't until I was on Main Street that I saw anything out of order. Even there the destruction was random and already being tamed by repairs. Buildings, boarded where the semi had hit them, suggested desertion more than destruction, and the handle of the sledge hammer sticking out of the pool hall looked like a practical joke.

At the end of the street, however, I saw the power that Two-Speed had brought down that hill. Hurricane fencing had been strung around the barbershop, and plywood fastened over the brick. Above the plywood the front of the building sagged as if it had lost all support. I stepped over the fencing and pressed my eye to a crack between brick and wood.

The inside of the shop looked as if a bomb had exploded there. The semi's cab had hit with enough force to throw the entire front of the building against the rear wall. Brick and broken glass were scattered over the floor. Pieces of ceiling lay over the bench at the back, and furniture—the plastic-coated chairs where men had read the paper and talked about hunting and fishing and farming—looked as if it had ricocheted off the walls like pool balls. Bent and tangled together, it lay anywhere, at weird angles, on the floor. The long mirror at the back of the shop had collapsed, a heap of bright glass on the counter. A big square of clean paint showed where it had been.

The second barbershop chair was skewed backwards. Two-Speed had hit it so hard that he bent it. It looked like a chair on some weird carnival ride, tilted back crazily, as if to spin a person into dizziness and fear. Just looking at it made me feel displaced. The cab of the semi had completely penetrated the building, embedded in its own destruction, bricks and plaster falling down around it, and Two-Speed had been ejected through the windshield, must have literally flown to his death across the space of the barbershop, shedding glass as he flew.

The street outside the barbershop was still stained brown where the firemen hadn't managed to wash all the blood away. A few cars moved peacefully down Main Street. Trees shimmered in the sun. I stepped around the corner of the barbershop and looked over the fields behind it. Here the land rolled a little, moving up from the small creek that ran just outside Cloten and formed the hill down which Two-Speed had come. I could see where the rolling ended and the land flattened out into the old slough country. Corn poked through the black soil. Everything shone. Within a month the corn would cover the rows, and there'd be nothing but green.

I left my car parked and walked the three blocks to the hardware store. The front was boarded up, so I went around and entered through the rear door. The dim interior was unchanged. Down the aisle I saw Angel Finn at the cash register reading the paper. Thin, white-haired, big-nosed, homely as a post, Angel ran a mecca of hardware, a store so complete with pipe fittings, hydraulic couplings, fine-thread bolts of various pitches, and other hardware esoterica, that people came from forty miles away searching for equipment and fittings.

At night, however, Angel haunted the river, sitting in his boat in the darkness while water backflowed and purled. I'd known Angel since I was old enough to go to town with my father for nails or bolts, but I'd first met him on the river one night at two in the morning when Luke and I were stumbling home after several unsuccessful hours of fishing. We were blundering through the woods when Angel came upon us, quiet as the owls that haunted the valley. We'd been talking and were startled to find him suddenly in our path, gliding toward us as smoothly out of the dark as something moving through water. We stared as he swam up, his white hair shining dimly.

"Well as I live," he said. "Jeff Gruber and Luke Crandall, making enough noise to clear the area of wildlife from here to Deadman's Creek. Been fishing, and catching nothing."

Luke and I looked at each other. "Not a thing," Luke said. "You heading in to fish?"

"I just might be," Angel said, sucking on his teeth. "Down here on the river in the middle of the night with a fishing pole in one hand and a bait bucket in the other."

He said it so good-naturedly that both Luke and I laughed.

"You scared the shit out of us," Luke said. "Thought you were a ghost, quiet as you came up."

"Practicing," Angel said. "Get as old as I am, you gotta start doing that. But you boys're quitting when you oughta be starting. They're gonna be biting now."

"How do you know?"

"Don't suppose I do now," he replied. "Suppose I'm just guessing. Still, if you boys ain't wore out."

"Sure," I said. "Why not?"

We fell in behind him, following a path toward a U-bend in the river where the bank dropped vertically down fifteen feet to the water's surface. Angel walked this path as if his feet and not his eyes did the seeing. We came out over the bank, heard the water chuckling and gurgling below us. As I stepped forward to stand beside Angel the air opened up, and the oily water glided beneath me, slick and shiny in the starlight.

"There it is," Angel said.

"What?"

"The river. Every time I come here, there it is. Always kind of surprises me, though. Surely it does."

He reached into his pocket, pulled a penlight out, stuck it between his teeth, and prepared his equipment. He hooked a three-inch minnow through the back, let it dangle in the air for a moment, then flicked it into the darkness. We heard it splash. Angel sat down on a stump. "One thing I know," he said. "You don't catch'em without a line in the water."

For perhaps an hour we fished in silence. When I felt the strike I wasn't even sure what it was—not quick and furious like a northern but instead a steady, relentless pull, as if the river had solidified and begun to pull the line downstream. The rod tip bent and stayed down, and I only slowly realized that something had taken the bait, something so big and powerful that the hook hadn't even slowed it down.

Then the drag on the reel jumped into the silence. The power of the fish ran through the rod into my hands. "I've got something!" I yelled.

Angel's voice was in my ear. "Better tighten it up. He's heading for the Gulf otherwise."

I clicked the drag up a notch—two, three—and still the line, glistening in the dim moon, spun down the line guides, sparked for a moment over the river, and disappeared. I could feel the fish now, the massive movement of its tail ramming through the water. Then the whining stopped, and the line went slack.

"Reel," Angel said.

I reeled, and was still reeling when the fish, heading upstream now, hit the end of the shortened line and nearly jerked the rod from my hands. Something wild in me reached out through the thin line to the animal struggling under the water. I forgot everything—Angel and Luke beside me, my breathing, my memories—as I matched the fish's movements and fought to bring it up.

When it weakened I maneuvered it downstream to where the cutbank leveled out and I could stand near the water. Angel stood beside me with a net and lantern. When the fish first appeared in the lantern light, its mouth tentacled, its head flat as a water-smoothed rock, with glittering eyes, it seemed for a moment to be the river rising out of itself, immensely old, and I felt the fear of something elemental and sacred, and stood rooted while Angel scooped it up with the net and lifted it into the air.

In the full light of the lantern the fish lost its power. It slumped against the cords of the net. My fear leaked away from me, and I wanted it back.

"God," Luke said.

Angel hefted the net. "Channel cat. Fourteen pounds, I'd say." He looked at the two of us. "You never get used to it," he said. "Or if you do you quit coming down."

The river filled the silence between us as we stared at the weakened fish, its gills moving slowly. Then Angel said, "Take'm off and let him go. He needs to do some growing."

I moved to the net, running the line through my hand. The catfish lay motionless except for its mouth opening and shutting and its gills heaving. Its oily smell permeated the air. I thought: I must look like a monster to it, moving through the air out of this light. I groped in its mouth for the hook. Carefully I pried it out, feeling the sandpapery gums against my fingers.

With the fish unhooked I reached into the net with both hands and found the fish's gills. I hoisted the animal out of the cords. Its eyes were round buttons on the sides of its head, foreign as stone, indifferent as sand. I stepped into the water, letting it soak through my boots and socks, and laid the fish down, preparing to move it back and forth to get its gills working. But at the touch of the river it exploded in my hands. I felt an instant of its body hardening, two ripples that passed between my palms, and then my hands were empty in the river. I stayed squatted down for a moment, reluctant to rise, letting the river flow past me.

"I've got a boat, boys," Angel said. "Any night. You let me know."

We had. Now, as my feet creaked on the wooden floor of the hardware store, Angel looked up from his paper. "Well, as I live and breathe," he said. "Jeff Gruber." He came around the corner and extended his hand.

"Angel. How've you been?"

"Surviving. You?"

"All right. Been fishing lately?"

"Been breathing?"

I laughed. "Haven't caught the big one yet?"

"Got a thirty-two pounder the other week. Put it back. Gotta let the children grow. Back for the funeral?"

"Yeah."

"Sure is something. Both of them. Like that. You talked to Luke?"

"No. I haven't even been home yet. Thought I'd stop in and see you. How about you?"

He stuck his hands in his pockets and leaned against the counter, his long legs sticking into the aisle. "Nope," he said. "It's not my place to be looking him up, and he hasn't been in. Family stuff. I'll be at the funeral. Like everyone else."

"This is big news, isn't it?"

"Surely it is."

"He hit your store, huh?"

"He did. Hit it good."

I walked down the aisle to the broken front of the store and looked at the damage. The glass had been shattered, the door ruined, the brickwork smashed, the display shelves under the window destroyed.

"What's it about, Angel?" I called back to him.

He came down the aisle, his shuffling walk not even making the floor creak. "Don't know," he said. "I wasn't here. I was up at the county park pulling my boat out of the water about the time he was loading, I'd guess. Sleeping when it happened. They had to wake me up."

"What're people saying?"

"Anything you can think of."

"Yeah. And what do you think?"

He shook his head. "Two-Speed Crandall," he said. "Who knows? You live in this town, you knew him. And still."

"Knew *of* him, you mean?"

"No. Knew him. Down to the bones. Just, there was nothing there."

I said nothing.

"Think what you will," Angel said. "But you put Two-Speed Crandall on a couch and let him babble long's he wants, and when you're done you're gonna know what everyone else does—that he could drink and he could drive truck and talk, but he didn't know squat about who he was. And neither will you. Because there's nothing there. Maybe you'll know why. But it won't change nothing. Figuring out there's a hole in a pail don't make it full of water."

"Two-Speed Crandall in counseling," I said. "That'd be something."

"And as successful now as it woulda been two days ago," Angel replied. "Least he'd stay put for it now."

I couldn't help but laugh. "Still," I asked. "What do you make of it?"

His eyes went beyond the plywood to the street before they realized they were deprived of space, but even then he went on staring as if he could see right through the wood. He sucked his teeth. "I think he aimed it," he said.

"Aimed it? You mean everything? Here too?"

"I'll tell you," he said. "He come in here one day so mad he was twitching. I figured he was just bad drunk, but it was more'n that. He had something on his mind, and that's the worst thing a drunk can have. I was standing up by the cash register, and he come through the door looking like a jack-in-the-box that'd just popped open, jerking and bobbing. 'Mr. Simon Crandall,' I said. 'What can I do for you?'

"And the oddest thing. He stopped right there and drew himself up. 'Damn right,' he said. 'Simon Lane Crandall. And maybe you think you taught my son something down there on that river? With that damn boat of yours?'

"I didn't know what to say. Who the hell swears at a boat? I just looked at him. Fore I could say anything, he goes on. 'I'll teach my own damn son,' he says."

"What was he getting at?" I asked.

"Don't know. He stood there in the aisle wobbling, and I decided he had a bad drunk and happened to find my door. I figure the best thing to do with a drunk is play along, so I said, 'Sure, Simon, he's your son, you can teach him whatever.'

"But that just made him madder. 'Damn right,' he said. 'I'm Simon Lane Crandall, and he's my son, and you stay away from him with your goddamn river and your goddamn boat.'

"Hell, I hadn't even been on the river with Luke for a

long time. He'd borrowed my boat a few days before—like he does every so often—but that was none of Two-Speed's business as far as I was concerned. But I wasn't about to argue, no sense to that, so I said, sure, I'd stay away from Luke if that's what he wanted.

"He stood there a while. Then he said: 'You watch yourself, Angel Finn. Maybe some day you're going to wake up and remember this, and you're going to say, "Oh."'"

"Well, what kind of a threat is that? Then he walked out the door. A sure enough case of paranoia. But I got to say, I kinda said 'Oh' when I come back from the river that morning and saw this store. I don't know why, but I think he aimed it. You got any ideas?"

I shook my head. "I've been gone," I said. "Two-Speed and my dad never got along. And they were Dad's cattle. And now this. But what would Two-Speed have against you? And I can't believe Dad could've somehow caused this."

"Can't believe Two-Speed could've planned it either. On the other hand, you can't hardly believe it was an accident, can you?"

"That's just it."

"One thing about it. Accident or not, it sure was big. Two-Speed might've not amounted to much living, but he sure made his dying big."

We pondered that thought for a moment. Then Angel said, "But big or little, dying's dying."

"Yeah," I said. "Well, I gotta go."

"Good seeing you. Say hello to your dad."

I didn't reply.

"Hell," Angel said then. "I never been with Luke anywhere *but* the river." He sucked his teeth and shook his head, then reached over and rapped the plywood on the windows with his knuckles. The sound boomed dully in the hardware-laden aisles.

Elizabeth Gruber

≈

LEO CAME UP FROM THE BARN to greet Jeff when he came home. He stopped working for the entire afternoon to spend time with Jeff. He told me he was going to do it. He didn't make a big deal of it, but I knew—he's trying.

But they're polite. They talk to each other as if nothing were wrong. Like a show for someone else to watch. Or for themselves to watch. As if the show were the real thing, something to applaud. They sat in the living room like strangers. Almost as if they didn't speak the same language, though they spoke about the same things—crops, weather, forecasts, the prices of soybeans and corn, the weights and conditions of cattle. Jeff still knows it all so well. Jeff asked about the cattle in the yard, how they were feeding out, how long before Leo sold. But he never asked about the ones that had died, never even mentioned them.

It's not that I think he should have to. There are reasons to be silent about anything. Leo taught me that. When I first knew him there were times I thought he was ignoring me, or was even angry with me. He has such a capacity for silence. It took me a long time to understand that. Not a fear or disliking of talk. Just a capacity to absorb silence, to move within it, to hear it as something distinct. Nuanced. Changing. It was after Jeff was born, in fact, before I really understood it. We were going through the usual hard times couples go through with a new baby. After a whole evening of dealing with Jeff's fussing and crying, devoting all our attention to him, we finally got him to sleep. I wanted, finally, to talk. I'd hardly said a word to Leo all day. But he barely responded to anything I said. Short answers, and then silence. It hurt me. So much that I began to cry. He looked at me, even then not saying anything for several seconds, before rising and coming across the living room to me. He sat down beside me.

"What's wrong, Liz Beth?"

"You won't talk to me. We haven't talked all day. The baby's been crying all day, and now that I can finally talk to you, you won't." I was distraught. It wasn't, probably, as major as it seemed then, but I cried uncontrollably once I began to talk.

He let me cry. Even then he didn't respond. Just let me cry—sat there, holding my hand. I couldn't see that it's what I needed. All I could see was that, even when I came right out and told him, he still didn't talk. I felt an anger larger than the loneliness I felt. I was ready to walk away from him, go to the bedroom and lock him out, make him deal with his own silence.

But his hands must have felt something in mine. I didn't know then—or it was my first experience—of how he listened with his hands. Because before I could get up and stalk away, he said, without even waiting for me to stop crying, "It's not that I'm not talking, Liz Beth. Maybe I'm not talking, but that's not it."

"What is it, then?"

"It's . . ." He was at a loss for words. "I'm just listening to it all."

"It all?! What all?"

But then I heard it myself. The house creaked in the summer wind. The elm outside shook and rattled. A hog feeder clanged. A last barn swallow, in the last light, twittered on the wire outside. Before he answered, I heard them all. Then he said what I hadn't heard.

"Jeff's breathing," he said.

Then there it was. From the crib in the next room I could hear the tiny sounds of the baby breathing in and out. That's what he'd been listening to. All along he'd heard it.

But between them now the silence is too much. It's not a silence that listens. It's a silence that won't ask questions.

Jeff sat in the living room and never asked his father about the cattle dead on that truck. Or about the rifle. He would have understood, more than I do, because he worked with the cattle, knew them like Leo knows them. A single question, and Leo might have spoken of it, to someone who could give him the kind of hearing he so often gave me.

And Leo, for his part, never asked Jeff about Jenny—though I know he was dying to. They talked about everything else. As if everything else were interesting. Then their conversation lagged. Jeff asked if there was work to be done. Leo was taking the afternoon off to talk to him, but he mentioned building fence. Jeff insisted they go do it. He found clothes in the mudroom, went out the door. They were talking of work as they went.

You never expect a child to learn the formalities of distance. The maintenance, the structures. You never expect it. A husband, you realize it's possible. You can create something from anger—a pipe, a rock, a running tractor. But children are so close. So close that when they're distant, they're beyond a mother's reach.

Ellen Easton Crandall

≈

I SAW JEFF AT THE FUNERAL. I was hoping he'd come back. This is all so strange and hard. And then, what I've found. I need to talk to him.

I remember how snow fell around us that time on the river. With Luke gone. Jeff told me of Chris, and his dream. I put my hand on his shoulder. Just lightly. Just resting. To hold him down. And to let him know I felt the dream. Inside me. I felt it like one of my own. We were close. Too close, I suppose. He looked into my eyes, and I felt this little surprise of hope. But nothing happened. Luke was off looking for deer. And then we got up and walked down the river together.

I was relieved to see him at the funeral. I was happy, even. For a moment. I'd thought the funeral would be spiritless. People coming just to see. And many did. But in the songs I felt the Spirit move. I think of LouAnn. Most people talk about Simon, but I think of LouAnn.

Only once was I ever together with Luke's whole family. One Thanksgiving LouAnn got them all together. Luke and I had been married for two years. He was in the living room with his father and brothers. LouAnn was in the kitchen preparing the meal. I thought I should help her. So I went back. We made small talk for a while. Then Simon said something from the living room, and laughed. LouAnn was chopping nuts for a salad. She stopped moving the knife when Simon laughed. She looked straight ahead at the wall. Then she said: "He'd be lost without me, you know."

I didn't know what to say. She swept the nuts into a pile with the curve of her hand, watching them push up into a little pyramid. Her hair was gray where it curled in wisps around her ears. She laid her hands flat on the counter, with the pile of nuts between them. From the living room Simon laughed again, alone. Then Matt joined in a little. Luke and Mark were silent.

"They're good sons," LouAnn said.

"Yes," I replied. "I know." I had to say something.

She glanced at me. Her eyes crinkled at the edges. Her face was serious, but there was humor in her eyes. "I hope *you* think so," she said.

I didn't know whether to smile or not. I ducked my head. Geese marched around the border of the paper napkins I held, holding flowers in their beaks. The truth is, I didn't like Matt much, and Mark I hardly knew at all. The kitchen was too quiet.

"Sometimes life's a sea of troubles," she said. She pushed the pyramid of nuts off the counter into her hand and dropped them into a bowl. "But my sons have been good to me." Luke told me once that his mother used to read to him. And tell him stories. She seemed so unlikely a storyteller. 'A sea of troubles,' I wanted to ask her. 'Do you mean like

Hamlet's sea of troubles?' But it seemed so unlikely she did, and I didn't ask.

We never really understand anyone. And when we most want to we don't ask the right questions. Or we pretend we understand. To keep ourselves from getting what we want.

Because it wouldn't be what we want.

I set the napkins on the table, listening to the men murmur in the living room and the whisper the napkins made when they touched the plates. I was young. I didn't know how to ask her the things I wanted to know. Or the things she wanted to tell me.

She picked the knife up and began to chop more walnuts. Over the *chuk chuk* of the knife, the men's tight talk reached us. I asked how she wanted fruit arranged on a plate.

I met Luke at college. I had a note on a bulletin board asking for a ride to Clear River. Luke called. It was a four-hour drive. We talked about classes and professors. Clear River and Cloten. Safe talk. When we got close to home he took a county road. So he could drive through the valley. He pointed out things I'd never known about the river. His voice changed as he talked. Became quieter. Like his mother's.

I didn't think I was looking for a man. I wasn't. When we started the ride he was so quiet, and when he did talk it was brash, as if he needed to impress me. But in the valley he seemed to be talking of things deeper than he knew. And when I got out of the car in Clear River he gave me a look that kept me thinking of him all weekend, in spite of myself.

Sometimes I think he revolves around me. Simon may have revolved around LouAnn, too. She thought he did. What powers that kind of revolution? Love like gravity?

Sometimes Luke seems so open to me. As if he can't keep from showing everything. And other times that openness seems like a mask to me. You can only see the curve of the moon when there's a shadow on it. When it's full it's a flat disk. You'd think that's all there is.

If LouAnn were alive, I might go to her now. After what I found. I thought of confronting Luke right away. But then thought I should wait until the funeral was over. My breath catches in my throat when I think of it. Especially with the baby inside me.

But maybe it's nothing.

It was so good to see Jeff at the funeral. And not only for myself. Sometimes, before he moved to Duluth, when he and Luke would talk, I felt there was a code to their silences. They'd skim over the surface of things with their words. Talking of nothing at all. But beneath the words, in things not said, was something said. Maybe Jeff knows, even now, Luke's silences better than I do. Or knows them differently.

Angel Finn

≈

THERE'RE CATFISH IN THE RIVER bigger than anything I've caught or seen. There're catfish big enough to swallow a man, hiding in the deep water that won't reveal itself through probing with poles or reading the current or lie of the bank. The big ones stay in those holes, and the water runs through their mouths like it's going through a pump or bellows, and the whole river feels their breathing. I've never seen one or caught one, but I think sometimes I've smelled one's oil rising off the water, or I've felt one waiting under me. And one time I was surely on the river where they stay.

I was coming downstream back from an empty night, nothing but mosquitoes and starlight, and the water coming big around the bends, and not a strike all night. I shut the motor off and let the current carry the boat, keeping it in the middle of the river with oars, thinking I might anchor and try a spot I was coming up on where the water runs hard up against a bank and cuts it deep, where I'd caught big ones before, but not big ones like I mean.

I come around a bend and found myself on a part of the river I'd never been on, and I've been on all of it from the county park upstream and downstream twenty-five miles either way. Funny thing was, I didn't think nothing but how odd that after all these years of fishing this river I could find a branch like this I'd missed. The banks were lower, not standing fifteen, twenty feet above the water, but hardly out of it. I went around a few more bends, and the banks got lower and lower, and the river wider, and I noticed the shore seemed to be moving by me faster than usual, slipping backward at an unfamiliar rate.

Then I come around another bend, and I was on a plain of water, but it was sure enough the river too, stretching away from me on either side maybe a mile, maybe more. I ain't been afraid on that river for a long time, spooked but never afraid, no more'n around someone I know well has odd moods and a temper. But I was surely afraid when I come around that bend. I couldn't tell anymore how fast I was moving because there was nothing but water around me, but I could feel the current under the boat through my feet kinda singing in the metal, and I knew it was faster'n any current I'd felt on this river. My heart kinda shriveled thinking of that much water moving that fast.

This makes no kind of sense that I can figure, I said to myself. The river ain't this big when she's flooding. What kind of branch could've I moved onto bigger'n the main one? But thinking got me nowhere. This was my river, I could feel it, this was the one I knew. But it was stranger'n I cared for, surely it was. I reached around and grabbed the motor rope and give it a pull to turn around and head back where I came from, thinking maybe I'd come back here in the day and figure what'd happened. But the motor didn't start, and that motor always starts, but it just spun and spun when I pulled the rope, and no ignition.

Angel, I said to myself, this is surely peculiar, it surely is, and if you can't get back to where you come from, and you don't know where you're going, maybe you ought to stay put for a while until you can figure something out, and you could maybe do a little fishing while you figure. I picked up the anchor and dropped it overboard. The rope uncoiled over the bow'n I thought, all right, but she just kept uncoiling snick, snick, snick till she was all gone, hanging straight down into the water, and me still drifting along.

That got to me. This much water, I said, can't be moving. But that argument didn't seem to make no difference, even if it was a good one. I still went drifting down, the anchor tipping the boat a little to one side with the weight till I hauled it back in, and the water so wide it had waves on it. Then I noticed these ice chunks floating with me, big chunks, some of 'em taller'n me. It was the middle of summer'n that just confused me more. I dipped my hand in the water, and the cold of it about snapped my fingers off.

But something hit me then. I said to myself, If this ain't the river but it is the river, then what is it? I looked up over the water, the black, chopped surface, with foam on the tips of the waves and ice shining like towers, white in the moon, off to a shore way off, just an edge of land going away flat, with no hills or bluffs, maybe some trees, but it was too dark to tell. Then I looked at the sky, and that's when it hit me. I grunted like I'd been sure enough kicked in the stomach.

This is the old river, I said. This is the one that was.

The River Warren.

The stars were the stars I knew, but odd, the configurations skewed, the lines from one to the other not quite right, things just a little twisted, the Big Dipper flattened out some, and the square of Hercules even more skewed than now. I was sitting, I don't know how, on the River Warren, that drained Lake Agassiz—the old river, the one that every time I went out I thought about, all that water pounding down, older than the names of the stars themselves.

Angel Finn, I said to myself, you are sitting in a boat on the biggest river ever.

And your motor don't work.

A wind came up blowing waves four, five feet high around me, me and the chunks of ice going up and down, peaking and troughing, and even then I could feel the current running, the pressure of that lake up north, and that wall of ice on its other edge calving these floes. I could hear them hitting against each other in the dark, the sounds coming from all around, dull booms and cracks and pitches, singing and groaning and sighing, and even screaming, near the boat and far away, and the sounds running across the water.

The smell of the wind was different than I knew—no algae or moss off the water—the smell of a cold land with musk and life in it. It was such a big water, stretching away from me, the peaks of the waves shining in the dark, under those uncommon, familiar stars. I knew if my boat tipped over or one of those ice calves slammed against it, I'd be gone in an instant, the cold and current taking me before I had a chance to swim to shore and find nothing familiar anyway, maybe mammoths pounding dust from the ground, moving in big herds, trumpeting. I didn't care. I was on the River Warren, the big river. The thought of drowning in it, even, seemed like a chance you don't never get, some kind of blessing.

I let the boat drift, using the oars just enough to keep it heading in the current. I didn't even think of pulling for shore. It was enough to be there, listening to the wild ice sing and seeing the stretched stars above me and feeling the boat slip along on the back of a water that old. I ran down that way I don't know how long, and then the river narrowed, and I saw away off the bluffs starting to rise up out of it. The ice disappeared and the air warmed and the valley rose up around me till I found myself on the river I knew, coming around the same bend where I'd gone into the Old One.

I've gone by that place a hundred times since at all times of the night or day, but I can't seem to get back. I don't know what the trick is, I surely don't. Maybe there's no trick at all, maybe there being no trick's the trick. It was a big enough gift the way it was.

Still, I could've dropped a line in the water. I was surely doing nothing else, and having a line in the water would've only made the sky and the ice banging and singing and the cold smells clearer and sharper like it always makes things clearer and sharper. And if I'd gotten a strike, I'm guessing I might still be out there, fighting that fish, or whatever it'd be.

Odd how you can forget your own advice. I always say you can't catch 'em without a line in the water, and then when the time comes I ought to be taking that advice, I'm not giving it.

But I know that river's there. The River Warren—it's there. Here. It's never receded, like I used to think. There's a way to it, and when the next time comes I'll be ready. A man could fight a fish for a long time on that river. Could fight a fish for a long, long time, if he once hooked into one. Maybe—who knows?—forever.

Jeff Gruber

≈

THE DAY AFTER THE FUNERAL Becca called. I was sitting in the kitchen when the phone rang, having coffee with Mom after fixing fence with Dad all morning. My mother said, "He's here. I'll put him on. But let me talk to Jenny first," and then had one of those one-sided conversations, full of questions, that adults have with children who can't yet speak.

"How're things going?" Becca asked when I took the phone.

"All right. The whole town came to the funeral. Afterwards everyone sat in the church basement and talked and ate."

"Did you see Luke?"

"Luke and Ellen both, for a bit. Not much. Matt and Mark were there, and some relatives I didn't know. But he mentioned going to the river together. So we're going to do that. It seems funny, though."

"Why?"

"I don't know. So soon after all this. But he wanted to do it. And Ellen encouraged it."

"You're staying a while then?"

"A few days, I guess. Are you and Jenny doing OK?"

"We're doing fine. I took her down to the lake today. She loved it."

"You didn't let her go in the water."

"Wading. She'd scream and run every time a wave came in."

"She could fall."

"She did. She thought that was the best part."

"I don't know if she should be going into the lake, Becca."

"She's fine, Jeff. She loved it. What are you going to do for the next couple days—other than go to the river with Luke?"

I gave up. "Work," I replied. "What else do you do here?"

"With your dad?"

"Don't get your hopes up. The first rule of farm work is the less talk the better. I learned that one a long time ago."

"You don't need to follow the rules."

"We'll see." Then I conceded: "Mom'd love to see Jenny. I can tell that."

"What about your dad?"

"I suppose."

"How are they?"

"My parents? They're OK. This is pretty hard on them. Dad had to take a gun and . . ."

"You've already told me."

That seemed to end the conversation. "Put Jenny on," I said.

Sounds of fumbling, of the phone being dropped—then I heard Jenny's breathing. I imagined her wide eyes. "Hi, sweetie," I said. "It's Daddy. You be careful in that water, OK?"

The drop into the valley was always a surprise. Corn and soybean fields ran flat before our eyes, and then suddenly the road flowed downward and the valley lay before us, thick with trees, interspersed with fields. In the early morning light the trees shone transparently green, as if the leaves glowed from within. Luke crossed a bridge over the river, the tires whining on the metal, and for a moment I saw the brown ribbon of water twisting out of sight around the banks, all that was left of the immense glacial river.

We turned off the highway onto a gravel road and followed the river past messy farm places and old houses tacked against the hillsides, dogs drifting onto the road to chase the pickup for a few futile feet before being lost in the dust, cats crouching in the roadside grass, startled into stillness, watching with wide eyes. Below the road the river came and went, hidden most of the time by trees, but occasionally revealing itself, dark brown in shadow, silver in the sun, flat surfaced, spilling into backwashes, disintegrating into flashes of light strobing between washed-out corn rows. In a field edged by trees a herd of deer stood, raising their heads to watch the pickup go by, and an egret, stone-still, stood on its thin legs, gleaming pure white over the muddy water.

Luke turned off the gravel onto a two-track that dropped off into the fields. Grass brushed the underside of the pickup as we followed the tracks toward the river. After a quarter mile the road entered woods, then dropped sharply down toward a long stain of mud lying in the tracks. "That's about it," Luke said and pulled to the side, leaving enough room for someone with a four-wheel-drive who might want to go around. We took bows out of the car and strung them.

We walked through the mud, staying as high as possible, then reached dry track again, which disintegrated into a number of faint paths leading in different directions. "How about the creek first?" Luke asked. "Then we could go down river?"

"Sounds good."

I followed him down a trail that led to the right. It all came back so easily—from the moment he'd picked me up— as if years hadn't intervened and death hadn't come. We talked of small things during the drive, and now we slipped through the leaves in a silence we had learned long ago here, and that seemed, allowing as it did for the unexpected to happen, as intimate as speech. Vegetation grew thick between the trees—ragged burning weeds, wild hemp, and thin-leaved preacher's lice, green and burrless now, but which in the fall would produce thousands of flat, two-pronged burrs, like men with raised hands.

A few birds called back and forth, and the creek gurgled. I heard the full sound of the river itself, the whisper of water against dead trees, the chuckle of small whirlpools. We came out on a low sandbar with willow copses in its center. Mosquitoes emerged from the vegetation and formed a humming cloud over our heads. We walked across the sandbar and stood at the river's edge, our boots nearly touching the water. A dead branch moved back and forth in the current, and behind it the river smoothed in a wake. Fifty yards across the river the opposite bank came straight out of the water, thick with trees.

For a while we stood in silence, letting the river's smell rise to us—the smell of fish, silt, mud, the smell of gravity and time, of things decaying and growing and borne onward. "Remember that tree?" Luke asked.

I knew immediately what he meant. One spring we'd taken a canoe to the boat landing at the county park three or four miles upstream from where we now stood. The river was flooded, spread over its banks, the entire valley bottom covered in water, like a lake with trees growing in it, and in the center of that lake the river ran like a pulse. We had stopped at a flooded field before we reached the boat landing, shoved the canoe over the road bank, and climbed in. We paddled across the field and into the woods, laughing as we maneuvered the canoe between the trees. We didn't pay attention to where we were and without knowing it went over the bank into the channel.

The canoe suddenly surged sideways as if a hand had come up from the water and pushed it. Through the thin aluminum floor I felt the force of the water, not fast but relentless. On either side of us, as we straightened the canoe out, trees drifted backwards. Around us the dark water roiled and spread.

"Shit," Luke said, matter-of-factly. "We're on the river."

Angel'd always told us: Stay off the flood. But we were surprised at its tameness. It seemed the same river as always, just more of it. Though we knew the water under us was deeper, on the surface nothing had changed. The canoe sat on a tight, thrumming surface as if suspended on a smooth sheet of moving, dark rubber. A wind blew up the channel, keeping mosquitoes away.

"This is nothing," I said.

We went with the current. A half mile ahead of us the river swept around a great bend, back toward the pickup. If we left the channel there we'd have an easy paddle across the fields out. We floated downstream, between trees that stood in water, marking the banks. We'd gone maybe a quarter mile when we came around a bend and found a cottonwood tree in front of us, uprooted by the flood and floating slowly downstream. The river had dozens of dead trees on every mile of its banks, bleaching in the sun, but we'd never seen one floating. The trunk rode barely out of the water, the top, green with new-budded leaves, thrusting into the air, and a few gnarled roots, caked with mud, sticking through the surface. Pools of water, like miniature lakes in a strange landscape, glittered in the crevices of the bark.

The whole thing rode at a forty-five degree angle to the channel. Luke and I stared at it, awed by its silence, moving in one great mass downstream, only a few of the leaves rustling in the breeze. We backpaddled, keeping our distance. Luke looked back at me. "Ripped right out of the bank," he said. "Look at those roots."

"The river just ate it away," I said.

"Can you imagine when that sucker fell in?"

I could imagine it, whistling in its own wind, toppling into the water, disappearing beneath the surface, then slowly rising, turning, settling.

"Should we go around it?" Luke asked.

"I don't know."

"Let's go around that end." He pointed with his paddle at the branches.

Beyond the tree's branches were forty yards of clear, smooth water. The whole thing made me uneasy, but I nodded. "All right. Let's go."

We dug our paddles into the river and angled the canoe across the current. By the time we rounded the tree we were only ten feet from its top branches. The leaves shivered in the wind. We were so close I could hear individual leaves, and water gurgling as the tree made small movements, shifting its weight in the current. We were only about halfway around when it began to roll.

The roots, coming around a bend, caught on the bank, and the current, bearing down with the weight of the entire river, began to spin the tree. I heard first a slight, musical gurgle of water being backed up. I turned to look, and a chill ran down my back. I saw the river fill against the trunk and then wash over the entire thing. The trunk disappeared under the water, but it looked as if, in one watery sigh, the river rose and swallowed everything but the uppermost branches.

Though I'd never seen it before, I knew what was going to happen.

"Paddle!" I screamed at Luke. "Paddle!"

I jammed my paddle into the water to turn the canoe away from the tree. Luke hesitated and glanced back, a startled look on his thin face. The canoe lurched forward. I raised the paddle to dig again, saw Luke turn back, the sun shining on his cheekbone, heard a robin song drift in the air.

Then behind me I heard a whisper, a sigh growing to a soggy groan, of submerged branches rising and rolling, water cascading off leaves, the tree shrugging the river off.

My paddle caught the water, and I looked behind me. A tower of branches rose there, rolling momentously toward me, coming down on top of me faster than I could make the canoe move forward. The tree, caught on the bank, was not only rolling but also straightening in the current, going to a right angle across the river. As it did it lengthened toward us at the same time that the force of the water rolled it. Undisturbed, it had floated heavy-side down, so that the longest of the branches were hidden underwater. Rather than going around it, we were actually going over it, and now the entire crown boomed out of the water under us, like an immense and tangled wheel.

I felt Luke's paddle catch, the canoe jerk forward. I couldn't wait the moment it would take to bring us into synch. I turned my back on the tree, loud as a waterfall over me, grunted as I drove my paddle into the water.

The canoe dove straight down.

I saw Luke shoot up as the front of the canoe shot above the river. At the same time I went down, and water, ice cold, rushed over the gunwale and into my lap. The branch that had caught the canoe skreeked along the aluminum. I sank even further into the river, standing in the canoe now, the water to my waist, and still I felt the canoe fading from my feet. I twisted, pushed with my paddle against a branch, heard Luke swearing as if from far away, heard the water running over the gunwales toward the front of the canoe, filling it. I pushed against the branch with all my strength.

The paddle slipped. I shot into the tree, flailed, grabbed the branch bearing me down. For a moment I pressed my face against the bark. If it drove us down further we could become entangled in the net of its branches. I screamed and pushed, straightening my arms with my knees bent as if I were doing a clean and jerk. Then I straightened my knees, driving the canoe even further into the water, down and away from the branch that held it. The tree rained water. The rough bark cut my hands. I felt the canoe slip. I arched even further, and with everything in me, drove it into the river.

It slipped forward, free, away from my feet. I lost it.

I threw myself backward, diving to where the canoe should have been if Luke pulled it forward as it came up with its own flotation. The cold floodwater rammed into my nostrils, suffused with mud and silt. I went blind, felt a moment of awful aloneness. The sound of the tree turning underwater came into my ears, a low moan, a bass almost beyond hearing. I knew it was all around me in the darkness.

I kicked away from it and swept with my arms. A branch scraped my thigh, and I twisted away. The icewater was a vise against my chest. I swept and kicked again, still underwater, my face to the surface. I felt the prow of the canoe rise to touch the small of my back.

I nearly screamed but clamped my mouth upon it, turned to my stomach, flailed in the water, groping for the canoe. I found it, held on, kicked again, raised my head for the surface, for air. It wasn't there. The canoe wasn't rising fast enough, and I had to let go again. I almost couldn't. Having this connection to someone else was almost more important than life. I gripped the canoe, my lungs bursting.

I let go. I shot straight up through the water, perhaps right into the tree, but toward air. I broke through the surface, water streaming from my face, into the mild, bright sun. Air poured into my chest, tearing at my throat. Then the canoe rose into me again, and I grabbed it as it lurched forward under Luke's stroke, felt it yank me through the water. A branch of the tree clubbed my heel, and I jerked into the fetal position. I had no strength to haul myself into the canoe. I held on and let it carry me along. Luke was submerged to the waist, as if he were paddling only himself along the river.

He took the canoe to the right bank and over it. I trailed like a rag. I dropped my feet, touched land. The water came only to my knees. I let go of the canoe. Luke turned and looked at me, then jumped out himself. We stared at each other. We had no words for what had happened. I looked back toward the river, saw the crown of the tree sweep downstream, still turning, its roots snagged.

"You OK?" Luke asked.

I tried to say yes but couldn't. I tasted the river. I nodded.

"Suppose we coulda' drowned?"

I stared at him. "Could've?" I hacked, rolled the taste of the river in my mouth, spit. "I damn near did!"

"I turned around and you were gone," he said. "I freaked, man. The damn thing just kept coming. Just kept coming and coming."

I nodded, remembering.

"Angel'd have our nuts if he heard about this."

Something about the glum way he said it, as if it were a real concern, made me smile. "Shit, Luke," I said. "You gonna tell him?"

"Hell no."

"I guess he'll never know, then."

"It looked so smooth, man."

"Angel says it'll fool you."

"It's old self."

"What?"

"Angel. He says sometimes the river thinks it's its old self."

"Yeah. I guess."

Suddenly Luke whooped. His voice rang down the river. I stared, then joined in, filling my lungs with air and shouting it out.

Then over our shouts we heard wood snap. It silenced us. Across the river the cottonwood broke loose from its mooring and began to roll again. It thrashed the water, lifting huge chunks of the river up in its branches and dumping them down in a cascade of silver light. One great limb snapped with a sound like a shotgun, but continued up out of the water, mangled and splintered, grotesque as the broken arm of a giant. It flopped over the top and crashed back into the river. Finally the whole thing settled, sank, bobbed, then drifted calmly downstream.

Now as we stood on the banks of the river the memory was alive between us, like a thread that held us, and this place, too, like a thread: the way the creek flowed, the snag white and crooked below the cutbank downstream, the pattern of sunlight on the water.

"I sure do remember," I said.

"I thought you were dead that time. I thought you were gone."

Because we were here, where we'd spent so much time together, it seemed easy to speak in spite of my long absence. "I nearly was," I said. "You saved my skin, paddling like you did."

"So you think," Luke said without turning to me.

"So I think? What do you think?"

"That you saved mine."

He looked at me then. His jaw was tight, his face dusky, defiant. Often, the more Luke said about himself, the more he seemed to challenge me to accept it.

I shrugged it off. "OK. We saved each other's."

"Hell," he said quietly. "I was just sitting there. Given up already. That was me. Then I felt the canoe jump forward. You kicking off that branch. Shit, man. Using the damn thing that's going to kill you to get away from it. I couldn't believe it. I started to paddle, and every stroke I took I was swearing at you."

"You wouldn't've just sat there."

"That's sure as hell what I was doing."

He shook his head slowly, looking over the moving water. He shrugged. "Let's go down to the cutbank. There's always carp under that snag."

We followed a faint trail that led off the sandbar into the weeds along the bank. As we walked, the bank rose until the river was a dozen feet below us. Another skeletal tree, white and twisted, stuck out of the water. It had been here for as long as we knew. The sun, behind us, threw our shadows onto the water. We stood above the snag. "Well, hell," Luke said. "They'll stay down with those shadows there. Guess we can stand still and wait."

We stood motionless, side by side, waiting for the stillness to settle into us, for the fish beneath the surface to lose memory, to know us as fixtures on this bank. A red squirrel chattered, silenced, chattered again. The river gurgled against the snag. Far away, over the fields, a tractor hummed.

"Hell," Luke said quietly. "I was so screwed up back then. When I saw that tree coming down I freaked and froze. Like I wanted it to happen."

I was silent, thinking. "Funny," I said.

"What's funny?"

"There were times back then I thought I wanted to die."

"You? I thought all you wanted to do was win wrestling championships."

"Yeah, well. That whole business with Chris. I never did get over it."

"I guess I'm not your brother."

"What?"

"You couldn't save him, but you got me to paddle."

His conversation was taking directions I wasn't used to. He'd matured—I suppose we both had—in the time I'd been gone. He'd always been a thinker, but he seemed more reflective now. But then, he'd just attended his parents' funeral. It would make anyone reflective. Still, this seemed a different Luke than the one I remembered.

"I suppose. When do you think those carp'll show?"

"This whole business. You try to." His voice trailed off. "Ah hell. I just never figured he'd do something like this. And take her with him. How could've anyone figured on something like that?"

The squirrel, closer now, chattered again, testing us. I didn't turn, but I imagined it clinging to a trunk, head down, one bright, suspicious eye on us. A pair of mallards suddenly appeared, low over the water, and followed the curve of the river out of sight.

"Snap, like that," Luke said. "Gone. Matt and Mark and me, when we heard, we all came to the house. We hadn't all been there at the same time for I don't know how long. Some Thanksgiving a few years back. But there we were. And we had nothing to say to each other. We sat in chairs and stared. Like some scene from a weird movie. Then Mark mentioned the Twins. Matt perked up, and we had this conversation about baseball. We laughed and joked. I bet Matt fifty bucks the Twins wouldn't win the AL West. That's what we talked about. The day our parents die, me and my brother make a bet on baseball."

"You've got to talk about something."

"That's not it. I'm not apologizing. It was good. Best time I ever had with them. Just talking about what came to talk about. Never did that before."

Beneath us, out of the murky water, a shape floated upward. It hung several inches below the surface, the water so dark and full of silt from the fields that I had trouble seeing the fish's outline.

"Go ahead," Luke said.

I raised my bow slowly, trying not to startle the fish,

drew the arrow nock to the corner of my mouth, anchored, let go. The arrow dove into the water. The fish disappeared, and the line hung slackly against the bank.

"Went over," Luke commented. "Forgot the refraction. Gotta aim where you think it isn't. Lost your touch."

"That'll keep 'em down for a while," I said.

Mosquitoes hummed around us, frustrated by repellent.

"Just talked about baseball," Luke said. "For once we weren't paralyzed. In that canoe that time, I just sat there till I felt you kick. Been paralyzed all my life."

"Pure bullshit," I said. "You've led your life as much as anyone."

"I don't know. I'm still hanging around Cloten. Coming down to the river. Getting by. Shooting carp for entertainment."

"And I'm hanging around Duluth. Not much difference. Besides, someone has to take over when Angel gives it up."

He smiled, for the first time since we'd arrived here. "Wouldn't be the worst thing."

The river flowed by.

"You married Ellen, right? That wasn't the dumbest thing you ever did, was it?"

I'd never known anyone so crazy about a woman. I remembered, when they'd first started going out with each other, how Luke couldn't believe it. He kept thinking something had to go wrong, that it wasn't really possible.

"She's something," he said. "We're going to have a baby."

"Well, congratulations! How long've you known?"

"About a month."

I held out my hand, and we shook, smiling at each other.

"So you're gonna be a papa. How's that make you feel?"

"Good. Truth is though, it scares me shitless, too."

"It ought to."

But a shadow passed over his eyes, and his face twisted. He looked away from me, across the river. The wind blew his dark hair into a tangle. He held the bow motionless at his side. Beyond him I saw the plane of the river shining in the sun, dark and light alternately, shadows of trees floating on it, stretching away. For a moment he seemed ancient and hurt, forgotten by time, a hunter standing on this bank forever in a green-lit, mosquito-heavy, endless morning. When he spoke again, without turning to me, he seemed to be asking a question he'd noticed floating on the water, or plucked out of the shattering light.

"How can anyone be a father?"

He turned to meet my eyes, and his expression contained more pain and doubt than I understood. He was unguarded and lost.

I thought of Jenny tottering over to me when I held my arms out for her, always on the verge of falling. I had no idea how to be a father. Never had. But Luke was asking something more than that, something more troubling that I wasn't understanding or he wasn't revealing.

"I don't know, Luke," I said.

An incomplete question, an incomplete answer. They mixed with the wind and the light, with the stir of transparent, thin-veined wings, the smell of things rotting and growing. The river flowed down, the sun lay on it.

Ellen Easton Crandall

≈

YOU CAN THINK TOO MUCH about the past. You can make it like a chain that stakes you. Then run around at the end of it and trample your life barren.

I've told Luke: Let it go. And he does, for a while. But sometimes it's like the past engulfs him. I know when it's happening. He seems to pay attention to things I do and say. But only to keep me from noticing what he's thinking about.

Maybe it's the baby. Sometimes I feel there's more to me than there is. I'll feel larger than my mere events. I'll know my body, but I'll know I'm more. Not believe. Know. Even now, when I'm so aware of my body, I'll float beyond it. Beyond anything staked and grounded.

In church, repentance and forgiveness make sense. When the songs are being sung, or the Gospels read. When I'm solid and weightless both, and the pages of the hymnal are light as angel wings. Repentance goes beyond feeling, beyond not-doing. It's knowing you're more than time, or anything that ends. Once you know that, repentance isn't just possible. It's already happened. You've let go your sins and wrongs. Allowed your past to rest.

Forgiveness is the same. It's knowing you're more than the things that have been done to you.

But if you wrong someone, repenting doesn't mean you'll be forgiven. And forgiving someone who's wronged you doesn't mean you'll bring repentance to their heart.

When Luke talks about the river, I hear it—his knowing that he's larger than he is. Or when he says he loves me. Something big comes out of him then. It's what I sensed that time he first brought me home from college, what I thought about that first weekend, waiting for him to pick me up again. But then, something small and uncertain, too.

Blame shortens vision. Sometimes small things happen, and Luke will blame his father. Then all forgiveness ends. He stakes himself to things that happened.

He was so happy when he heard about this baby. I'd never seen him so happy. But something changed. Nothing against me or the baby. But some gravity pulled him away from me. Even when my own gravity was strongest.

He went fishing one night alone. I've gone with him, but often he'll go alone. He needs to do it, and that's all right. This last time, though, I woke up, and he'd returned. He was in bed beside me. But he was cold. Stiff. I could tell he was wide awake, thinking and hoping I was asleep. Something about him made me afraid to even speak. Afraid to say his name.

Usually after he goes to the river, things are good. But something that night was terribly wrong. We lay awake, both of us, for I don't know how long, though he thought I slept. Everything was so still, me and Luke so still beside each other. I felt the little burbles of the baby floating inside me.

The next morning Luke paid attention to me in the way he does when he wants to direct attention away from himself. I couldn't ask him about the river, or what had happened there.

Then, after the accident, when I opened that closet door, a few days after Luke and I had gone to his parents' house, I remembered that night. I felt that same coldness. Like something stilled within my life.

Pop Bottle Pete

≈

I WALK FUNNY. I GO SIDE TO SIDE. Skeet walks straight. Sometimes when I pick up bottles, he walks by me. His legs go reach, reach. Finding some? he says. I nod. I watch his legs. I used to walk straight too. My legs went reach. But now I go side to side.

Sometimes he'd be there and sometimes not. Sometimes my sheets wouldn't get wet. Sometimes they would, but he wouldn't come. The wind would go against me until the sheeby-jeebs made me go back inside. But if he came he'd always look for me. He could see me, even with the dark inside me. And he didn't think. He'd always say, Peter. And come over.

We'd talk about assholes. And scumbags. And fucking morons sorry Peter. About all of them in town. And we'd talk about driving the big truck, and I could pull the horn. Someday you and me will go trucking, he said. Take you someplace, teach you how to use that thing. That's not an icicle. He always laughed then. He liked to laugh. Me too. But not if Mom woke up.

We talked a lot. More than ten. Then once I saw him coming. He always walked like I do now. Side to side. Not straight. The cold was way in me. The wind had snow to help it. Wa-a-a-a-a, it went. And the snow put cold in me. But he was coming. On the sidewalk.

Then he stopped. He reached for something on the sidewalk. I couldn't see him then. The dark went in him fast. The hot in my feet was all out where they went in the snow. But I waited. He didn't come.

If I went on the lawn the light would be there. Then people would see me and think. My feet wanted to go back in the house. All the hot was gone from them. But the dark stayed in him and he didn't come. If the dark goes in you too far people can't see you ever. My heart went like a horse.

I crossed my fingers and shut my eyes. I ran onto the lawn. I put my hand down by my thing. So if the light came in me people wouldn't see it. Because that's what makes them think. My feet went on the lawn like when I hammer. Hammer hammer hammer they went on the lawn. They didn't have any hot in them. I wanted them under the covers. To put their cold in the bed.

I opened my eyes. Oh no. My feet had run off Mom's lawn. They were running on Mr. Dietrich's lawn. And the light was coming in me. But I could see him on the sidewalk. The dark was going in him fast. I started to cry. I'm not supposed to go on Mr. Dietrich's lawn. I went wa-a-a-a-a like the wind.

I got off Mr. Dietrich's lawn. Onto the sidewalk where he was. A big tree made a lot of dark, and I got in it. He was in it, too. Except his head. I looked at his head. It was blood blood blood. He had a stocking cap on but it was blood blood blood. And on the sidewalk too.

The blood was smoking. I stopped crying. The dark was in me again and people wouldn't see me and think.

Get up, I said. You stay out in this too long you could freeze.

He didn't get up. His eyes were shut. He was sleeping.

Simon, I said. Get up. Asshole. Fucking moron sorry Peter.

But he didn't. The blood smoked. It was letting all its hot out. The sidewalk was taking all his hot. He was getting where people couldn't see him ever.

I pushed him with my foot. My foot couldn't feel him. Simon, I said. Scumbag. Get up. Get up get up get up. Fucking right.

The dark was in him too far. My voice wouldn't go in his ears. I cried again. My bed had too much hot. If I put him there he would be all right. But Mom would say why were you outside Peter? I told you not to go outside. And look at these sheets. Now I'll have to wash them.

I pushed him with my foot. My foot wouldn't feel anything. I sheeby-jeebed. I cried.

I pulled his hand. The dark made him heavy. I pulled hard. He slid. His head went slide and bump on the sidewalk. I pulled him by the tree. I knew where he lived. Because once in the summer I had cans and bottles. It was hot and I was feeling like an egg. Sizzle sizzle. And I saw him by a house. Straight from ours. But further. I saw him by it. Then he went into it. I remembered.

I pulled him by the tree and made him sit by it. I had to kneel. My knees didn't like the sidewalk. Fucking asshole scumbag moron, I said. Sorry Peter. Shityeah. I cried.

Because his house was further. And the lights. And people thinking.

I made him sit by the tree. The tree held him up. He was dark and it was dark. I got on my hands and knees. Like playing horsey. And my heart went like a horse. I pushed against him. I pulled. I went up and down. His head went on my back. I made it go further. I went down. Like playing horsey drinking. He went on my shoulders. I pushed him against the tree. I made him stay on my shoulders. I turned around. My hands went up the tree and my legs went push. Push push. My hands went like a bear on the tree.

My breath went like a train. The cold went in me but I sweated. Like summer but not. He wanted to get off me. He wanted the dark to be in him. He tried to go back on the sidewalk. No, I said. You stay out in this too long you could freeze. Fucking right. Asshole.

Then my feet went hammer hammer hammer down the sidewalk. In the light and in the dark. To where his house was further. I had to hold him with both hands. I couldn't cover my thing. If people saw me they would think. I cried because Mom wouldn't like it.

My legs went reach reach. Fast. Like I could do then. Straight. He wanted to make me fall. He wanted to go on the sidewalk. His breath went in my face. It smelled funny. Moron. Sorry Peter, I said.

I came to a street. I stopped and looked both ways. Like Mom says. No cars. My legs reached, my feet went hammer on the street. I was cold and hot and the wind was crying.

There was another street. Then his house. Where he went in that time. I walked to it. The cold was biting at my thing. I cried because the cold was biting at it. Stop it, I said to the wind. Stop it stop it stop it. But the wind went wa-a-a-a and bit some more.

My knees went bend. My face went on his steps. His head went bump on me. I pushed him off. I rolled. I got up and held my hand down to cover my thing. But it hurt and hurt. The sweat came out of me but the wind was cold. It tried to go in me further than ever. And my hot tried to come out.

Asshole, I said. Fucking moron. Sorry Peter. Scumbag. I climbed up the steps. I made sure not to step on him. I saw my hand where it was going knock. All red. Wa-a-a-a, I cried. But I knocked. Knock knock knock.

Then hide. Because if she saw me she would think. Then Mom would be mad. And people might take me away. And I couldn't find bottles in the summer. Or pick rocks and make them into mountains. Then I'd never get a Walkman. Or be able to buy Coke.

My feet didn't want to run. I made them. Run feet run. Around the corner of the house. In the dark. Make it go in me hard. Stop my huffhuff breath. My horsey heart. Shhhh.

I sheeby-jeebed and sheeby-jeebed. But I didn't cry.

She opened the door. Her breath made a loud sound. Her clothes went swishswish out the door. Jesus Simon, she said. Her hands went touch all over him.

Then she said, Trying to kill yourself again. The drunken hue of resolution. Well, you picked a good night to do it, but the currents turned awry. Let's get you inside.

She pulled. Her breath went uh uh uh. He wanted to stay on the sidewalk. But she made him come in with her pulling and her uh uh uhs. He went ahhhhhh when his head went bang on the door part.

You'll live, she said. But I wish to hell you'd make up your mind. Then she was inside. And him, too. But the door was open. So I didn't move.

I heard her on the steps again. She stood. I made my breath all stay inside. So she wouldn't know. She stood long and long and long. I heard her standing there. I thought my breath would go out loud.

Then she said, Thanks, whoever you are, out there.

Mom says always say you're welcome. But I didn't. Because how did she know I was there? But I almost said you're welcome. Because I'm supposed to.

I guess he's got a friend somewhere, she said.

She shut the door then. Mom says be polite. I wasn't polite. I hope it didn't make her think. When she shut the door I ran. Across the lawns where the dark was. I held my hand down to cover my thing. And to keep it warm. But my hand was cold and the wind bit at me. My feet went hammer. Like they weren't there. All the way home.

I made the door go quiet. So Mom wouldn't know. I got into bed. I felt like a big rock. Except I went shake shake shake. Rocks never go shake. They have winter in them always, so they never go shake. But I went shake, and the winter was in me like I was a big rock.

I went shake shake shake and I cried and cried. I guess he's got a friend, huh? I said. Fucking right. I guess he's got a friend.

Luke Crandall

≈

I WENT TO THE RIVER WITH GRUBER, and we got to talking about things like we always used to, but I couldn't quite get at what I meant about being a father, not even with him. I was thinking of how Ellen stood in front of me with her hand on her stomach and said: "I'm pregnant, Luke. We're going to have a baby." I didn't even know what she meant at first, not because it was a surprise but for the opposite reason. We'd planned it, and when you do that, when you tell yourself you'll be ready for it when the time comes, then you can't be quite ready when the time comes, because it's your future, right there, right now, and you've already agreed not to escape it.

I watched her hand go around in little circles on her belly, and I thought: She's always going to surprise me with the things I expect. How's it possible I knew this was going to happen, but when she says it, I'm surprised and can't get my mind around it?

I first saw her at a party in Clear River the summer I got out of high school, a keg out at the boat landing. Some friends I knew from up there told me to come out. I didn't drink much. I swore I wouldn't turn out like Dad. But when

I did drink I drank too much, and I drank too much that night. I had to piss, and I walked down to the river, away from the crowd, and pissed by a clump of willows. I came out from behind them and looked toward the river, and I saw this woman's head framed against the stars above the opposite bank, all black and smooth from her hair combed straight down. I walked toward her, and she seemed to come out of the river, black rising out of black, first her head and then her shoulders and then the rest of her.

She looked too lonely for belief. But just from the way she stood there, not even turning around to see me, just looking at the river going by, I thought, drunk as I was: She's going to laugh at me. She seemed to be standing on the water, the light from the fire not making it that far, and the dark welding everything together.

I walked up to her and said, Mind if I join you here? And she turned the most amazing face on me, and it broke into a smile, and then she laughed, and it surprised me even though I knew it was coming. You're so drunk you can hardly stand, she said. She lifted a plastic cup of beer to her mouth and took a sip and brushed the hair back over her shoulder, and the moon above us sat behind a line of barred clouds, and she crossed one hand below her breasts and held the cup away from her and said: I don't think I'm interested in what you're looking for, but if you want to stand here I can't stop you.

Nothing like indifference to make you feel worthless. I didn't know what to do. I looked at the river, and it seemed to rise and tip like a big-beamed scale. I was afraid I'd fall over right there. I turned away, still hearing her laugh in my head and seeing how she'd turned toward me, not alarmed, but expecting to be amused, and her white teeth flashing and the sound of her swallowing when she tipped the glass. I walked to the fire, not looking back, and when I got there I turned to see, but she was either gone or the willows hid her, and I couldn't help but think she'd just sunk into the river the way she'd come up.

So when she came to my car out of the dorm, carrying a suitcase, that weekend in college when I answered a bulletin board card asking for a ride to Clear River, I thought: It can't be. I turned my face away from her, then looked again, her coming down the sidewalk, all bright in the sun, the suitcase making her tip as she walked, and her black hair hanging straight down behind her tipped face, trying to look through the window of the car to see who was giving her a ride. Jesus, Luke, I said to myself, it's her—your river woman.

But she didn't recognize me and I've never reminded her of our first meeting. I was just one of how many drunk men who talked to her that night? I've never wanted her to remember. I swore to myself on that ride that I wouldn't mess this up if I could help it, that having a chance to see her again was more than I had a right to hope for. If it was just chance, which I suppose it was, then I wasn't going to throw it away.

Not that I thought I'd ever marry her. But I guess I didn't do anything too terribly wrong on that ride home and back. I was careful, trying not to make an idiot of myself. She agreed to see me again when I asked, and something just kept happening. I couldn't believe it. I was afraid to push her, afraid anything'd make her up and leave. But one night she was in my apartment and she just didn't go home. I could've been expecting it, if I hadn't been so scared of losing everything, but I was completely surprised. The old lady whose basement I lived in had a rule that all women had to be out by 11:30, and Ellen knew the rule, and the time came, and I said: It's 11:30, and she said, I know, time to go to bed, isn't it? I thought she meant she'd leave so I could sleep, and it took her coming over and kissing me and starting to unbutton her shirt for me to realize what she meant and get unparalyzed.

I suppose, if you're surprised by who a person is, then everything that person does will kind of surprise you. So when Ellen stood there with her hand on her stomach and told me of the baby, smiling and half-doubtful, waiting to see what I'd do, I thought like I had so many times before, How does she do these things? How can there be a child inside her? Before I could go to her and put my arms around her, I had to say to myself: My child. I'm its father. I'll be its father. I had to will it, even if I had no idea what it meant. Then I walked to where Ellen was turning my future under her hand and pressed myself into it.

Ellen Easton Crandall

≈

AFTER THE ACCIDENT, Luke and I went to their house. We were both stunned. We thought we should take care of business. And we hoped for some clue to what had happened. We found nothing. Old tax records, old checks, boxes of paper. Dust and rubber bands and paper clips and grocery receipts. Like an X ray of their lives.

We threw so much away. It seemed so useless. So much stuff kept. For what? Now I wish I had it all. To sort through and ask it questions: how they lived, who they were.

When I knew about the baby, I went to her. We lived in the same town, but we hardly ever talked. But I thought: She is my mother-in-law. So I stopped by to visit and tell her. She was so happy that I did.

She wouldn't stop smiling. Every time I looked at her, I'd find her smiling at me. Like we had a secret together, the baby, even though everyone else knew, or would.

Before I left, she said: "I'm going to do something for that child someday."

"Of course you will," I said.

"No," she said. "Not like that. Not 'of course.' Something special. I'm going to *do* something."

She was too fervent. It made me embarrassed. I wanted to flatten it out, to say something like: Just being a grandmother will be special to the baby. I wanted to make the ordinary special.

She took my hands. She gripped them so hard they hurt. "Yes," she said. "Something special. For my grandchild."

Then she stared past my face. Staring at nothing. Her face twisted. As if she'd been stabbed inside. "LouAnn?" I asked.

Her face settled. She looked back to me. Smiled. But it was strained. I thought she was going to cry. "You'll be such a good mother," she said.

I'd been embarrassed for her, and now I was embarrassed for myself. "I don't know," I said. "I hope so."

"Oh, you will be, Ellen. I just know."

I didn't know what to say. She didn't let go my hands. We stood there. My wedding ring dug into my middle finger from the force of her grip. It pressed against the bone.

Then she said: "I tried to be a good mother."

She had this way of saying things I couldn't respond to. "I'm sure you did," I said. But it sounded like I was saying she hadn't succeeded.

She didn't seem to notice. "I'm so glad Luke went to college," she said. "I never did. I wanted to, but . . ." She stopped, shrugged lightly. "I married Simon. And then." She made a little, dismissive gesture with her lips.

Then she went on: "I used to read Shakespeare to myself when Simon was gone. I acted in high school. A little. Did you know that? I used to read Shakespeare to the boys when they were little. To get them to sleep. I thought that some day they'd remember it."

The ring pressing into my bone hurt so badly I could hardly listen to her. I twisted my fingers. I didn't want to jerk away, but I thought I might have to. "You raised a good son," I said.

She gave my hand an extra squeeze, then dropped it. Relief made tears start in my eyes.

"I'm so glad Luke has you," she said. "You're good for him."

It embarrassed me again. But she brightened. "But for my grandchild," she said, "I'll do something special. I'll know what it is when the time comes."

"Yes," I said. "I know you will."

I walked down the sidewalk toward home. I turned back once, and waved. She was still standing in front of the house, watching me. I was relieved to be away from her. There was too much intensity, too much attempt at closeness. She made me feel claustrophobic.

Now I wish I'd paid more attention. Tried to understand her more. Why was she in that truck? She never rode with Two-Speed. Even if it was an accident, what were they doing together? And if it wasn't an accident, was she part of what it was? She once said to me that Simon was lost without her. Then who was pointing the direction that morning?

I've heard a rumor that she was leaving Simon. I don't know if it's true—that she was leaving that night, and he found out, and that's why all this happened. It could be true. LouAnn, as far as I know, consulted no one. But I can't help but wonder, though I hate to, just the opposite. Something special, she said. Something special for her grandchild. What was it going to be? Or was she doing it when she climbed into that semi, with the weight of all those cattle?

Jeff Gruber

≈

ANOTHER CARP DRIFTED UPWARD, stayed for a moment near the surface, then sank to darkness. "Me a father," Luke said. "Makes you think. What do kids want from their parents? I mean, what do they really want?"

"Is this a test?" I asked, trying to make light of his seriousness.

"F for you, my man," he said. "Now listen up, because here's the answer. It's not all the shit people say it is. Kids want to know they've changed their parents."

"Is that right? Well, now I know."

He looked at the opposite shore, not responding to my joking. "It's true, man. They want to see it. Change. That nothing'll ever be the same for their parents. Just because the kid was born."

I thought of Jenny, of whether I could ever be who I was again, now that she was born. Probably not. She'd worked a spell on me in the hospital when I first held her. She'd slept in my arms, and time had gone by, and I was willing to let it go by forever. And every smile since then, every cry in the night—all working change in me.

I decided to take Luke seriously. "I guess you're right. If it's the right kind of change."

"If it's not the right kind, it's not a change."

"No?"

"Just more of what was. Ellen says when she was a kid she used to try to imagine her parents before she was born. Couldn't do it. Says she'd always end up laughing. Couldn't even believe her parents existed before she was born. Because they didn't. They were someone else till then. Like your parents. Your dad. Can't imagine him without you. Never could."

"Yeah, I suppose."

"You suppose?"

"So what are you getting at?"

"What am I getting at? I'll tell you. Mom and Dad, they were so caught up in each other, me and Matt and Mark could never get a wedge in anywhere. Never did manage to change them. That's what I'm getting at."

Luke had never talked this way about his parents before. Only a few times had he even mentioned them.

When he spoke again I could hardly hear his voice over the slow current. "Right up to the end," he murmured. "That's what I was trying to do. Just a kid, trying to change his dad. Make a difference."

Then he abruptly raised his voice, dropping the seriousness. "Ah hell. You're never free of your old man, are you? Just like the Road Runner's never free of Wile E. He can always outrun him, but he can't get rid of him. Wile E.'ll be back. If not in this cartoon, the next."

He lifted his bow and drew it back, aiming at something

I didn't see, until the arrow was almost parallel to the water's surface. He anchored the string, then released. The heavy arrow shot over the bank and arced through the air, trailing cord. The arrow curved into the water. The water exploded, and an enormous carp shot high into the air and stood for an eternal moment, its tail dancing on the surface, shaking off flecks of light. Then it fell back through the surface while drops of water rained down and ripples spread and smoothed.

"Shees," I exclaimed. "You almost hit that thing. I didn't even see it."

"Missed him on purpose," he said. "Just wanted to scare him a bit."

"Right. Missed him on purpose."

He ignored the jibe. "I wouldn't mind being that carp. Big and fat and in my element. Sucking all the easy stuff off the surface. And then, once in a while, an arrow comes zinging at you. Out of nowhere, bam, like that. Always missing, but not gonna miss forever. That old carp, he'll stay down a while, wondering what he just missed, and not sure he wants to know. Wouldn't be bad, being a carp."

We rode home in silence. I'd been wanting to ask Luke a question since he'd picked me up but couldn't find the right words. I fingered the scar in my palm and watched the land. Luke turned off the highway onto a gravel road that led to my parents' farm. Rows of corn flickered past us, and a cloud of dust billowed behind the car. Tractors crawled in the fields. I decided to just come out with it.

"This whole business with your dad," I said. "My dad's

cattle were on the truck. Was there a connection, do you think?"

He turned his face from the road and looked at me. "What kind of connection?"

"I don't know." I stumbled to explain. "I guess, maybe it was just an accident, but . . ." I didn't know how to suggest that his father might have committed suicide and murder, didn't know what he himself thought had happened or how he'd respond to my fumblings. "What I'm wondering is, could it have something to do with Dad's cattle?"

"I don't follow."

He hit an intersection without slowing down, and the hump where the two roads met sent the pickup heaving into the air. The way he drove sure hadn't changed.

"It's probably nothing," I said, ready to be done with the question. "It's just that our fathers never got along."

The meaning of my question finally dawned in his face. His foot came off the accelerator. "Shit! They sure didn't," he said. "I never thought of *that!*"

He braked and stopped at the edge of the road. I'd never known Luke to stop driving just to think. He stared through the windshield as the cloud of dust slowly passed over us, obscuring the fields of corn. For a while the pickup seemed to be moving backwards through it.

"I can't believe it," Luke muttered.

"Hey, it's nothing," I said. "I shouldn't have asked."

"It's OK, man. It's just." He shook his head.

The air cleared. The fields appeared through the dust, the bright green of the new corn gleaming against the black soil.

"The first time I ever heard of your dad, mine was swearing about him," Luke said. "Never did know why."

"Loading cattle. They'd get pissed at each other. Almost a ritual."

"Yeah? Well, it didn't take much to piss Dad off. What was it this time?"

I didn't want to mention the cattle prod, didn't know what memories it might call up. We'd never talked about these things. "My dad didn't like the way yours treated the cattle when we were loading. They'd have this confrontation."

Luke was silent. I suspected he knew the prod was involved and that I'd deliberately not mentioned it. "Anyway," I went on, "Mom thought maybe our cattle were on the truck for a reason. And this is probably nothing too, but then I saw Angel, and he wondered about his store. And the bank got hit."

"Shit!" Luke whispered. "Wait a second, man. Wait a second."

The change that came over him alarmed me. The color drained from his face, and his dark eyes, staring at me, widened and deepened.

"No way," he said. "There's just no way."

Suddenly he opened his door and got out of the pickup and strode without looking back to a dredge ditch bridge in front of us. I watched his thin figure recede, pinned to my seat by the force of his reaction. Finally I opened my door and stepped into the dusty grass of the road ditch, walked around the hood of the pickup, and followed. When I reached the bridge Luke was leaning over the cement railing, looking down. I stood beside him. A ribbon of water ran between the sharply sloped banks. I looked away from it, over the fields.

"I'm thinking too much," I said. "I should've kept my mouth shut."

"No, no." He shook his head slowly back and forth. Far away over the fields a hawk circled. "It's OK. It's just, you're way ahead of me here. I mean, I knew all that—the cattle, the store, the bank. I just didn't put it together. It was just him and Mom, you know? I thought maybe it wasn't an accident, but I never thought . . . Shit, man, that's too much control."

"Seems like it, doesn't it?"

"I'll give you he hated the bank. He was always asking for loans for some scheme or another. Gonna make us rich. Wile E. all over again. Mom'd say, 'Don't go, you know they'll just say no,' but he couldn't ever hear her. 'I got things planned this time,' he'd say. 'Things're gonna fly this time.' And he'd march out the door. And we knew there'd be a drunk soon. Sometimes Mom could get him to hold off it for two, three days, but it'd eventually come. And then, watch out. Ah, hell, yeah, he hated the bank. But he hated everyone in town at some time or another. Said they were all assholes and morons who wouldn't know a good idea if it bit them. But saying he did all this, planned it—shit, man, it's like one of his crazy dreams."

"But you do think he could have dreamed up something like this?"

"Dreamed it? Oh sure. But you're talking doing. Dad

didn't do, man. Not like that. Not *planning* and then doing. With him it was all just right now."

He bent down, picked up a stone, and dropped it. I didn't watch it fall, but heard the silence, then the splash in the water below.

"OK," I said. "Just wondered what you thought. You used to say that just when Wile E. was flying highest, that's when he'd hit the cliff. I just tried to put too much together. Angel told me your dad threatened him."

"Dad threatened Angel?"

Again he'd interrupted me and again was staring at me in disbelief. I couldn't keep up with his mood changes and wished I'd never brought the subject up. I found myself dismissing it all, protecting Luke even though I wasn't sure from what.

"He was drunk," I said. "It was nothing. He was mad about Angel's boat for some reason. And the river. He was drunk, that's all."

"When?"

"I don't know—not too long before the crash."

He turned away from me and strode to the other side of the road. For a moment he leaned over the railing there, looking into the water, then flung himself away, raised his hands to the sky, and dropped them. "Christ!" he shouted. "I don't believe this. The boat?!"

He turned a full circle on the road, his feet scuffling in the gravel.

"That's what Angel wondered," I said quietly. "What about the boat?"

He raised his hands, palms upward, then dropped them to his sides. He shook his head. "Nothing, man. Just stupid, I guess. Dad didn't like the river. Didn't like water. When I started going down there, it was Angel and his boat, so I guess he didn't like Angel. Just like he didn't like it when you and me started doing things together."

I didn't say it, but I thought: That'd be another reason for him not to like Dad, though. Maybe it wasn't just the cattle and the barn. Maybe it was me and Luke.

"Well, like you say," I said, "he hated everyone in town at some time or another."

"Yeah," he murmured. "He did. All this shit. I can see him thinking about it. But doing it? Man, if he did it like you're thinking, then he wasn't who I thought he was. Or else." His mouth dropped open. A new realization hit him, or a new question. He was whiter now than he'd been before.

"What?" I asked. "Or else what?"

He didn't answer immediately. He tried to smile. When he did speak his voice was tight and pinched, sardonic. "Or else he changed. Wouldn't that just be it? He actually changed?"

I had no idea what he meant, no idea how to respond or what I'd be responding to.

"Jesus!" he said.

He shook his head, his lips thin, his face pulled tautly over his cheekbones. "I'm gonna see if there're minnows in this ditch."

"Go ahead. I'll stay here."

He disappeared under the bridge. After a while I walked

to the other side of the road and looked down at him. He was squatting by the water, near a wild rose just beginning to bud, trailing his hand in the stream. He wasn't moving. I watched the water make a small wake behind his hand, then turned away.

Ellen Easton Crandall

≈

IN MY DREAMS, CHRIST COMES TO ME. She comes in the form of an old woman. She shows me wounds. She lifts her hands, shows red marks and blood. And the wounds on her feet, too. As if to say: This is what happens when you come into the world. You get wounded.

She does this silently. Spreads her arms, points, and shows. It's a dream, but more than a dream. I think she can't speak. Christ? She nods her head. Then speaks.

And then you know what happens? she asks.

I shake my head.

Oh, but you do, she says. Give it a try, take a guess.

I don't know, I say. After the wounds? What? Death? Then resurrection?

Oh, she says. That. She grins. She's enjoying herself. Well, that's what I did. Wounds, then death, then resurrection. But no. Think. That's not normal, is it?

No, I say. I don't suppose.

Of course not. How many people have you seen crucified?

It's not too many, is it? I reply.

We both laugh then.

No, she says, laughing. Not too many. Pretty rare.

Well, what then? I ask.

You get old! she shouts. She can't restrain herself. Her laughter bursts like a balloon blown too far. I stare. Then her laughter catches me. I feel like a bell that's been rung. I peal. Laugh so hard I hurt.

Isn't that great? she gasps. First you get wounded, and then . . . and then . . .

She's laughing so hard she can't talk. And then, she says again. And then you get old.

You do, don't you? I cry. You get old.

Oh oh oh, she pants.

We settle down. Politics, she says, wiping her eyes. Back then, who'd believe a woman? But even worse, who'd believe an old fogy doddering around? Tell me that?

No one, I say. Right?

Exactly. Your old fogys with vision, they get established. Make a business of their thinking. Or turn into kooks. Am I right? People say: My God, he was saying that same thing thirty years ago. Let's hear something new already. Am I right?

Yes, I say. I guess.

You guess? Another five, ten years, the Pharisees would have asked me to join. I could've said no. But just being asked! Or else people would've expected better parables, better miracles, better truth. So it's in, spend three years, get things rolling, then take your wounds and beat it. That way people're still saying: This is something new. This is something different.

Yes, I say. I see. It was brilliant.

Brilliant? Maybe by human standards. But after all, I had to sacrifice myself. And even then it wasn't perfect.

Not perfect?

Well look. Once you get past thirty-three, you're on your own. No model anymore. You got to make it up. Use your imagination. But hardly anyone sees that.

So, I say. People get wounded and then . . . they get old.

She slaps her thigh. You got it. Isn't it something?

It's pretty funny, I say.

Funny? It's not funny at all. That's what's funny. It's a hoot.

She starts laughing again. Then she blesses me and disappears. I wake up thinking: I'm not old yet.

I'm in my room, and Luke is sleeping beside me, and my sides hurt, as if I've been laughing.

Hey Luke, I say quietly.

He goes on sleeping.

I rise on one elbow. Guess what? I say, close to his ear.

M-m-m-m-m-m. But he goes on sleeping.

You get wounded, I say. And then you get old. What do you think?

Uh-h-h-h.

I kiss his cheek. Lightly. My lips just touching him. Me too, I whisper.

I lie back on the pillow and stare at the ceiling.

You got to use your imagination, Luke, I say quietly. You got to make things up.

Leo Gruber

≈

HE KILLED THE TRACTOR YESTERDAY. Shoveling corn into the hammer mill as if he could change the world by shoveling. There's nothing like the silence after a hammer mill stops. We stood there, both of us, looking at the tractor and the plugged-up mill. As if it would restart itself. I could hear his breath, hard, like when he wrestled.

He used to look into the audience when he won a match, until he found me. I'd stand. Cheer and whoop. Make as much noise as I could. But I could see his eyes. They wanted my cheering, sure. But they defied it, too.

He had that look when he turned from the silent tractor.

"Well," I said. "Let's get it unplugged."

I walked to the latch and opened the door to the hammers. They were jammed full of corn. I reached in and removed a fistful, threw it on the ground.

Then he was next to me. "I jammed it," he said. "I'll take care of it."

I stepped aside.

Sometimes the sun is just rising and falling, nothing else, bright and empty.

Arlene Schuh

≈

I KNOW ONE THING THAT NOBODY ELSE in this town knows, and that's because I've chosen not to tell, because when the person the story's about really doesn't want it known I keep my silence, it's not all blab blab blab with me. If you don't want a story known, then you do what you can to stop it, and if you don't do what you can then it's out and free game, and no one can deny you self-pity, but you should've worked harder in the first place at keeping it under wraps. So I know this thing that I've never told, because, all right, I'll talk about anyone, but I'll keep my silence too on anyone, I don't care how insignificant, if I think the silence ought to be kept, and it's only accident that let the story out, only some sleepless old bat awake at her window when by all rights she ought to've been snoring alone in her pillow.

Maybe it don't matter anymore, what with Two-Speed gone now. Anyone can make up their mind about that and probably will no matter what I say, so I can't see it makes any sense for me to argue one way or the other. So here: Two-Speed Crandall ought to've been dead a long time ago, ought to've froze to death that time he pulled that idiotic stunt under Hank Tyrrell's pickup. Luck of a drunk, people said, when he didn't freeze to death walking home with all that blood lost, and maybe so if you can call Pop Bottle Pete luck, though he's for sure himself the unluckiest man I know.

I was awake and looking out my window, just looking out at the nothing-happeningness of this town at two in the morning, a cold night, looking at the wind make the trees go all creepy and spastic and the snow strung out in long streaks when it shot through the halo of the streetlights, and across the street the kitchen light burning in LouAnn Crandall's house, waiting for her husband to come home. If anyone'd been out there and looked up, they would've got the spine knot of their lives if they could've seen through my windowpane, the gossip queen staring out from the second floor. Course you can't see through a windowpane into a dark room, and anyhow, no one ever looks up out here, cause there's nothing to draw anyone's eyes up, nothing but the sky, so people tend to keep their eyes down, just to believe they're getting somewhere by the stepping of their feet, just to see something change when they move. I could stand on the edge of my roof in broad daylight with nothing on, now that'd give people something to talk about, except no one'd look up and notice long's I kept my mouth shut, which some people'd say is about impossible with me.

I was looking out at the cold, looking at the windsweep of the trees and the snow and the little perimeters of light the bulbs made against the darkness, when I saw out of the corner of my eye, going through the halo of those lights, what looked like a big, hunchbacked man, shuffling along in a hurry of feet. You can believe I stared, but by the time I turned my head for a better look he'd faded into the dark between the lights, and the snow so thick and white falling between where he'd been and me that I thought I'd been seeing things, and it wouldn't be the first time, Arlene, that your eyes've played tricks on you, I told myself, but if this was a trick then your eyes are getting too good at it, and you better find a way to unsmart them.

Then in the next halo of light, pop, there he was out of the darkness again, shufflerunning along, and I saw this time that it was two men, one on top of the other, and that the hunch I'd thought I'd seen was just one of them. Then I saw just before they got lost in the dark again that the bottom man was naked, holding his arms up to keep the top one on, and nothing on his feet, and big and potbellied and hairy, and a ghosty feeling went through me, and I thought, My Lord, is that the Abominable Snowman running through the streets of Cloten? Is that the Big Man that the Indians know about come to snatch a citizen and carry him away?

Then out of the light he came again, just one post away, running out of the snowstreak, humping along, and all I could see was the Abominable Snowman, like he was running right out of the things I'd heard and read about him, out of the old stories or wherever time keeps him however far back you want to go, and it caught my heart like the spook houses of my girlhood caught my heart but also like when a church service grabs you just right, and you know what it's all about, and you don't want to sing or praise, you just want to stand there in your own silence and feel the big silence around you echo with itself.

God help us, I whispered. Glory be. He was running down the sidewalk into the wind, and I could see he was sure enough naked, I won't go into that, but it had some bulk swinging between his legs, the snow plastered against him and caked into his hair so that his whole body was one white sheet, snow on top of his head, coating his eyebrows, covering his chest, his arms, his legs, his big hairy belly sticking out looking for all the world like a snowball just stuck to him, and shuffling along under the weight of who he was carrying, his big feet going plop, plop on the sidewalk.

He was close enough now I could see him in the dark when he left the light, a big white thing moving down there in the snow streaking the other way. He looked like he was floating through the storm, like he was going to rise right up the planes of the angling snow and over the roofs and barren trees and away, and I held my breath, waiting.

Then he was in the light again, and for the first time I could actually see his face and try to make it out, though I'll admit that when you see a naked man running through a blizzard, even if you're not sure it's a man, and you've been widowed as long as I have and waking to an empty bed in the dark, the face isn't the first thing that holds your attention, and I've got to say it looked mighty cold taking the full brunt of the wind like it was, and the snow looking sharp and long and knifey cutting through the light. But I looked at the face as he went directly under the lamp post, and for a second I couldn't see nothing but the Snowman, the hair and eyebrows and even the eyelashes so coated with snow, and snow sticking to his chin, that he looked like he was furred in snow. But then something about the shadows coming down from the light straight above or maybe something about the way he moved, I don't know, made me see, and I said out loud to myself: "Why, it's Pop Bottle Pete." My face was close to the window, me peering out trying to see everything, and when I spoke out loud like that the window frosted up, and for a moment I couldn't see anything.

By the time I had the window cleared off he was turning up the sidewalk to LouAnn Crandall's house, and at first I didn't know what was going on because, if you can believe this, I'd totally forgotten he was carrying someone else, the way the snow was covering them both and me all caught up in the illusion that it was the Abominable Snowman, so that the second man I'd seen before had turned back into a big hump of snowfur. And even now when I knew it was Pop Bottle Pete my mind couldn't let go of the Snowman, so I wondered why he was going up to LouAnn's house, the light from the window through the thin curtains glowing onto him, and me with this spooky feeling that he was going to go right through the door, a chunk of unstoppable ice.

Then all of a sudden he bent and broke into two pieces, and I screamed, I actually screamed, and I jerked my hand to my mouth to stop it and held my hand there and screamed into it and almost bit myself trying to stop it. He bent way down and broke, and the top part of him rolled right off the bottom part onto the steps, and his big rear end was pointed up at my window as he went to his knees. Then I realized that Pop Bottle Pete had brought Two-Speed Crandall home, and it was only later when I heard about the Hank Tyrrell thing that I put it all together and realized Pop

Bottle'd found him, though what he was doing out in a blizzard stark naked is something I'll never know, and I'll bet his mother doesn't know, and if she did she'd have a fit.

When he rolled Two-Speed off his shoulders he knocked a lot of the snow off, so when he stood and turned to look down the street I could see sure enough that it was Pete, with that same look he has when he's searching for bottles, up and down the street to see if anyone was coming. Then he reached up and knocked on the door, his hand big and slow, making me think of a Chinese gong, looking just that big and slow as it moved in the swirling snow, and I almost thought I'd hear it through my window, *bwo-i-i-i-ing* as it hit the door, the whole house over there shaking and vibrating, the roof collapsing, and Pop Bottle, if that happened, would still be standing there waiting for someone to answer.

But he only knocked twice and then disappeared around the corner of the house, and I could just barely make him out, crouched in a shadow. I thought I saw him shaking but I don't see how I could have noticed a thing like that, dark as it was and across the street and all. I was thinking what a story this'd make when I finally made sense of it all, when I'd picked up the strands of it from other people. Maybe that kind of thinking sharpens your eyes too much, and you'll see someone shivering when you couldn't really see it, or maybe you'll hear things that're beyond hearing. So there was Pop Bottle Pete crouched in the shadows shivering, and LouAnn stuck her head out the door and then fell down on one knee and kind of slid toward Two-Speed with her hands down like she was going to scoop him right up and carry him inside the house. She flicked the outside light on before she came out, and I could see through the slanting snow how she touched him all over and then jerked when she came to his head and then reached out to touch him again and then looked at her hand, and I could see that it was red.

Then LouAnn looked straight through the snow at me, and I almost jerked away from the window, how a person will, but I held myself still because I knew I was in the dark and she was in the light, and the pane of glass was keeping me hidden, but it was awful to just stand there while someone stared back at me, and even though my mind was saying, you're invisible, my heart wasn't believing it. She wouldn't look away. She must've been thinking about what to do, how to get him into the house and whether to call for help or what, and while she was thinking she just happened to look up and hold her gaze where I was, but it was all I could do to stand there. I thought, My God, Arlene, she's waiting for you to come down after all these years and help her out, she's seen you all along but she's been too polite to let you know, but now she needs your help and she's trying to tell you, looking right at you up through the snow from the light, kneeling and trying to say: Come down, Arlene, and help me, because this is beyond politeness and way beyond pretending.

I was trapped, and I'm not proud of it. I thought I'd have a heart attack my chest was pounding so hard. Dr. Piersoll has told me that since menopause my cholesterol is too high, it was a terrible situation I was in, because I knew she couldn't possibly be seeing me unless my clothes were somehow reflecting light, but it didn't seem possible, I'd looked at that window from the street myself just to be sure. But it sure looked like she was seeing me and waiting for me to do something, but on the other hand if she wasn't seeing me and I moved, then she might see that movement through the window because she happened to be looking at it, and then she'd know I'd been spying all along.

I wanted to run down my steps and across the street and help that woman, but I couldn't move, because if I did it'd be like admitting years of doing nothing. She knelt in the snow and I stood in my bedroom and we stared across a blizzard-filled street.

I didn't think she'd ever drop her gaze. I swear she was pleading with me while the wind drove the snow in white lines through the dark and into the light, and Two-Speed bled on the doorstep, and Pop Bottle Pete shivered in his hiding place, and I stood stock still and prayed I wouldn't have a stroke, though if I had it probably would've served me right.

When she finally turned away my knees about buckled. I backed away from the window and into the darkness of the room until I felt the bed touch the back of my legs, and then I stopped. I could still see, like it was a little scene far away, the doorstep framed by the window, and LouAnn standing up and taking Two-Speed's hands and pulling, and him not moving, and her pulling harder, and I realized I was all tensed up pulling with her, and then I realized I was crying, standing there in the middle of my bedroom crying without making a sound, crying because he wouldn't move and I couldn't, and I felt like my whole house was just a big lot of empty space, nothing but a perch for an old bat to watch from.

I don't know where she got the strength, because I know how heavy dead men are, and Two-Speed was close to it, but somehow she pulled him over the sill and into the house. And then, I've never understood, she stuck her head back out the door and stood on the steps for a while, and then held her hand up like she was waving to the empty street, and she spoke some words. She didn't know Pop Bottle was hiding along the house, that was clear, so she couldn't've been talking to him, but anyway she said some words, maybe a prayer of some kind, and went back inside the house. She shut off the outside light, and then Pop Bottle, all white again from the snow that'd gathered on him while he waited, came out of the shadow and went loping like some crippled, hurt animal across the lawn toward his house. He held his right hand on his groin, and the other swung back and forth, and he went galloping off, furred with snow.

Then I got down on my knees in that big old house with only me in it, and I prayed, with tears falling down my face and onto my nightdress, and my hands at my sides and my face to the ceiling, that God would forgive an old woman who'd gotten so lonely and wretched she couldn't even walk down her steps and across the street to help a neighbor even lonelier, and in need.

I knew then that I wouldn't talk about what I'd seen, not just because I'd come by the story dishonestly, but because, all right, you're as much a part of a story if you don't do something when you should've as when you do something you shouldn't. It was all four of us that night, Pop Bottle Pete and LouAnn and Two-Speed and me, and I knew because I was part of it that they wouldn't want it told.

I still say, how do you know how to run your life unless you know how other people've run theirs, and how do you know that unless you listen and talk? But if the watching and the listening and the talking get bigger than the living, then you've gone over some kind of border. Maybe LouAnn didn't know I was there. But maybe she did, maybe she knew from way back and just went on living her life and letting me watch, waiting for the time when she'd need me, maybe even feeling comforted knowing I was watching, that someone would see when she needed help.

Lord! And then when the time came the help didn't, because the watcher'd convinced herself it was possible to just watch and listen and not be involved, never realizing even if you're not involved you can be involved.

They're dead now, and Pop Bottle Pete has done to himself what he did to himself, and maybe I couldn't've done anything to change anything, but that's not the point. The point is that if you watch long enough you can become an old bat behind a dark window who can't move even if someone is watching back, and waiting.

Pop Bottle Pete

≈

MY TOES CRIED. I couldn't make the warm go into them. And my thing too. Right at the end. They got black. Because I couldn't make the warm go into them.

If Mom saw, she'd know. When she was gone I turned on the oven. I tried to put them in there. It's like a red snake in the oven. But it couldn't make the warm go in.

I cried. Because if Mom saw she'd get mad. She'd say, now everyone's going to think. And they're going to take you away.

I cried. Away is bad. No friends. I couldn't pick up bottles away. Or rocks. Or have money to buy Cokes. I couldn't stand outside and wait. And talk to Simon about trucks. And assholes. And fucking morons sorry Peter.

And Simon. He'd say, where's Peter? If he fell down, the dark would go in him. No one would see to pick him up.

I went in the garage. I got the big scissors. The one for trees. It goes smile when you open it. Then chop. The branches on the bushes go fall. I snuck in the house. Mom was in the kitchen. I went tiptoe ouch upstairs. To my room. I shut the door.

I looked. My toes were black. Two of them. And three. One two one two three. Bad toes, I said.

I sat on the bed. The big scissors went smile. I put it on a toe. I closed my eyes.

Chop.

I tried not to cry. Because Mom would hear.

I opened my eyes. Oh no. Blood. The toe went on the bed. In the blood. Like a little branch. A black branch. I tried not to cry and opened the big scissors again. It went blood smile.

I put it on another toe. I shut my eyes. Chop. My toes were like branches in the summer. Fall fall onto the bed. I was like a tree.

But trees don't bleed. I tried not to cry but I did. Don't cry, I said. But I cried. Me didn't obey me. I cried and cried. Mom came. Her feet went pound pound on the steps. Her voice went Peter Peter Peter.

One two one two three. On my bed. Just my thing left. Then Mom wouldn't know. And no one would think. And they wouldn't come. And I wouldn't go away. Me and Simon would still be friends.

The wind had made my thing so it wouldn't work any-more. It melted for always. The big scissors went smile smile. But oh no. My thing hung down. It hid under my belly. I couldn't see. I had to hold it out. I couldn't make the scissors go chop.

Mom's feet went run hurry in the hall.

I let go my thing. My hands went hold tight on the scis-sors. I put its smile down where I couldn't see.

The door went open and Mom screamed.

Chop.

I dropped the big scissors. I put my hands on my ears. Then I screamed and cried. To chase Mom's screams out of my ears.

I looked at the bed. And floor. Toes. One two one two three. But no thing. Just toes.

I missed. I took a hand off my ears and felt. It was still there. I cried and screamed. Because now Mom would know. And everyone would think. They would take me away and I wouldn't have no friends.

Dr. Piersoll

≈

MAYBE IF YOU'RE A PRIEST the things you hear in a confessional will tell you more about the quirks and weirdnesses of people than if you're a doctor. I'd like to sit down with a priest and compare notes, the dark of the confessional with the light of the examining room. Most of it would be boring. I get mostly bad backs and high blood pressure, and I can imagine the drone that a priest must have to listen to, the common liaisons and sins that seem so uncommon to the person confessing them.

Still, there must be times when something entirely new is told within a confessional, something that revives a priest's amazement at the inventiveness of human degradation, just as there are still times when I'm amazed at injury or pain. This latest thing with Two-Speed Crandall amazed me in that way, and it follows hard upon the heels of another odd story, the time that Peter Janisch amputated his toes with a pruning shears. My old med school pals would probably tell me that two stories like that in a year in a place like Cloten have got to be more than coincidence, and they'd wonder how I stand the excitement.

Ernestine Janisch's husband left her when Peter was two

years old, unable to believe that he had fathered Peter, or more likely saying that as a way to avoid the responsibilities. Since then, Ernestine has lived on the edge of hysteria, afraid that Peter will leave too, or that he will prove a danger to himself or others, and the state will cart him away. She spends much of her time on the phone, asking if anyone has seen Peter, and eventually someone will report that they saw him in a ditch somewhere looking for bottles. Many people in town won't even wait for Ernestine's call, but if they see Peter somewhere they'll call and report, just to ease her nerves. In the summers Ernestine tries to find Peter jobs picking up rocks for farmers or baling hay, and some farmers will call when they need those jobs done.

In the winters, though, Peter holes up in the house, so how he frostbit his toes and penis without Ernestine knowing makes an interesting question. When I saw Ernestine and Peter in my office, she was actually wringing her hands. "You won't report this, will you, Doctor?" she kept asking me. "They'd say he's a danger to himself, and they'd take him away. But he's not a danger. It was just an accident. I'm sure it was."

Every time she asked that Peter cried. I asked Ernestine to calm down, and she finally settled herself in a chair in the corner of the examining room, watching me through the lenses of the old-fashioned cataract glasses she wore. She looked like an owl perched there.

I got Peter onto the table and unwrapped the bandages Ernestine had applied to his feet. I almost whistled when I had them off. He'd done a fantastic job, very clean and neat, three toes on one foot and two on the other. Ernestine hadn't brought the toes in, so I'm not sure they would have needed amputation, but if they had I couldn't have done a better job myself, and it surely would have cost Ernestine more money. There's a strange humor that happens sometimes in an examining room, the same kind that makes people laugh at funerals. If Ernestine hadn't been there dabbing at her eyes and blowing her nose, I would have asked Peter if he'd ever considered medical school, good as his job was. But I was pretty sure Ernestine wouldn't see the humor.

The tension of Ernestine sitting there watching me with those big eyes, and her sniffling, and Peter's slow, heavy breathing, got to me, though. I worked for a while, stopping the flow of blood, then asked: "I don't suppose he sterilized the shears first?"

Ernestine was so relieved to be able to talk that her voice almost burst out of her. "Oh no," she exclaimed, her voice rising with conviction. "I'm sure he didn't."

I nodded. "Wash his hands?"

"Oh, Doctor, I don't know," she said. "I don't think so." She blew her nose loudly.

I nodded again, gravely. "Would have been best if he had."

"Oh, I know, Doctor," she said. "And I would have told him to if I'd known. But I didn't even know he was thinking about it."

"It's all right," I said. "But next time, huh?"

"Oh, of course," she said. Then she stopped. "But Doctor. Do you think there'll be a next time?"

Her eyes widened even further. I felt a bit cheap and apologetic. "I doubt it, Ernestine," I said. I worked a while longer, scrubbing antiseptic into Peter's toes. It must have hurt a great deal, but he never pulled away. He just watched me work, his face revealing nothing, just as it had revealed nothing when he walked into my office unaided.

"Ernestine," I said, "did you know you could get contact lenses?"

"Contact lenses?"

"For your cataracts. Those heavy glasses aren't necessary. You might like contacts."

"Do you think so?"

"Yes, I do."

"I've been wearing these glasses so long.".

"I know how it is," I said. "I've got an old Buick that's falling apart, but I just keep driving it. You get used to things."

"Oh, you do," she said sadly.

"So, Peter," I said. "Are you planning to do this again?"

"He isn't!" Ernestine cried out. She looked at Peter. "Petey," she said, "you're not going to do this again, are you?"

Peter didn't say anything. He sat there slowly. He's the only person I've ever known who even sat slowly. His breath came out slow and steady as an old steam engine, and he didn't even flinch as I finished with the antiseptic. I'd considered giving him a local, but I knew he was terrified of needles, and I decided it would be kinder to go without, though I hadn't expected the kind of calm he displayed. He seemed indifferent to everything I did.

"It's frostbite," I said. "See these patches on the balls of his feet? Do you know how he got frostbite?"

Suddenly the silence in the room was so great that I noticed the fluorescent lights buzzing. I realized that Peter's breathing had stopped. I looked up at him and thought I saw a glimmer in his small eyes. I'd never seen him smile, but I think he almost did; I have no idea why. Then he started to breathe again, and his whole body seemed to relax. His foot sagged to the side so that I had to hold it upright while I worked.

"No, Doctor," Ernestine said. "He must have been outside without shoes and ..."

She stopped.

"Without clothes at all?" I asked. "You said his penis looked bad, too?"

"Yes," she said, despairingly. "He tried to cut it off, too. But he missed. I screamed, and I think it startled him. Doctor, what if he had?"

I didn't think that Peter's having or not having a penis would affect future generations or his prospects for marriage one way or the other, but I kept that thought to myself. "I don't know," I said. "Let's just say it was a good thing you were there."

"Oh it was, wasn't it?" Ernestine said. "If I hadn't ... oh, it just was."

"How did you get frostbite, Peter?" I asked.

He didn't answer, just shook his head, but I had this odd feeling again that he wanted to laugh.

"Ernestine," I said. "I need to look at his penis. It might be best if you left."

"But I help give him a bath."

"That's fine," I said, "but this isn't a bath."

It was me more than Peter. I didn't feel right examining

that part of a grown man, even if it was Peter Janisch, with his mother looking on. And I wanted Ernestine out of the room for a while. She got up slowly and left, glancing back cautiously before she shut the door. "Peter," I said. "No one's going to take you away. You're going home. All right?"

He sat on the examining table, absolutely immense and corpulent, gazing at his feet. Finally he looked at me and nodded.

"Good," I said. "You understand that. Now then. How did this happen?"

He stared at his toes again, then looked back at me. He shrugged a big shrug that pulled his entire huge torso up and then let it fall. It recoiled inside his shirt like waves.

"Well, that's quite an answer, Peter," I said. "But it doesn't tell me much. I really need to know how you frostbit yourself this badly."

He nodded then, vigorously, and actually grinned. "Frostbite," he said. "Shityeah. Frostbite."

I stared at him. I couldn't imagine Ernestine teaching him to talk that way. Perhaps some farmer he'd worked for. I wasn't getting very far.

"Could you take your pants down, Peter?"

He undid his belt and shuffled his bulk around until his pants were down around his knees. I stood up and took a look. The tip of his penis had been frozen, but it looked like it would be all right. "Well, Peter," I said, "you're lucky you've got good circulation there. Lucky you missed with that shears, too."

"Shityeah," he said. "Fucking lucky."

I stared at him for a moment and almost asked where

he'd learned to talk that way, but decided it was no concern of mine. "Pants up," I said. "I'll bring your mother back in."

"Is he all right?" she asked before she was even back in the room.

"He's fine," I said. "He'll be sore for a while, but OK."

"Is he . . . a danger to himself?"

"Well now," I said. "If someone else in this town were to frostbite his toes and develop gangrene in them and then had the sense to amputate them before it killed him, I'd wonder why he hadn't come to me first, but I'd give him credit for saving his own life. Let's just give Peter the benefit of the doubt like we would with anyone else and let it go at that."

I thought she'd fall down in disbelief. "Ernestine," I said. "You should quit worrying so much. It's hard on your heart. Peter's biggest danger right now is his weight. You ought to put him on a diet."

"Oh, I know," she said. Then she added, "He likes Milky Ways, though. And Coke."

The truth is, it would be best if Ernestine outlives her son. I hate to imagine what would happen to him if she went first. But I knew she'd never put him on a diet. So I let it go at that.

I hopped around the office a little, demonstrating the crutches we found for him. He was as happy as he gets, trying to work those crutches. Then, me on one side and Ernestine on the other, we guided him out the door, the crutches looking like they'd snap under his weight.

I prescribed some anticoagulants in case the frostburned tissue didn't circulate blood as well as it should, and also some pain relievers, though Peter seemed impervious to pain. Ernestine walked out, clutching the prescription.

As she was about to leave the office, I stopped her. "Ernestine."

"Yes, Doctor?"

"Think about contact lenses."

"Oh, I will."

No you won't, I thought as she walked out the door.

Pop Bottle Pete

≈

IT WORKED.
   I fooled Mom.
   I even fooled Mister Doctor.
   No one will think. No one will come.
   I won't go away.
   Mister Doctor thinks I got bit.

Luke Crandall

≈

WHAT DID I KNOW ABOUT being a father? Ellen said, however you're a father it'll be the best, because it's you. Of course. But of course not, too.

Dad was afraid of being afraid, and that's the biggest bullshit there is. It's like a mirror reflecting itself. There's no way to break into it. It'll keep you running from your life just to keep from knowing how scared you are. And shit, you might climb into a semi and run it down a hill and kill your-self, because if you can prove you're not scared of death, then you're not scared of anything, maybe—not being alone, and not the man who's not afraid of you, and not your dreams or your wife or your son.

I wanted to see some change in him. I wanted to see his bullshit turn into something real. He made the world mighty big when he got dreaming out loud, and himself big enough to handle it. All the Road Runner has is speed. And he's been given that. But the Road Runner show's not about the Road Runner. It's about Wile E. He's the one who in-vents rockets and motor roller skates and sailboats with electric fans, all this shit that can't work but does. Wile E.'s the one with the hunger.

But Wile E. can never go fast enough, because the Road Runner always has as much speed as he needs. But Wile E. doesn't give a shit about actually catching him. He just wants to make plans. He just wants an excuse to dream something up and make a threat. Dream and threat, threat and dream. That's what Wile E.'s about. Shit, if he can buy sailboats and electromagnets, he can sure buy a hamburger for lunch. Wile E. wants to be hungry, because without the hunger he wouldn't have the dream, and without the dream he wouldn't have the threat. If he'd ever catch the Road Runner his whole world would fall apart. As long as he's dreaming and threatening he doesn't have to notice that the world's full of hard places and holes, even when he hits them. Doesn't have to notice that he's scared.

At night sometimes I'd wake up and look at Ellen sleeping. I'd wonder what it was out there ahead of us, for both of us. I couldn't get a grasp on it. If I couldn't figure out what it meant to be a son, how the hell could I be a dad? It reached a point where I thought I had to do something. It just didn't turn out like I thought it would.

I borrowed Angel's boat. I told Ellen I was going to spend the night fishing. At dusk I took the boat down to the landing past the bridge on Old 16. I put it in the water and tied it, then unhooked the trailer from my pickup out of the way of anyone else using the landing. I stood for a while, listening to the water come around the bend. I let the first stars come out, standing inside the mosquito sound. Then I drove back to town, thinking nothing, keeping my mind empty.

When I got back to Cloten I thought of Mom, how she'd be waiting up for Dad. I thought of going to their house and telling her not to bother tonight. Then I got pissed off. She'd been doing that forever. Let her wait, I thought. Let her wait all night. If they won't change anything, I will.

I drove around town, wasting time, up and down the streets like I'd done in high school, but not looking for anyone now, not expecting anything. Just thinking, here I still am. Go away and come right back. The pickup's mufflers echoed off the buildings. My lights showed me nothing I hadn't already seen.

I got sick of it. I parked the pickup by the city park, where I could look up the street and see the bar. I slouched down and waited. Cars went up and down the street, and light moved through the cab. People came out of the bar in groups and went to their cars, waving to each other. Their arms looked like antennas. The town got darker, and the stars got sharper in the gap between the streetlights. I waited for the bar to close.

Finally he came out. He didn't wave to anyone. He came out the door and walked down the sidewalk. No one called to him. I thought: You bastards, you could at least wave after spending an entire night with him. Then I thought: Hell, the son of a bitch doesn't wave either. He can't stand their guts and they can't stand his, and that bar's just a place where they don't have to admit it.

He came down the sidewalk toward me. I slouched down further, though he might've looked right into my face and never seen it. He turned and headed to where Mom was waiting. I started the pickup and let it idle for a while. Through the trees of the park I could see his silhouette weaving away from me. I waited for him to cross the next street, then put the pickup into gear.

I followed slow, my lights off. No hurry. In spite of the drink he walked right along and made a couple blocks before I pulled alongside and rolled my window down. He never looked up to see who it was.

I pulled the pickup over to the wrong side of the road so I was only a few feet away from him. "Dad," I called. "Dad."

He went on walking like the words hadn't reached him or he didn't understand them. Then he stopped. He swung his face around to me, blank as an old pail swinging on a hook. He frowned. "The hell you doing out?" he asked.

He wasn't as drunk as I thought. Good. I wanted his mind working. For a moment I didn't answer him. That's right, I thought, challenge me. The night's mine, Dad. The bullshit's ending.

"Get in," I said. "I'll take you home."

He came to the pickup and looked in, leaning his elbows on the door. He nodded, curled his tongue against his teeth. "Aha," he said. "Had a fight with Ellen, didja? Never let a woman kick you outta bed."

There was a time when he could outcon and outbullshit anything I tried. But he didn't know how much I'd learned. Part of me breathed hard, but the other part ran along smooth and quick. I couldn't tell which was the real one, the watcher or the doer. But that just made me sharper.

"Leave Ellen out of it," I said. If he thought he had one up on me, he'd get in. If not, he'd turn stubborn, and I'd have to knock him out before he'd come with me. "You gonna stand there all night?" I demanded.

A double whammy. Make him think I'm mad at him about Ellen so he'd think it's true, and then make him think I'm trying to cut him down to get back at him. It'd make him generous.

"Oops," he said. "The pretty girl's untouchable. I did forget, didn't I?" He grinned, holding the door for balance, then walked around the front of the pickup, opened the door, and hauled himself into the seat. It's damn near not fair, I thought. Unless he can actually piss me off, I've changed the rules, and he doesn't even know it. But the rules'd always been his, and the game too. The only difference was that this time he hadn't badgered me into playing it. But he didn't know that.

His face was green in the dashboard lights as he glared across the seat at me. "Well?" he demanded. "We gonna sit here all night? Let 'er rip, boy."

I watched myself put the pickup into gear. I watched myself watching his greenlit face and then looking away through the windshield. Something changed inside. When I'd first thought about this night it'd been the doing of it that mattered, the getting him alone and away from all his crap and defenses. But suddenly, how I did it mattered, not just the doing.

"When ya gonna learn?" he said as I pulled onto the street. "Let a woman get to ya, and you're whipped."

"Fuck off."

People throw the phrase around all the time, but to use it when it's just the right one—the watching part of me jumped with excitement, almost not able to just watch. "You leave Ellen alone, hear?" I stared at him, but he just grinned.

"Hear?" He grinned some more. I turned the dash lights down, and his face faded. "You don't seem too damn tired," I said. "I got Angel's boat down on the river. You might's well help me haul it out."

I made it tight, like a demand, like I was still trying to get back at him, making him do something he didn't want to do. If I'd asked he'd've said no. But now he could show how unperturbed he was, having the upper hand.

It should've been the oddest thing in the world that I'd want his help hauling a boat out of the river. Even drunk he should've wondered. But I was on a roll, and the oddity slipped right past him, he was so damn eager to beat me at this game he thought we were playing. You trained me too well, I thought. Wile E.'s son, brighter than the old coyote in his cave. Bright enough to stay on the ground. To not try to fly.

"Sure," he said, leaning back on his seat. "Me, I'm eager to please. Whatever you say."

On the eight miles to the boat landing he dozed and I thought. I wanted everything to be so he thought he was doing it all on his own. When I was a kid he'd stop talking in the middle of a sentence when we drove across a bridge. He'd stare straight ahead and not talk again until we were on the other side. Didn't even know he was doing it. His hands'd grip the wheel. I often wondered what it was like for him, driving those loaded semis, all that weight, over some of those old river bridges. Must've terrified him, though he'd never admit it. Tonight I'd use that fear—because he'd have to prove to me that it wasn't real.

I drove down the gravel embankment to the landing.

Dad didn't wake up when I shut the engine off. I opened the door and heard the river running on. From where I stood the surface of the water was a flat plane of darkness. I went around to the passenger door and opened it. I watched him for a while, slouched, the alcohol smell sweet against the cool river air. I shook him. "Let's go."

His eyes turned to me uncomprehending. I remembered the look from when I was a kid, how he hated to be woke up. There'd be this moment of waiting, to see if he was going to blow up. I didn't let him have the option this time. I took control. "The boat," I said. "Let's get the damn thing out of the water and get back home."

"Damn the boat," he said. "Take me home right now."

I felt a new surprise. I felt cruelty like cold ventilation under my ribs. It swirled inside my chest, but I didn't recognize it. It wasn't a need to cause him pain. If I'd felt that I would've known. What I felt was just this: He'd do what I wanted him to do. I forgot for a bit why I'd brought him here, the questions I had, the answers I wanted. Love, anger, fear—they all left, taking their excuses and alibis with them. The river ran behind me. Air moved. He was going to do what I wanted. Ellen talks about free will, and standing there looking at Dad I realized why God—if Ellen's right—gave it to us. If He hadn't, He couldn't've borne thinking about us. I looked away from Dad, knowing he had no choice.

"The boat first," I said. "Then home."

"No," he muttered. "Gotta go. Peter's waiting."

That almost threw me, just when I thought nothing could. "Peter," I said. "What the hell you talking about?

What Peter? It's past one in the morning. No one's waiting for anybody. Let's get that boat out."

"No. Peter's waiting for me. If I don't show up . . ."

"You're drunk. You don't even know anyone named Peter. And if you did, he sure as hell wouldn't be waiting for you."

"No. You know. Peter what's-his-name."

"I sure as hell don't. And neither do you." I pulled him out of the cab. When his feet hit the ground he stood, and I kept pulling him so that his feet had to move. He was three or four steps away from the pickup before he jerked away from me. "Goddamn. What the hell?"

He lifted his head like he smelled fire in the air. He realized he was alone—with someone who couldn't be conned. The river worked on him. It flowed into the moment. He knew this was my place. I saw that he knew.

But he had to think I didn't see. Anger will hide almost anything. It's a genus in itself. I waved him back like I didn't want him close to me. I strode across the gravel to the boat trailer. "Shit," I said. "You're too drunk to be any good. Stay there. I don't need your help. Get back in the pickup and wait for me."

I reached for the cable that winched the boat onto the trailer and gave it a pull, not looking at Dad. I was so sure. He never could stand being told he couldn't do something. I heard his steps behind me and smelled the smoke and whiskey of the bar swept toward me on the breeze. His shoulder brushed against me. "I'll get that," he said, reaching past me for the cable.

"It's got. Stay put. I'm going to pull the boat closer."

I turned and walked down to the water. I heard his feet behind me, following like a string follows a fishing arrow, flopping around, but staying right on course. My chest felt like a balloon filled with ice water. I knew what was coming and how it would happen. I grabbed the rope holding the boat and hauled it in until the bow scraped the shore. He reached past my arms and grabbed the rope too, his face right next to mine, his heat on my cheek.

I dropped the rope and stepped away. "Well shit," I said. "If you want to do something, get in there and raise that motor."

He did exactly what I knew he'd do. He stood stock still and stared at the boat. Even dark as it was I could see his face working.

"I ain't getting in the damn boat," he said.

"Fuck! Make up your mind. The damn thing's grounded. There's nothing to be afraid of."

It came down to that one sentence—the mention of fear, and how it'd be used. I let it slip in and let it work. I moved to the boat and ignored him, as if I were disgusted. As if his fear made him useless.

"Afraid," he muttered. I was nearly to the boat. "Afraid," he said again. The river lapped the toes of my boots. I started to climb into the bow.

"Stop," he yelled. "I'll pull the goddamn motor up."

I stepped away.

I held the rope in my hand and as he pushed by me, splashing water, I reached into my pocket and found my knife. I took it out and opened the blade. I watched him stumble over the paddles that Angel keeps in case the motor quits. When he bent down to grab the motor and pull it up, I cut the rope. I heard the quiet crackle of polyethylene threads parting. The motor chunked and locked against its pin. Dad began to turn around. I threw the cut rope into the boat, lifted the bow, shoved, followed my shove and stepped in, gave a push with my foot against the shore to send the boat into the current—and we were on the river.

Dad fell when I shoved. His feet went with the boat but his body stayed where it was and gravity pulled him down. He stumbled toward me and collapsed. He hit and rolled onto his back, and his legs went up in the air like they were jerked by strings. I was still leaning forward with my foot over the water, the boat gliding from my push. The river chuckled and gurgled. I could feel it through the hull, deepening as we drifted into the channel. Between Dad's legs, like some kind of weird frame, a crooked V, kink kneed and upside down, the surface of the water glistened black, as if his legs were collecting it and funneling it into his groin.

We drifted sideways downstream. The shore slipped past. I let my foot hang over the water and looked down at that face that had been the largest thing in my childhood, lit with dreams or darkened with threat. I looked down at that face and saw nothing but an old face slack as a fishing line collapsing after the lure's hit the water.

I looked at it and felt nothing. He had a life preserver under him, and it looked like everything had been drained out of that face into the life preserver. The current swept the boat along. I felt the nothing that I felt and said: "We're on the river, Dad."

Then I said: "There's no bullshit out here, Dad." I stepped over him, dropped the motor, looked quick to see that the gas was hooked up, and pulled the cord. The smell of burnt gasoline erupted into the air, a slick of oil gleamed behind the boat, and the engine splatted into life.

I took the tiller, twisted the throttle full on, and turned upstream. The boat swung big against the current, the prow cutting a circle like a clock hand marking time against the shore. Dad turned over on his stomach and crawled away from me. The roar of the engine echoed off the banks. I straightened the tiller out, and we charged upstream, all noise and spreading wake, the landing slipping behind us until it disappeared around the bend, and then nothing but the dark banks and the stars and the river coming down, cut by the prow.

Dad hit his head on the aluminum bench in the middle of the boat, then crawled onto it and turned, facing me. He looked past me, at the river behind me and the trees thickening on the banks, as we turned away from the road and entered the deeper woods. His mouth hung open. I looked away from the sight of it.

Too easy. I'd learned all of his rages, the way he kept other people off balance—learned them like a trapeze artist learns the swing of the bars. Push one here and push one there. Loop and circle. Let one go, pick up another.

Dad took me to a circus once. He and I'd gone downtown to pick up groceries and cigarettes. In the window of the Super Valu was a poster showing a clown in a striped cap and a big tent with flags flying over it. I stopped in front of that poster. Dad ran right into me. I stumbled but kept staring at the poster. He laughed: "You wanna see the circus?"

Sometimes he'd be like that. He'd notice everything and cut right through the bullshit to the heart.

"You wanna see the circus, then by God we'll see the circus."

He slapped me on the back, but on the way home I thought it'd never happen. I tried to put it out of my mind. When Saturday came I never mentioned it. It was better he'd forget than that he'd refuse. But that evening after supper he pushed back from the table and stared at me. "You wanna go to that circus or not?" he demanded. I heard the joking in his voice and knew things were OK.

Mom was happy. When things were good with Dad, Mom thought they'd always be good. She couldn't see it was all chance, that the circus happened to come to town on a day when Dad was good, that's all. Of course, none of us saw it then.

It was the best evening I ever had with him. Nothing ruined it. The tent turned out to be smaller than I expected, and the animals weren't as fierce, and it was only Cloten, after all, but none of that mattered. Dad bought pop and caramel corn, and we ate from the same box and drank from the same cup, and Matt and Mark were too old for this, so it was just me and Dad.

I remember the trapeze act the most, because he went silent when he watched it, never turning his face from the top of the tent. I felt his focus, like something I couldn't break and didn't want to. The bodies flashed and dropped and stopped their falling and looped back up. They caught each other's wrists and ankles and flung each other out to other arms that weren't there but would be, arriving out of empty space. On the walk home, when we passed under the street lamps, Dad's face was quiet in the blue light, his eyes turned inward—an almost reverent stillness that relaxed his walk and made him drift.

"The acrobats were something, huh?" I asked.

"Something's not the word," he said. "If a guy could fly like that, son."

"What?" I asked. "If a guy could fly like that, what?"

"Well," he said. He looked up at the stars, like he might see acrobats swinging from them. "Then, well, he'd be flying."

"Yeah," I said. "Flying."

"What a job. Get paid to fly."

But even then I knew what he didn't. If one of those trapeze artists had fallen like a sack of wet sand, maybe Dad would've seen that nobody flies. They just pretend to. Now I was gunning a boat up a dark river, thinking how I swung on Dad's emotions, never missing a beat. But I didn't see how the trapeze artist is trapped. He's got to be in the same split second of time and space again and again. He looks free, but he's trapped, and even though the circus moves from town to town, he's in the same space in the same tent, and once the pendulums start and he makes that leap, he doesn't have any choice, but moves the only way that gravity allows.

Dad's old white face stared at me like a pocked moon rushing down a curve of black water. We thudded up the river, the motor thrashing against the current. Dad didn't know what was going to happen, and that's the one thing he always hated more than anything. All his uncontrol, his shouting and yelling and threatening and drinking—just a way for him to be in control.

And now he didn't have any of it. I gave him nothing. I ran the motor full speed upstream, watching the shores until I saw the willow hung out over the water above the white snag. I stopped the motor there. The boat drifted a few yards on its momentum, then slowed in the current and began to drift backwards. I threw off the anchor. The rope slithered over the bow. The anchor caught. The current sang in the hull.

The silence left me stunned. Then the willow's leaves chittered in the breeze, and the deep woods sighed. A night-feeding fish broke the surface upstream. The sound came down with the current, taking its time. I let quiet settle. I let starlight fall.

Dad sat upright on the seat, his hands clutching the hull like his arms were two rods he'd bolted down to steady himself. Now that the boat'd stopped moving he was more afraid, feeling it sway.

"The river, Dad. Here we are."

He didn't reply.

"The water's at least fifteen feet deep here. I stuck a long pole into it once and couldn't find the bottom. Best place on the whole damn river. The way that tree leans into the water, and the sound of the leaves. Hear 'em?"

"What the hell are you doing?" he asked.

"Hear them?" I asked again. I shifted my weight, and the boat rocked. He gasped and gripped the gunwales. "The boat won't tip over," I said. I rocked it hard, side to side, sloshing water against the hull. Dad grunted, his arms stiff as girders. "See?" I said. "It's stable. And anyway, there's life preservers."

I stopped rocking and talking, and the silence dropped like a membrane over us. We were as alone as two people could be. "Dammit, Dad," I said. "We haven't done anything together since you took me to that circus."

He forgot for a moment where he was. His eyes sharpened, and his face cleared. "The circus," he said. "God, yeah, the circus. Those acrobats are something else."

He was gone. Just like that. Gone. Even here, dreaming of something else—Wile E., even as he hits the rock, thinking he's got the Runner in his frying pan.

"Right," I said. "The acrobats. They damn near fly, don't they?"

He missed my tone. Of course. "Jesus," he said. "Yeah, they damn near fly. Made you feel like you could fly too, if only—" He jerked his head up and suddenly realized again where he was. "You could," he finished.

"Dammit, Dad. They can't either. They're not flying. They're falling. Even when they're flying, they're falling."

"So what?" he asked.

He brought me up short. I didn't know how to answer. "So they're falling," I said. "That's what." But it wasn't what he meant. He meant, what's wrong with falling if it lets you fly, and what's the big difference? It was just one of the times I can see now where we might have talked that night but didn't. Even though I thought that's what I wanted.

I shifted in my seat, and the boat rocked. He froze. He was as caged by his fear as if I had a steel box around him. I came back to that fear. It was there, easy and convenient. "You're scared, Dad," I said. "Of all this. I remember how you used to get driving over a bridge."

"The hell you talking about?" he demanded.

I had him reacting to me again. The smooth, cold part of me knew it. "You know what I'm talking about," I said.

And then, I'm not sure, I didn't intend to, but there it was, coming out of my mouth: "Say it."

"Say what?"

I hardly knew why I'd asked for it, but I wanted to make him say it. "Say you're scared, Dad. Just that. Say that."

"Goddamn. Don't you . . ."

I stood up, rocking the boat so far that the starboard gunwale nearly dipped to the water. I flexed my knees and brought it back the other way, the hull banging and splashing, water spewing white around the prow. Dad's neck corded. His face looked like pasteboard gouged by a chisel.

I leveled the boat. My heart was empty. "You're scared," I said. "Just say it. That's all. Then we're out of here."

It wasn't why I was here. But somehow it all came down to that. To something I didn't even know mattered.

I bent my right knee, letting my weight slowly carry the boat over. The gunwale rode down near the water, which ran silently on. Dad watched the water come closer. His eyes got big. When the water was only four inches below the gunwale, he shouted: "Stop! Stop it!"

I let the boat level itself. Dad sat rigid and sweating. "You're crazy," he said hoarsely. "Start that engine and take me home."

"Listen, Dad," I said. "What do you hear? Nothing but

that tree shaking. And water flowing. Your voice's just swallowed up out here. Say you're afraid. I want to hear you say it."

"Start that damn engine."

I'd never heard my voice so cold. "Start it yourself. Come over here and do it."

I stood on the river and looked at him. Beyond him the dark banks narrowed and disappeared into a bend. The trees were thick against the stars high over them. The river flowed under my feet. I felt larger than any of it. I knew he wouldn't move. He couldn't. He glanced at the engine. His face worked. Such a simple dream—six feet to an engine.

"Dammit, Dad. Look at you. You got no excuses not to start that engine. It's just fear. And nothing to threaten any-body with. Jesus!"

For a while there was nothing to say. Then I went on. "So what, Dad? Who gives a shit if you're scared? Except you? You're the one who makes it a big deal."

I stood in that boat like I was hanging from a scaffolding in the sky. So much bigger than Dad. He was shrunken, shriveled up. He sat on the seat, but from where I stood he looked like he'd stuffed himself into the triangle of the prow, collapsed down to nothing there. This wasn't what I'd come out here for. I'd come out to make sense of things, to make him stay put for a while, to get enough control to where he had to talk to me, where he had to answer questions. I had the questions. I wanted him to answer them. But things'd changed. I got on the river, and things changed. Or maybe things just reasserted themselves. Something as big and in-different as the river itself was running through me. I could've told Dad he didn't have to be scared anymore. I even wanted to. But I stood above him, above the river, feeling how he saw me dark as the trees, dark as the sky.

"Just say it," I said. "Say you're afraid. For once in your life. I'm so sick of watching you dance all around it. Say it and we'll go home."

He shook his head.

Jesus. He shook his head.

In a battle of wills, the worst thing is winning. And that's what it got turned into. Just a battle of wills. Everything else got thrown out. Everything. When he shook his head I felt my will tighten down like a screw against him. Everything else I might have hoped for, every other reason I had for being out there with him, was squeezed out of me. I had no reasons anymore. The only thing to do was turn away. But where do you find the will to turn away if it's all used up in the battle?

I sat down on the aluminum seat where I'd been standing. I reached down and pulled one boot lace and then the other, then removed my boots. I took off my socks and stuffed them into the boots. Then I took off my shirt and scuffled out of my pants. The wind ran down the river. My back prickled. I was so quiet that everything around me seemed loud. The leaves on the willow shouted. The boat rumbled and groaned with each chuk against the anchor rope. The current bellowed and sang. Through my bare feet against the hull I felt the current making me vibrate.

I picked up my clothes and threw them into the current. The boots filled and sank, the pants and shirt floated away. The pants rode high for a while, the legs like an old building with decaying towers drifting through the dark. I took the life preservers and set them on the water like I was setting a baby in a basket there. Dad's face turned paler than I thought possible, so white it looked transparent, like water just beginning to freeze. I let the life preservers go, and they floated away like flat river animals with several tails.

I stood again. Balancing on the seat one foot at a time, I removed my underwear and dropped them in the river too. They floated away, high and white.

"What the hell are you . . . ?" Dad began. But I held up my hand and silenced him. That's how it was. Just my hand, and I silenced him. I had the power. I stood there. The wind lifted the hair on my body. I let him look.

"You're scared, Dad," I said. "And not just of this water. All sorts of shit. That's why everybody's half-scared of you. But I'm not. Not anymore. You know that? I'm not scared of you."

I wasn't just talking. I knew it was true. I wasn't scared of him. But hell! I was sure scared of something. How else would I have let it go where it went? Let it become just his will against mine? And I knew, even then, what I was scared of, one of those flashes that runs through you, but you don't let it work. I was scared of myself.

My words came out quiet and ready. "All your threats and dreams, Dad. You're even scared of them. And your kids. So damn scared you had to scare us to not know it. And everybody else, too. You got that whole town bullshitted. But not me. Not anymore."

I still had my hand out. Turning his nerves to strands of ice.

"Matt used that cattle prod on me once," I said.

He sucked his breath in. For the first time since I held my hand up, he reacted.

"Yeah," I said. "But I'm not sure it was as bad as you always threatened it'd be. Your threats were always so goddamn big. And your dreams. So big. You'd get into my head with either of them like nothing else could. But you never did anything, Dad. Either way. You never did anything."

We stared at each other. Frozen. Like nothing'd ever melt or move us. Rocking in the boat.

"Say you're scared, Dad. For once in your life. Knock off the bullshit."

He said nothing.

All his talk all the time. And now, nothing.

"All right," I said. I began to lean, pushing the right gunwale toward the water.

His stillness broke then. His mouth opened, and a tremor ran through his arms like a crack in ice spreading under weight. It ran again.

But he kept his silence.

I drove the gunwale down. The boat dipped, bobbed, sought its keel. I pushed it down the other way, grim and hard, using its momentum. Dad and I had our eyes locked on each other when the river poured in.

It shocked even me when it came—a tremendous surge suddenly pouring over the gunwale, sucking at the boat, engulfing it, smooth as a muscle, glistening in the starlight. It took the boat beyond my control. I almost lost my balance as the gunwale sank beneath me. I stumbled, caught myself, flung my weight hard the other way. The river rushed in, too fast, beyond me. It spread in the boat, coiled and foamed, hissing.

I couldn't get the boat back. Couldn't take it away from the river.

Dad screamed.

I'd forgotten him. But his scream scared me more than the water did. I jerked, threw myself almost out of the boat on the side away from the pouring water, trying to use my weight to counteract it. My shoulders strained as I stopped myself, and I was bowed over like a swimmer on a starting platform, gripping the boat's edge with both hands, my head so close to the water I saw small whirlpools circle. My weight barely pulled the boat level. It rocked and sloshed, and the water in the bottom ran up the sides, curling white. The top of my head dipped into the river. I strained, my shoulders popping, to come back into the boat.

"No! No! No! No!" Again and again. Dad was screaming. Again and again. His hands were locked on the sides of the boat. He stared at the water, screaming like a kid. It didn't seem possible for a man to scream like that. His mouth was open, but the sound seemed to come from somewhere else.

I heaved myself backwards and fell into the bottom of the boat, into the sloshing water. It moved like a small flood over Dad's boots. On my hands and knees I stared at those boots. As the boat settled low in the water, his words changed. "All right! I'm scared! I'm scared!" And then, as the water stopped moving, his voice hushed as if he were in a trance. "I'm scared. I'm scared," saying it only to himself. Whispering it. "I'm scared."

Then silence.

Slowly I looked up from his boots to his face. He didn't see me. He looked right over me at the black path of water.

"All right," I said. "No more. No more."

I don't know if he heard me.

"Jesus, Dad," I said. He still didn't look at me. I had goose bumps all over my body. I couldn't bear to look at him, at the way his face'd gone blank, his eyes reflecting nothing but water.

I stumbled to my feet, stood for a moment staring over his head, then let myself fall backwards away from him, deadweight, into the river.

The current clutched me, carried me. In the instant, liquid silence I lost all direction, but then felt the current against me and turned to face it. I spread my arms like a bird. It felt like a bird of death, wide-winged in the cold darkness. I pushed hard, headfirst, into the moving water. I stayed down, stroking upstream, feeling the flow. The river filled my ears and eyes. It drove Dad's screams from my head and washed his face away. I had no idea where the boat was. Didn't care. I didn't care whether I was keeping up with the current or not, didn't care how deep I'd gone.

I stayed down. Dad's screams receded completely. His face, and then the whole world, fractured, then fractured again, and the pieces drifted away. Darkness and silence were left. No bullshit. Nothing. I thought I could just quit stroking, let the river roll me. Snag me in its silence. I could let the current carry me. Deeper and deeper, until there was no coming back.

I released my breath and pushed myself down. Like a

big fish seeking the bottom mud, the deep, never-lighted waters.

Then I remembered Ellen. How she swelled and seemed to float on the bed when she slept. I was a father, no matter what I did. Even if I went down to the bottom and burrowed into the mud there and sucked mud and river into me and was never found, not even by Angel, the far away hum of his motor passing back and forth—even then I was still a father. Even then the baby was going to be born, and I was always going to be its father, all of its life.

Fear shot through me. God! I was so far down. I suddenly realized how far down, the weight of the river like a cold clamp on my chest. Inside the silence I heard my own heart beating, felt my own warmth. I straightened, kicked toward the surface, without air. My chest swelled. I fought the river off. It grew against me, a great balloon of pressure, forcing its way in. I clamped my mouth shut, fighting it. I kicked and pumped. Up and up, without even knowing for sure I was going up. My heart echoed inside my chest. I began to lose consciousness, and fought against that loss, but I didn't even know if I was kicking anymore. The smell of the river filled me. I had to breathe.

Then I shot through the surface, choking, breathing water and air both. The river broke off me, streamed down my body as I lunged into the night. I gagged, gasped for air, filled my lungs, coughed the river out, gagged on it again. I forced a long breath. It felt like a necklace of burrs drawn down my throat. I trod water in the large night, the stars above me like burrs that I breathed.

Then I realized the current was taking me. I'd surfaced only about ten yards from the boat. All that time under water, and I'd hardly gone anywhere. But already I was moving away, in the little time it took me to draw breath. I wanted to just stay there, the river's head, watching the boat riding low in the water, so low Dad seemed to be sitting on the river. But I couldn't. I set out hard for the boat, stroking overhand.

I hardly made progress. I was exhausted to begin with, and the current never stopped. I paused once to see how far I'd gone, but it cost me two yards, and after that I fought the current with everything I had, looking up only enough to keep myself headed toward the boat. I thought I might have to go to shore, walk upstream, jump back in and take the current down. Just when I was about to give up and do this, my hand struck the hull. The boat boomed. I found a grip, pulled myself up, and rolled into the boat, bringing some more of the river with me. I lay in the bottom, the water running over me, looking straight up at the stars. The boat sank lower. It was a good boat, but there was too much water in it. The motor could pull it down. I'd gone too far, risked too much.

"Jesus, Dad," I said. "I didn't . . . can we . . . ?"

I didn't know how to finish, or even what I wanted to say. I ran a hand through my hair and pressed some water out. My hair felt like seaweed.

Dad looked like an old sack that'd been hung over a fence until the spaces between the threads were as big as the threads, and you couldn't tell whether it's threads or spaces that're forming the little shape that's left. The beginning of all this seemed like some other night, some other life. I shivered. I didn't see how I'd ever get warm.

"Dad? Dad?"

He raised his head slowly until his gaze met mine. Then he stopped as if a joint in his neck clicked and locked. His mouth moved. Like an old man's mouth. He groaned.

It was the opposite of the scream, almost inaudible. Full of sawdust. He didn't even know he was doing it. His eyes stayed on mine, but he still wasn't seeing me. His groan went out, echoed off the banks, crossed and recrossed itself.

Finally he heard it. His mouth snapped shut. His teeth clicked against each other. His eyes changed, and he saw me.

He'd gripped the sides of the boat so hard his fingers'd locked. Now he concentrated, like he'd forgotten how to make his muscles work, and he had to think each movement through. He pried his fingers off the gunwale. I wanted to help him, but I couldn't move. Mechanically his fingers opened. He sighed. The smell of alcohol washed over me. I realized it'd only been an hour or so since I'd picked him up. His arms bent like robot arms and came together. His hands kneaded each other. We both watched them, as if some magic thing were going to come out of them.

He jerked. A spasm went through his legs. His boots kicked water. He jerked again, and I realized he was trying to stand. He put his arms on the seat and pushed.

"Dad," I said. "Dad."

He went silent with effort. He was so worn away that I could hardly look at him. But I couldn't not look either. I saw a wasp lay eggs in a caterpillar once. The caterpillar arched. It raised its head and tried to turn. But it was fat and soft, and the wasp drove a sharp point into it. The caterpillar squirmed on its twig but held on while the wasp pumped above it, pouring in eggs that would hatch and eat the caterpillar alive, from the inside out. The caterpillar was helpless, squirming on its twig, though it refused to fall. The wasp, black and potent, pumped above it, its wings hard and veined in the sun, and its eyes like scoured silicon. I wanted to crush them both, for what they were together—too hard and too soft, too helpless and too powerful, too alive and too dead. I wanted to crush them, and I wanted to turn away. Instead I watched while the wasp heaved its abdomen, and the caterpillar lifted its head in silent consent and complaint. Then the wasp flew off, and the caterpillar crawled away to eat until its death was born—and I walked away from both of them.

Now I watched Dad with almost the same feeling. He struggled to stand in the boat. I didn't go to help, and I didn't go to hold him down. I hated how helpless he was, how he moved almost worse than a baby. But there was something implacable behind his movements, something more powerful than I'd ever seen in him. I couldn't move. Even though he was in danger of swamping the boat, I couldn't move. And I couldn't turn away. His hands pushed on the seat, and his knees unbent like sticks held together by wire. He swayed. The boat sloshed. Slowly he rose upward against the dark river behind him. I thought he'd fall. But he rose until his head blocked the stars. He spread his feet to steady himself.

Then he went still. Not even sober, and in a swaying boat, and scared more than he'd ever been—and yet he went still. It wasn't an act, and it wasn't to hide anything. It was something he'd never shown me before. He pushed himself upward on his own fear. He stood on his terror. I could see it in him yet, but he controlled it. He went still. Stood on the river.

He looked at me. We were right there, together. He looked at me, and we were together. Like I wanted. And he was going to say something. Even in the darkness I saw words form behind his eyes. For a second he was like the trapeze artist who looks across empty space and swings into it, making the decision to trust the catcher. And once he makes that decision, it's the catcher who's scared. I'd never realized that before. But I was ready. I waited for him, and I was scared, but ready. His throat convulsed. He tried to speak. But something happened to the words. He seemed to swallow them even as they came up. He tried again, couldn't. Confusion came into his eyes. The space between us seemed to grow. I thought he was going to try again, and I waited, wanting him to try, even though I was scared.

Then something hard and blank dropped over his face. The old protection. He could stand on the river, but he couldn't speak. He couldn't go that far. "Fuck you, son," he said. His voice was nothing, just old and tired. "Now start that engine and take me home."

I was chilled to the core. He'd come so damn close. And then let it all go. Let it be nothing but him showing me he could stand on the river, that he wasn't afraid even if he'd said he was. Just a negation. Just a stupid proof.

I turned and jerked the rope on the motor so hard I thought I'd jerk it right out of the pulley. The engine shattered the possibility of talk. Hand over hand I hauled in the anchor, pulling the dripping rope up until the slug of metal appeared. I set it in the bottom of the boat, hardly caring anymore if we sank. I sat down, twisted the tiller, and roared through the darkness downstream.

Without speaking a word, we hauled the boat out of the river, found the drain plugs, winched the boat onto the trailer, drove up to the gravel road, then to the highway into Cloten. We both stared straight ahead into the lights. I let him off a block from home so Mom wouldn't know he'd been with me. We had a pact of silence. That's all we had.

I took Angel's boat home with me, because I'd thrown my clothes in the river and didn't want to risk someone driving by and seeing me unhooking it, naked like that—the whole town'd be talking by morning. I parked in the alley behind my house and walked in the shadows to my door. I stood in our bedroom door and watched Ellen sleep. Even from there I could feel her warmth. I could smell the heat of her body.

I began to shiver so violently that the room blurred. I smelled her warmth and my own cold—like I'd brought the river inside myself to this room where she slept with our child inside her. I'd come back. I had. But I was chilled to the heart. My own shivering couldn't warm me. I walked across the room and got into bed. Ellen's pregnant warmth was like fire against my skin. I felt like a fish, with veins of cold blood, stealing warmth from a being I couldn't possibly love.

Jeff Gruber

≈

WHEN ELLEN CALLED AND ASKED if she could talk to me alone, I didn't know what to think. She wouldn't say what she wanted, only that Luke was going to be away. I drove into Cloten on the old, familiar roads, past farmsteads I'd known all my life, some abandoned now, the houses gray and empty, weeds filling the building sites and cattle yards. The memory of Ellen's face close to mine that winter day kept returning to me—her hand on my shoulder, her eyes looking into mine, the intimacy of the dream I'd told her, our mingled breath, and the silent owl passing back and forth.

She answered the door before I had a chance to knock. "Jeff. It's good to see you."

We hugged each other. I felt something subdued and quiet in her hug, a gravity in the way she held on just a moment longer than familiarity required.

"It's good to see you, Ellen." I stepped into the living room, small and neat, with a worn carpet, a few chairs, an end table piled high with baby books. On the wall opposite the door hung some photographs of Luke and Ellen, and Ellen's family, and one old black-and-white wedding picture of Two-Speed and LouAnn emerging from church, their faces young and smooth, Two-Speed looking skinnier than he ever did in work clothes. He stared straight out of the photograph as if challenging someone beyond its borders, unaware of LouAnn, who held his arm and glanced sideways up at his face. From across the room Two-Speed seemed to be looking right at me. While Ellen got soft drinks from the refrigerator, I went closer to the picture. From there I couldn't tell where Two-Speed's eyes were directed. He might have been looking anywhere, and he seemed more confused than challenging—the same expression Luke often had when he was unsure of something he was saying.

Ellen returned to the living room, and we sat on the couch with our glasses, catching up on each other's lives. We talked about common acquaintances from Clear River and Cloten, and I told her about Lake Superior and how the ore ships would sit unmoving for days, as cold and gray as stones grown from the water. We avoided discussing Two-Speed and LouAnn. Since I'd arrived in Cloten, that was all anyone had talked about, and it was good not to. The room seemed to wrap around us, as the snow had that other time, a close, unconscious intimacy, and I found myself not wanting to know why she'd asked me in but to let the afternoon go by with small talk, and the noise of ice clinking in our glasses, and our eyes meeting. But in a lull in the conversation, I saw her looking out the window, her expression suddenly remote, a strand of hair lying carelessly on her cheek.

"Luke said you had a good time on the river yesterday,"

she said quietly. Her tapered fingers slowly rolled her glass, leaving narrow tracks in the condensation.

"We did. The same old stuff. Shoot at carp, tramp around."

"Luke will sometimes spend all night on the river."

"He doesn't take you?" I teased.

"Sometimes he does." She smiled briefly. "And I like it. But not the way he does."

"It's the Warren."

"What?"

"Luke's never told you about the River Warren?"

She shook her head. "Should he have?"

"Of course! It's the biggest river that ever flowed."

"Well, you better tell me then!" She laughed, brushed the strand of hair back.

"It's the name of the old river, the one that formed after the glaciers receded. When they melted they formed Lake Agassiz. It pretty much covered North Dakota and parts of South Dakota and Minnesota and spread out over most of the middle of Canada. It'd make Lake Superior look like a pond. And the River Warren drained it. It was immense. That's what that little river really is. It's why it has such a big valley. The Warren cut it."

"How do you know all this?"

"Angel Finn, mainly. Get him on a boat, he can't stop talking. And all he talks about is the river. No matter where he starts, the River Warren's where he ends. And then, I picked up rocks from the time I was a kid. Every spring, go out and pick up rocks. They were dropped by the glacier, and every year they come up. Like the land grows them. I knew that glacier a little better than I wanted to, in some ways."

She laughed again, and it felt good to hear her laugh.

"Angel says he wants to fish the Warren," I said.

"It must have been some river."

"Sometimes it still is."

"I wonder why Luke's never told me all this."

"Probably because you never asked."

She didn't smile at that, though. Instead a far-off, pensive look came into her eyes before she looked down at her glass. For the first time since I'd come in the door a slightly awkward silence overcame us.

Then she said: "The way you talk about this land, Jeff. Why did you leave?"

"I've told you."

"I know." She reached out and placed her hand on mine. She remembered that afternoon on the river as well as I did. We were quiet, remembering. Her fingers were cool from the glass she'd been holding. "But tell me again. I'm not sure I understood."

"I'm not sure I do either, Ellen." I'd never admitted that to anyone. I looked into her eyes, clarified by sunlight coming through the window. She was curious, in the best of ways, willing to listen without expectation or judgment. Her curiosity was a power that made me want to tell her everything, like I'd told her the dream.

"I know what happened wasn't Dad's fault," I said. That, too, I'd never said to anyone. "It happened. That's all. There were all sorts of ways it shouldn't have. But it did. No one's fault. I know that. But when I'm around Dad..."

Then I didn't know how to finish, not even with Ellen. I stared at the ice cubes in my glass, then back to her, shrugged.

"I like your father."

"Most people do."

She gazed at me, her lips slightly parted, her face beautiful in its openness and in the sun slanting through the window.

"Do you blame him?" she asked quietly, as people do when they near the truth about another. "Because you blame yourself?"

I shrugged again. I'd considered it before. "Probably," I said. "Sometimes he just seems trapped."

"How do you mean?"

"The way he works. But more. A lot of people work all the time. It's just that the land seems to've trapped him. The farm. It never gives up. It keeps growing things, and he keeps working it. Even after Chris died. It didn't seem to make any difference."

"Do you think he feels trapped?"

"Funny. He once said something to me about that. Before Chris died. He said the land will get a hold on you. Said once you love it, it's got a hold on you, so you better learn to love its hold, too. And Angel says," I slipped into an imitation of Angel's slow drawl, "if you don't know land or waters, and too many sonsabitches don't these days, you'll never be free of nothing."

It broke the seriousness that had settled on our conversation, and we laughed again. Her hand still rested on mine, no longer cool, warmed by my skin. She squeezed briefly, then withdrew hers.

"Maybe Dad and Angel are freer than anyone," I said.

"Maybe that's what Luke's looking for on the river. Do you think?"

"I don't know."

"Did he tell you about the baby?"

"Yes."

"Did he seem happy about it?"

"Yes. But he also said it scared him. As it should."

I smiled, making light of it, but she didn't respond Whenever we talked of Luke she grew quiet, almost like the hush of woods when the wind drops. She looked through the window. Outside, a boy on a bicycle went by, weaving and pumping to go fast. Then he stopped pedaling, let go the handlebars, and raised his arms straight out from his sides like wings, his hair blown backwards.

"Trapped and freed," she said, in a subdued voice "Sometimes, with this baby, I feel that way. Completely trapped, completely freed. Do men feel that way, Jeff?"

She turned to me again, and I was surprised to see that her eyes were filling. She tried unsuccessfully to smile. I turned sideways to face her, took her hands in mine. "What's going on, Ellen? Is Luke feeling trapped? What are you trying to tell me?"

"I don't know. I don't know what he's thinking." She withdrew a hand from mine and dried her eyes with the back of her wrist. "I'm sorry, Jeff. Maybe you can tell me. I want to show you something."

She led me through the kitchen to the back entryway. A new pair of hunting boots stood near the door, hardly worn. Ellen turned around in front of the closet.

"I found something a while back." She opened the closet door. "Above the molding over the door. Reach up there."

She stepped out of the doorway, and I did as she asked. My hands closed around an object, round, long, and smooth, as if, groping in the darkness, they had found a memory turned solid. My fingers recognized it immediately, before I saw it. I brought it down and backed out of the closet. Two-Speed's cattle prod, nicked with use, dented, worn smooth on the handle, gleamed in my hands.

"I was putting a coat away," she said, "and it fell down. Luke must have brought it back from their house after the accident without telling me."

"Why would he want to keep this?"

She shook her head. We were as close together as we'd been on the river that time. I had the sudden urge to kiss her.

"I don't know," she said. "It scares me. Of all things to keep."

Her face was open and vulnerable. I had to look away from it, back to the prod in my hands. Why would Luke keep it? What did it mean? We all made the prod mean something. 'It was probably Two-Speed's prod,' my father had said years before, and in that one short sentence had made the prod mean everything. It gathered up and held so much: my own memories of Two-Speed in the barn, my father yelling at him; all the town's suspicions and stories;

Luke and Matt and the angry, crying cicadas; and Luke's hands on mine, keeping me from breaking it.

Yet the prod itself meant nothing. Ellen understood where the real questions lay, and refused to ask the wrong ones.

"It's not that thing that scares me," she said. "It's that Luke brought it here and never told me."

We both looked at it as if we were archaeologists trying to decipher the meaning of an artifact, a shard of pottery, while knowing that the shard, even classified and tagged, would never mean what it meant to a child who carried water in an urn, or to the mother who asked him to, or to the father who drank from the urn in a field. The prod's meaning all lay in Two-Speed, and that was beyond recovery. Maybe it had always been beyond recovery or access, even by Two-Speed himself, as Angel Finn believed.

And now the meaning lay in Luke. He seemed, as I gazed at the thing in my hands, as foreign and distant to me, as inscrutable, as the stone cliffs on Superior's north shore. I felt distant from myself, blank in my own eyes, as if they, too, were filled with pure horizon. I let the prod fall down to my side. A far-off scream boiled in my ears, and it was the scream of cicadas, which was the same sound as Luke screaming, and as my own scream as I rolled through thistles and wild roses toward a ribbon of water. I felt unsteady, as if the land under the house were rolling, and time and dream had ruptured, turning back on themselves.

Then Ellen touched my shoulder. I remembered our conversation.

"Why wouldn't he tell you?"

"That's what I need to know, Jeff. Every time I go by that closet, I think of it in there. It shouldn't be in the house."

"Why'd you put it back?"

"You would ask that." She touched me again. "I don't know. I was hurt. Confused. I needed to think." She let her hand fall.

Silence. I heard the refrigerator hum in the kitchen, smelled the perfumed lotion she used on her hands lingering in the air between us.

"Something happened between Luke and his father," she said.

"What?"

"I thought maybe he told you something."

I shook my head.

"He went fishing with Angel's boat one night. I felt something different in him when he came home. He seemed troubled. Especially when any mention of Simon came up. I don't know what it was."

"Angel's boat?"

"Yes."

"Angel told me that Two-Speed was angry one day about his boat. He thought Two-Speed was just drunk, but he didn't know."

"Why'd Simon run that semi downhill, Jeff? And why was LouAnn with him? Does it have something to do with Luke? And this?"

"I don't know. Maybe only Two-Speed knew. Or LouAnn. Or Luke."

She shook her head, defiant. "No. I won't go through life not knowing the people I live with."

She didn't intend it, but the words struck me with the force of an accusation. What did I know of my father? What did I know of what was in his mind as he stooped to pick a rock from the fields, or in the long hours when he had nothing to do but watch the land unfurl under the tires of a tractor? Did he spin back to Chris's death, worry it, toss it around like a picked-bare bone, trying to find something, still, that might absolve him? I had no idea what he'd gone through. I had only blame, and I had to have blame, because it gave the loss, however perverse, some meaning. But when I couldn't bear to blame myself any longer I blamed him, and I blamed him for not shouldering it for me. I didn't know him. Should a father take a son's guilt? Was that something he ought to have done?

I was lost in realization and questions. Ellen turned and went back to the living room. I followed slowly, the cattle prod still in my hand. She was sitting on the couch. I sat down beside her, dropping the prod onto the couch cushions.

"It's all just crazy, Ellen."

"It is. I know."

For a moment, as we looked at each other, I saw something inexpressibly sad and beautiful in her face, and then what had happened to us on the river, in the isolation of snow, came back in full force, and she leaned into me, while I trembled as if I were freezing, and kissed me on the lips. It was electrifying. I lost my body's limits, my heart's limits, as they dissolved into hers. It wasn't just the press of her lips, full and warm and soft, or her waist which my arms encircled; it was years of built-up emotion suddenly discharged and heightened both, as if my longing and doubt and wonder flowed into hers and returned to me mingled and changed. I grabbed the back of her head and pressed us together, pressed myself into her smell, feeling her hair and skull in my fingertips, breathing her breath, bathed in a sea of emotion that surged through both of us, rocking and swaying us.

Then we pulled away and stared at each other.

"We can't do this," she whispered.

The words were unconvincing, her face open as still water to the moon. I reached for her again.

But she put her hand up, from an interior resolve I hadn't sensed, and placed it on my chest.

"I'm going to have a baby, Jeff."

She turned her head down, not letting me see her face. I reached out, cupped her chin, tried to bring her face back up, to see what I knew was there, her own longing.

"Look at me, Ellen."

She wouldn't. She shook her head, the sunlight through the window turning strands of her dark hair silver.

"It's something we can't afford, Jeff," she said, almost inaudibly.

Then, briefly, she turned her face up again, and I saw what must have been on my own, longing to be known and revealed and taken out of herself and reaffirmed, all. She was almost unbearably beautiful. She reached up to my hand, still on her chin, and grasped it, brought it down, and we both looked at our hands holding each other's, afraid to look anywhere else.

"Do you still dream that dream?"

Without knowing, she made me think of Jenny, who had stopped my dreaming.

"No. Not anymore."

"I think of that day often. When you told me. The snow."

"You're the only one I ever told it to."

She squeezed my hand.

Our eyes met. "You should go."

She tried to smile.

"Should I?"

"Yes. You should." She stood, and pulled me up. Before she could stop me I took her in my arms again and felt her body against mine, unresisting, the swell of her breasts and the curve of her hips, and the tight rounding of her womb. She melted against me, for the briefest of moments, before I felt the small muscles of her back tighten, and she created a little space between us.

"Go now," she said. It was plea and command both. I backed away from her into the couch and knocked the cattle prod to the floor. I hated the thing. I hated its ugly, blunt prongs and the memories it carried.

"What are you going to do about that?" I asked.

"I don't know."

I swung the prod up, hardly knowing what I was doing, then brought it down across my knee with more force than I'd ever used to slam anyone to a wrestling mat. The sound of the prod shattering was like the crack of a splintered tree limb. Shards of plastic sprang upward past my face, arced, ricocheted off the ceiling. Batteries flew. Plastic rained down, scattered on the carpet, formed displaced combs in Ellen's hair. The prod lay in two jagged pieces in my hands.

Ellen stared at the broken thing. She looked betrayed. Then the look disappeared like a cloud shadow running over a field. She broke into laughter. For a moment I was dumbstruck, before her laughter caught me up. I threw the two pieces of the prod on the floor and laughed, too. Ellen reached out with a foot and ground one of the pieces I'd dropped into the carpet, and we laughed at the way it splintered into a hundred fragments as she spun her foot on it. I wanted to hold her, wanted to so badly, to feel her laughter in my chest, but I didn't. I reached out and gently untangled the pieces of plastic from her hair, showed them to her, and dropped them on the floor.

By the time I had the last one out we'd gone silent.

"I guess you know what you're going to do about it now," I said gently.

"Yes. He'll have to fight me now."

If there'd been any doubt that I loved her, it was erased by those words.

"If he gets upset," I said, "you tell him Gruber'll come back and throw him around till he's got some sense."

"Thanks, Jeff." Her eyes were moist, but there was determination and strength in her face. Part of me hated to see it. It meant I had to leave.

I walked out her door. The air outside was suffused with the smell of new-mown hay.

Arlene Schuh

≈

THERE COMES A TIME WHEN YOU can't stay cooped up any longer, when you realize you're turning into an old bird, and if you don't do something about it you're going to molt and fade away. So I bought a pair of tennis shoes, and I don't go too fast, and I'm pretty sure people're talking about me, saying, What's she up to now, all of a sudden got a health craze does she, all of a sudden working up to be a track star? But that's all right, let them wag their mouths and guess and fill their time with me and my white tennis shoes. It's about time, maybe, they had something to talk about me besides my talking.

I walk out to the cemetery to visit Frederick's grave. I walk through the rows of stone and think it's not such a sad thing they're gone, really, but it's good to be not-gone, too. Though I do wonder what kinds of stories the dead have to tell each other. I go by and look at Simon and LouAnn's graves, too, though last time some teenage kids'd knocked their stones over. You'd think they'd have more respect for the dead, especially the newly dead, though I'm not sure why it matters if someone's dead long or short.

I go by Peter's house. Everyone in town knows about his

toes and how he had frostbite in them. His mother probably told a couple of her friends and asked them to keep quiet, she ought to've known better, but on the other hand his limp is pretty obvious and there had to be an explanation, I suppose. But I'm the only one knows how it happened. I'm not even trying to guess why Peter was out that night or what he and Two-Speed Crandall had going.

You don't guess when you're close enough. Or if you guess you keep it to yourself, you don't spread it around and let other people guess off your guessing until the skew of it becomes larger than the straight, the story bigger than the happening. Course, the story's always bigger than the happening, but smaller too, and there're times when you got to keep the bigger smaller than the smaller, and this is one of them, if that makes any sense, which it probably don't.

I don't tell how I saw Peter carry Two-Speed out of that blizzard that time and dump him on the doorstep. I walk around town with those white shoes going flash flash flash, and for the first time I can remember it feels good to know something without telling it, to talk to someone and know what I'm not saying. It's not that I'm giving up listening and talking, I don't guess I'll ever do that, I'm just holding a secret that ought to be held, and it feels as good as telling a story that ought to be told, but different.

The town's settled down some since the accident. I walk down Main Street, and Angel Finn's hardware store has a front window again, and there's talk that the barber shop is going to be rebuilt right where the old one was, that'll give those men something to talk about, getting their hair cut right where Two-Speed come crashing in. They'll be remembering that for years, the old ones telling the young ones for who knows how long? I've been tempted to go to Peter sometime, to find him in the ditches and let him know that I know, that he's not alone and it's OK, and comfort him or something, but I suppose that's just Arlene thinking, the fixer-upper, and I let her think for a while and then forget it until I remember it again. Pete wouldn't understand, and the last thing he'd want would be someone knowing anything, especially me. Even he might've heard of my reputation, and he'd be spooked for weeks thinking someone was going to cart him off.

I've given up on thinking that knowing something leads to doing something, though I know too well that sometimes it should. But you can't do much for a man who saved the life of someone who later decided he wanted to die. And why Simon Lane Crandall wanted to die—and I swear he did—I don't much speculate on. People must be wondering, that Arlene, what's come over her, she lived right across the street from them, and this is the biggest news for years, and here she is keeping quiet on it, she must know more than she's saying and that's why she isn't talking.

I got to admit I don't mind fostering that rumor just a bit. When I see Thelma and Janet down at the Super Valu, or even Skeet Olson, him and me run into each other once in a while now, even walk along a bit together, though I sure can't keep up with him, I swear he's practicing for a marathon or else he's trying to get as far away from Gracie as fast as possible or maybe when you got legs that long you can't go slow, I don't know.

Anyway, I was saying when I run into Thelma and Janet

or Skeet Olson or anybody, I don't mind being obvious in my listening, and maybe I act just a bit distracted like I know something but won't tell it. But what am I saying maybe for? I know I do, and I smile just a little when they throw out a theory, just to make them think I know their theory's wrong, and I even had Thelma say to me once, Come on, Arlene, you know something you're not saying, what've you seen that we ought to know, and I said, Thelma, I'm telling you the God's truth, I don't know no more than you do about why Simon Lane Crandall run that truck down that hill. And ain't it funny, I think to myself later, watching my feet flash and breathing hard, that here when I tell the truth they think I'm not, and it used to be when I half made things up just to give things some flavor and interest, they all thought I was telling the absolute truth. Leastways they always repeated it like they did.

I got theories, sure. The funny thing about Simon Lane Crandall is that he never did much of anything while making it look to everybody else like he did all sorts of stuff. Half the people in this town live their lives the reverse, doing all sorts of stuff and trying to make it look like they're doing nothing. So why can't someone go the other way and do nothing while working hard to make it look like they're doing something?

Maybe Simon one day realized he hadn't never done nothing but make people think he'd done something, and when you realize that, and you got all the things you're supposed to've done hanging over you, they build up to a kind of pressure even though they ain't real, and something's got to give. There're all sorts of things Simon Lane Crandall could've done other than what he did. He could've taken up fishing or rock collecting. I know that sounds dumb, but only because of what everybody thinks he did, which he probably never did, and the kind of man who did the stuff he was supposed to've done but didn't isn't the kind of man who takes up fishing or rock collecting. But Simon, I'm saying, maybe wasn't that kind of man. But by now I've got even myself confused.

And LouAnn? I just don't know. I still swear there was more going on with her than anyone thinks. Lord knows a lot can be hidden in a house, and there ain't no one who ever had a good grip on what goes on in a family. I swear she was leaving him that night after he went out to load those cattle, though I got no evidence for that at all, and I've only just suggested it to a couple people to see their reaction and never pushed it much. But maybe not. Who knows why she was in that cab with him? That's maybe the real tragedy here, that no one in this town even knew her well enough to guess.

Anyway, I'm trying to be less sure about people than I used to be. The past is fine and all, but we got to live with the living and only put up with the dead. Peter Janisch is one of the living, and Simon Lane Crandall isn't, and whatever they had between them Peter doesn't have no more. Sometimes I'm mighty tempted to tell people what I saw that blizzard night, just to see if, putting it together with things others'd bring out, it'd make some sense to why Simon run that load down. But when I'm tempted to talk, I just start to walk again, saying how I best be moving, and those shoes flash so bright and white I can't hardly stand to look at them, so I look up instead, to notice where I'm going.

Luke Crandall

≈

WHAT HAPPENED ON THAT RIVER isn't what I intended. Things changed. Things got out of control. It's like the river heaved itself up and said to both of us: Look here—you come out here and expect things to go your way, you better think harder. It's pretty obvious that when you get on a river you go its way, not yours. I had the feeling almost that the river was saying: Make a choice. To both of us. Make a choice. Bringing us to the point where we had to decide something. And the thing is, he was going to talk. He was going to say something. And then didn't. And I didn't help him. Maybe if I would've he wouldn't've run that semi down that hill.

But maybe this was coming for a long time. Maybe he just needed the excuse. Leo Gruber's cattle, Angel's store, the bank that never gave him money—I can imagine him planning a way to get them all, and maybe he just needed the reason to go through with it and leave them all talking. Just like he always wanted. Sometimes he'd be in the middle of a scheme, and he'd say to Mom: When this one works, they're going to talk about me for a long time, I guarantee you that. And she always believed him. Wanted to so damn bad she did.

And now they are. Everyone's talking about him.

I always thought if you were a Wile E. you were a Wile E., but I don't know now. He was the Road Runner, maybe, to my Wile E., and I was the one making the schemes and plans to catch him. The Runner's always out of reach of Wile E., but if Wile E. realizes that, he's no longer Wile E. Maybe I'm finally realizing it. Never could reach him, never can.

Anyway, it's hard to be a Wile E. with Ellen around. She left the pieces of that prod lying on the floor. I came in the door, and there they were, pieces of plastic sticking out of the carpet. It made me mad. What right did she have? If you build up enough anger you can throw anything away, and I felt myself building up to it. A genus in itself. Throw everything away.

I picked up a piece of that broken prod, and thought: This is it. This is the end. And fine with me. But when I stood back up, she was standing in the kitchen doorway. She said, "Luke." Just my name. Didn't move toward me or away. Just stood there. I looked at her and realized if I tried to bullshit now, she'd be all over me.

Jeff Gruber

≈

I STAYED AN EXTRA FEW DAYS to help Dad bale hay. I was
ready to return to Duluth—yet I wasn't. What had happened between Ellen and me, and the things she'd said,
troubled me. It wasn't the kind of thing one merely puts
aside and forgets. I knew I had to go back to Jenny and
Becca; I had no doubts of that. In fact, in many ways I
wanted to see them more strongly than ever, felt confirmed
in them, having withstood a breach in our relationship. But
only withstood—not closed or sealed that breach. In those
first days, working with my father, I realized I would probably never seal it, never cause it to disappear, that it would
stay with me, held open by memory, for a long time, while
the relationship with my family grew around it, perhaps un-
weakened by it and yet containing this small and secret
opening through which, sometimes, I would see another,
fading world, mine and not mine.

I might have tried to call Ellen—I wanted to know how
she was and what had happened when Luke came home
and found the broken prod, and I wanted to know, still,
what had happened between us—but I didn't know what I'd
say, especially if Luke answered the phone. She'd probably

told him I'd broken the prod. Without knowing how he'd reacted, I couldn't call him.

In time, I thought, he'd call me. In time, perhaps, Ellen and I would talk with the ease with which we had before. We all needed time—and distance.

And—I don't know whether it was breaking the prod, or Ellen, or both—I found I could work with Dad without the old bitterness. Since Ellen had said those words about knowing the people she lived with, I'd been thinking a lot about my father, and for the first time what I didn't know about him seemed more a mystery than an accusation, and I was part of that mystery. I realized I'd been jealous of Chris after he died, for taking so much of Dad's attention. It was strange and frightening, that realization, so much more complex than I'd known, like a wild new country of the heart seen from a distance.

But I didn't have to explore that country just yet. It was enough for now to know it was there, perhaps in some tangled way the same country of the heart that Ellen lay in. It was enough to miss her, and Chris, and Becca and Jenny all at once, to feel the heart's illogic and flow, and to know that it could bind them all together, the heart's own watershed.

It was enough for a few days to lose myself in the steady chunk and grind of the hay baler, the rhythm of the bales being spat onto the rack, where I picked them up and stacked them five high while Dad drove. Together we unloaded them, he on the rack, I in the hay loft, connected, such as it was, by the work, the bales he put into the elevator, the bales I removed and stacked again.

Dad and I were in the pickup together, pulling an empty

rack to the field after lunch, when I asked him to pull to the side of the road. He did, without asking why. I got out of the pickup and stepped into the road ditch. Below me the dredge ditch opened up, the thin water in its bottom glimmering, flowing out of the fields toward the river.

The grass came nearly to my waist, thick, woven, interspersed as it had always been with wild roses, milkweed, thistles. It shimmered as the wind moved through it. I walked to where the ditch flattened and then sloped sharply down to form the dredge ditch. For a moment I felt my knees buckle as I started down, but I regained them and descended.

I stood with my feet nearly in the water and remembered. But I remembered with the calm of knowing that accidents are accidents even if, in looking back, they could have been prevented—and always, in looking back, they could have been.

For years I'd sorted and resorted all the ways I might have prevented Chris's death: by paying more attention, noticing more quickly, shouting louder, moving faster—so many things other than being on the hitch of the dump rake as it left the ground, so many things other than being helpless and with nothing to hold onto, so many things other than losing my balance at the one moment of my life when I most had to keep it, and falling, while over me the steel teeth of the rolling rake filled the sky. So many things other than being alive, and unable to save him.

I sat down in the grass. It swayed over my head. The sweet scent of roses mingled with the bitter scent of milkweed. The shallow water ran at my feet. I heard Dad's steps, and his shadow blocked the sun on my neck. He sat down beside me.

We watched a dragonfly hover over the water.

"I haven't been back here since," I said.

He didn't reply. The dragonfly darted and shone, wings quietly clattering.

"There was nothing we could do, was there?" I asked.

After long moments he replied: "No, Jeff. Just things we could've done."

Water flowed and wind moved, and the dragonfly took its shining light and the half-solid arc of its wings to some other quiet place.

"Remember Two-Speed's cattle prod?" I asked.

We were sitting side by side, watching the water flow.

"What about it?"

"I broke the thing. Luke kept it and Ellen found it. She showed it to me, and I broke it across my knee."

Dad nodded. "I wish I'd done it years ago."

Above us a meadowlark released its song. The melody burbled down into the ditch, caught us in its flow, passed.

"Suppose we ought to get back to work?"

"I suppose," he said. "Wait much longer, we'll lose leaves."

We climbed the ditch together and stood on the road looking at the crops covering the land. Near a fence post a pyramid of rocks was piled. I nodded at it. "That pile's gotten bigger since I left."

"It never ends."

"I used to hate that job. But it doesn't seem like it'd be so bad to me now."

"You can always come back."

I knew he didn't mean just to visit. I nodded. I wasn't ready to think about that.

We were standing near the bale rack. I hit it lightly with my palm. Dust puffed up and drifted away in the breeze.

I remembered being a kid, riding on top of the loaded bale racks, delighted at the way they'd shift like an animal under me, as if they could fall any moment.

"Jenny'd love to ride on top of a bale rack," I said.

Dad looked at the ground. I couldn't see his face behind the bill of his cap. He looked at the ground for a long time.

"I suppose we're losing leaves," I said.

We walked to the pickup. Before we opened the doors we both paused and looked around, seeing the same things as far as two different people can—swallows, dust, sun, insects blazing in the light—hearing the sounds of the fields, smelling blooming flowers and cut hay, all of it bound together within the round horizon.

Pop Bottle Pete

≈

IF I DON'T WAKE UP NOW, he stops. His horn goes wa-a-a-a, wa-a-a-a. Then he stops. Wave wave he goes. At me. I look at the bottles. And cans. My bag is full. Enough to buy a Walkman. They go jing and jang when I shake the bag. His truck goes stab stab at my eyes with the sun.

Peter, he calls. Come on.

I look at the bag. Enough to buy a Walkman. I don't know what to do. Come on, he calls again. He waves. His hand is like it has a rope. It pulls at me.

I drop the bag. It opens up. Cans and bottles go out. They go out and out. They go far away, where I'll never find them. I don't care. I look at his truck. Then I walk. I walk like I used to. Without side to side. Up from the ditch.

The truck goes bubba bubba bubba. I touch it on the head. When I go around. It goes purry in my hand. Bubba bubba, it says. The ditch is clean. No cans or bottles. Ever. I go to the door, and it opens. He's leaning over, and he pulls me in.

Here, he says. He hands me a Coke. It's cool. It makes me cool inside. Like ice.

Ready? he says.

Ready right let's go asshole, I say.

Fucking right, he says. Then he laughs. Peter, he says, this town needs more people like you.

Then the truck is laughing and the cows are singing and the wind goes drumdrum in the windows.

Take her, Peter, he says.

Fucking right, I say. I grab the great big wheel. Bouncy bouncy bouncy on the seat. I turn the wheel. Turn and turn.

I look in the mirror. Back there isn't there. Just sky. Just blue.

The truck is laughing, and the tires shouting, and the wind goes drumdrum, and the cows sing hah lay lo-o-o-o-o-o-o, lo-o-o-o-o-o-o yah. Like in church.

But sometimes I still wake up. I try not to, but sometimes I do. I go out and wait. Just in case. Once I went up to where he is. I walked right on the street. No one saw me. I didn't care if they did. Or if they thought. They made him into a stone, but it's not him. It has marks that say his name. And shiny. When cars go by, they put their light in the stone.

I pushed and pushed. Uh uh uh. Then crash. It fell.

I went hide. In the dark. By a tree. The wind said sssssss sssssss sssssss in the tree. I touched where my heart is. It went bubba bubba. Like his truck when I don't wake up.

But no one heard. My heart went bubba bubba loud, but no one heard.

A car went by. I made the dark go in me hard. No one saw.

When the car went by, all the stones had light inside them.

I went to the road. Where there was sand. And rocks and stuff. I dug in it. Like my hands were shovels. Dig dig.

It didn't like to be dug. It scratched me and made my blood go out some.

People give me dollars to dig big rocks from the fields. But rocks don't like to be dug. They want to sleep. Always. They don't like having light inside them.

I made a pile. Big. Then I took it to his stone. And hers. I threw the dirt on. Then more. More than my fingers times. Until the pile was all on them. And the shiny was gone, and there couldn't be light inside the stone. And the marks couldn't say their names.

When I don't wake up the light is everywhere, and back there isn't there, and the cows sing and sing. When I do wake up the dark goes in me so hard that no one sees me.

The wind went ssssss sssssss in the tree. Sssssss sssssss it went.

Sssssssss sssssssss sssssssiiiimmmmon.

Then in the rocks it moaned. Peeeeeteeeeer.

It called our name. The wind. It called our name.

I looked at the stones. That couldn't say nothing now.

There, I said. There.